EMBER

BY

M. T. WALKER

FOR CAT

**THANK YOU FOR ALWAYS
PUSHING ME AND HELPING
MAKE THIS A REALITY**

Content warning

This book contains the following:

Profanity
Graphic violence
Blood and gore
Mistreatment of individuals, including
children.
Forced Captivity
Child death
LGBTQ characters

CONTENTS

CHAPTER 0
OBSERVATIONS

Watching...so near...so far away...so odd it must be to be only one. The infant seemed so peaceful, as though it would never hurt anything. So sweet. Ah there it was again that feeling of sentimentality. As always, the burning chill followed. Always...always...

The infant was awake now...eyes of deepest green... How fate had chosen this was incomprehensible, yet it was not our place to judge, will do as we are supposed to.

An elegant dance of vibrant light and heat. The infant was now a boy, and his insight was deep...deeper than it should be. So much potential...so much strength. Already runes covered parts of his body. Yes, he would work well. Such an interesting route that this one would take. One...such a strange concept.

The deep chill that never leaves and the swirl of snow. Now there was a second boy...far more power in this one. Greater than all. Perfect. The first however was troubling now...older and the burden seemed to begin breaking him. How much longer could he bear it? Must watch and secure if need be.

Deep and dark yet with beauty of a bright and primal nature. Ah the brothers were powerful indeed. Such an odd term... brothers...to be alike another yet not be them...so strange. Another was making its way into vision now. This one was like the brothers, yet different. It was older...like the first one. It hadn't been seen before but now was clear. Change in balances...must be monitored.

Adrift in a sea of endless white and blazing light. They were nearly ready now...good there was little more that could be done to suppress what was coming. Still the one was cause for concern. The breaking hadn't spread but it hadn't ceased either. Continue to monitor...might have hand forced in the matter. Hope it didn't come to that...directive was to watch only.

CHAPTER 1
JOLEEN

Silence that was so deep that it seemed to absorb everything around it into a void. Silence so complete that not even breathing could be heard. That was what Joleen had been attempting to find for herself.

It was truly amazing how, even as a princess that things like this were so difficult to find. Though the argument could be made that it was her position that was the cause of much of her trouble.

Joleen's bedchamber looked like what you would expect of a princess with an aptitude for magic. Bookshelves holding a fair number of tomes, a grand four post bed and other furnishings made of an exotic wood, that she neither knew nor cared what it was. The ceiling had depictions of great heroes and mythical creatures on it. The floor had a mosaic arranged in a pattern of a bright gold dragon. Several locations gave off clear evidence of enchantments.

At the age of twenty-two she often attracted suitors due to her beauty and status as the princess. Many noblemen cast lecherous gazes at her and nearly as many had attempted to convince her father that she should be married off to them.

When she was younger it had flattered her, but the guards always stepped in to "escort" her and later she learned that none of these men cared for her in the slightest.

After she came to this realization, she learned to shut down her inner maiden and channeled the same strength that her younger brother showed. Her hair, like all the women in her family, was deep golden blond with steaks of the pure silver and her eyes were deep green like emeralds.

She had been sitting alone in her room for some time now attempting to focus her mind and relax. Being the eldest of three children she was technically the successor to the throne, though she had no real interest then the position.

That didn't stop countless ministers and delegates from searching her out when her father was unavailable. Besides her lack of interest and what was required of her were separate issues.

It had turned into something of a sick game of her trying desperately to find some place that they couldn't find her or at the very least a few minutes of peace, while they in turn seemed determined that she works every waking moment of her life.

Most of the time she simply gave in and performed the tasks as she was expected to but occasionally, like today, she'd had enough and went to great lengths to avoid people.

She had used some magic to put a seal on the door preventing most from entering the room. She had spent several hours in here today trying her best to calm her mind and focus on some of the things that she personally liked.

The image that the people of the empire, even the nobles of the court, had of her and the real self that she hid were very different. None would have expected that she truly enjoyed the martial training that she was (secretly) given from a young age or that she held a strong love for the simple "girly" clothing that the commoner girls often wore.

She simply didn't care how elegant or "regal" something appeared. What was the point of looking so distinguished if you were holding back a grimace of discomfort? Also, if you routinely dressed in that manor then you were likely trying to distract from something else.

Regardless she pushed these feelings down and acted as someone of her station should...for the most part that is. Her elegant dress, bone creaking corset and other similar implements of fashion torture were lying in a heap on a chair.

She was currently nearly naked, wearing only a specially designed pair of undergarments, specially designed tight-fitting pants cut at the knees and a snug short cut top that was holding her chest in check, having no desire to attend to the niceties for no reason.

On those few occasions when she really wanted to escape the prison of formalities that was her everyday life, she would join her youngest brother on some day trip. The thought of how scandalized the nobles of the empire would be if they knew always amused her greatly.

Like the rest of her family, she had been trained in several self-defense techniques. Unlike everyone but her youngest brother Joleen genuinely loved the feeling of the physical exertion, not that she was the most graceful of people.

So, she continued to train herself in secret in her own room where no one would know. It was likely that her brothers knew, but they had never said anything to her about it. So, they most likely supported her. Chances were that there were one or two others in the palace that knew as well and simply kept it to themselves.

Fighting was not really Joleen's strong suit. Even her magic affinity tended towards healing and other support. Part of this was due to her build but mostly it was due to her being a bit on the clumsy side.

In the middle of a complicated series of movements meant to test agility she lost her balance and landed solidly on her bottom. In fact, which was another reason that she kept up this training. It certainly wouldn't do for her to trip and embarrass herself when in an official situation.

Joleen stood up, rubbed her sore backside, and continued through the training, working up a heavy sweat. After some time, she picked up a small wooden sword that her youngest brother Meterove had made for her when they were younger and proceeded to use it in her training.

Well, she called it training in her head, but it was nothing more than her daydreaming about spending her days more like her brother. She prayed that no one ever saw this, it was just so childish, pretending to be killing monsters with a wooden sword.

After she had spent nearly an hour training herself physically, she began magic drills. Casting spell after spell she tried her best to strain her mental fortitude and exhaust her mind, trying to push beyond her limit.

An aurora of many hues of blue and green hung around her as she fired off constants spells before she finally could take no more and collapsed onto the floor panting. The cool mosaic on the floor felt nice considering how overheated she felt. She lay there till she felt that she could stand then got up and walked to her private washroom, stripping along the way.

The washroom was about twenty feet by thirty feet in size, though it was technically four rooms in one. One held a hot bath, one a cold bath, one a shower and then there was a changing room at the front.

Joleen showered, then briefly entered the cool bath to cool off before drying herself. After doing her usual shower routine Joleen hung up her towel and exited the room intending to clean up the dirty clothing that she had forgotten only to find it nowhere to be seen.

Joleen froze, suddenly noticing a figure over by the table next to the window and faced the person in question. His name was Narok, he was the current Captain of the Royal Guard as well as a childhood friend.

He was a few years older than her and while he wasn't exceedingly handsome, his features seemed to ooze kindness and friendliness. This tended to make him more desirable than the better-looking nobles in the eyes of the other ladies of the court.

He leaned against the wall his brown hair cut short and his deep grey eyes locked on her one eyebrow raised as if judging her. Adding to this feeling was the arms crossed over his chest and his feet crossed at the ankles.

With the force of a lightning strike the realization that she was fully nude hit her. It was as if time slowed to a crawl and her mind fired off countless thoughts one after the other.

I have to cover myself!

I can't believe I didn't think to get dressed first!

Is he judging me for forgetting to get dressed?

Wait...is he judging my body...he better not be...but what if he is...

Finally, logic took over and routed the embarrassment. She could not undo this situation and it was not like they had never seen each other naked before. Though they had been little kids...

Trying to bury the resurgence of embarrassment Joleen decided to try her hand at a game of chicken. Doing her best to keep her voice even and praying that her face was not as red as she thought it was, Joleen said

"Enjoying your view over there?"

Narok's face did not change much though it seemed as though he was trying to make more of a show of critiquing her and with the air of a judge evaluating a show dog, "You could say that..." He uncrossed his arms and used his hands to make "frames"

Damnit! He's calling me on this one! Well, I cannot let him win!

Joleen walked over, taking care to swing her hips just a bit more than normal and stood directly in front of Narok leaving barely an inch between them. "Since you've already evaluated me visually perhaps, you'd like to find out if it feels the way that it looks?"

There you bastard! Now what are you going to do!

Joleen was confident that Narok would back down now. There was no way that his sense of duty as a guard would allow him to touch her. It was her victory! After he surrendered, she would claim the right to remove this memory! It was a risky bit of magic but there was no way she could let that memory remain!

Just as she was planning on how she would gloat Narok said something that defied all expectations.

"Well based on what I found when I entered there is a good chance that you may have injured something, and I would be NEGLIGENT in my duty to not give you a THUROUGH check BEFORE escorting you to a more experienced person to make sure there are no injuries."

Being blindsided by this turn of events Joleen's façade crumbled around her and she surrendered the game as well as gave into the embarrassment and covered herself. "You're an ASS!"

Finally, a grin split Naroks face and he walked over to Joleen's wardrobe and gathered a few items out of it before returning to hand them to her.

"You need to be a little more aware Jol. What if someone other than me had come in? You know I am not the only person that is excluded from your barriers. I cleaned up your mess this time, but you really need to be more careful. Oh, and don't worry, even though you lost this round I will still let you do an alteration on my memory so stop looking at me like that."

Joleen reddened a bit more before letting go of her anger and embarrassment all together and quickly getting dressed. Once that was done, she was about to alter Narok's memory when Narok spoke, "Oh before you do that, I have a message to relay from your brothers."

Joleen paused then lowered her hand. It was true that magic that dealt with the mind was hard to control at best and that it was possible that Narok might forget his reason for coming. If he had been sent by her brothers, then she did not want to have to deal with their indignation later, or worse awkward questions about WHY she had altered his memory.

"So, what did Jolson and Meterove want?"

Narok's demeanor changed suddenly, and he stood at attention and saluted her delivering the message in the crisp manor of a soldier reporting to his superior.

"Prince Meterove and Prince Jolson request that I escort you to their location at the earliest opportunity."

Joleen dropped her hand. Of course, Narok would do this. There was no way he was going to let her off the hook THAT easy. He would make her sweat for a while knowing what he had seen.

Did he have an idea of what he would find when he came here? Was all this planned from the start? I'll find out when I go to erase that memory.

Sighing Joleen narrowed her eyes at Narok, "Well, lead the way...oh and you're still an ass."

Mostly keeping his proper demeanor Narok saluted again, though this time he had hint of a smirk and began to lead Joleen through the palace.

CHAPTER 2
PATHS

Her mind was buzzing now with thoughts about what on earth Jolson and Meterove wanted. Whatever it was, they wanted to keep it low key so that no one would know what was going on.

What mischief were they plotting? Or had they already done said mischief and were looking for her aid in covering it up or fixing it? Well, if it was mischief most likely it was Meterove's doing.

As she passed the windows she glanced outside. Far below she could see the orchard where Joleen assumed that Meterove and Jolson awaited her arrival. It was one of their favorite places to meet up since they had often gone there since they were children, and few would assume ulterior motives other than leisure.

She could also see the city. The city was shining brightly today. She had a momentary urge to act a bit like her brother and take the "express route" down and jump from the window and use the various fixtures as landing points. This held extra appeal considering the grief that it would cause Narok.

However, if someone were to see her do this the gossip in the court would reach her father and that was not something she wanted to deal with.   She quickly if a bit reluctantly suppressed that urge Joleen went on her way glancing out the windows as she walked.

Whenever she looked out on the city, she was struck by just how beautiful it was. This was one thing that connected her to her late mother. She too had loved the view of the city from the windows and would often sit on a balcony drinking tea with Joleen at sunset.

The oldest building in the city by far was the palace. It was the only building in the city that was made of green marble. It was polished to the smoothest texture, so that it stood out amongst all the other buildings in the city.

It was also higher and longer than any of the other buildings. Carved out of the side of the great mountain Erizne, it was a single piece of marble, testament to the skills of the elders in craftsmanship.

There were a few other buildings in the city that had some green marble but most of those had a direct tie to the imperial family. That particular shade of green was used in the imperial crest and was rarely gifted to others.

As she approached a doorway two suits of armor that were on either side of the door came to life and reached out and took hold of the large rings that were in the middle of each door and pulled them open. She continued down halls like this for some time. Every time that she reached a door the same thing happened.

The doors were also very wide. Ten men could walk through the doors at once without touching. The door itself was made of solid oak and was about a foot thick. These oversized doors were left over from times when sieges were a very real fear.

In an emergency a rune could be destroyed on the doors shrinking them down to the same size as those that led into the rooms along the hallways. The theory being that a contingent of soldiers could easily go through before destroying the rune making the door harder to breach.

While there were numerous upgrades that could be made to the palace most that were not strictly magical in nature went unused. The past emperors as well as her father felt that holding strong to tradition was important in the palace.

Eventually she reached the grand staircase. Here she turned aside to go over to a glyph for no one in their right mind would actually use the staircase unless there was no other option. There were seventy-two flights of stairs scattered across ten different floors, but this was the main one that would take her directly to the first floor. Nowadays these stairs were there only to impress visitors.

Spatial magic was used to give the impression that it was one long straight staircase despite there being a number of landings and turns. She reached out and touched the glyph and after it flashed with a white light, she and Narok were at the bottom of the stairs. There was another door down there that opened the same as the others did. Now she was in the entry hall.

This was one of the few sections of the palace that was open to the public, though only for certain events. Here in this large room, which was lit by a dozen golden chandeliers, was enough wealth to make even the richest outsider feel as though they wore naught but rags. It always bothered her just how blatantly this room showed off their wealth.

The walls had priceless pieces of art that were from days long in the past: golden vases that were ten feet high, great tapestries with jewels sewn into them, and the floor was tiled with gold and silver. The stairs were a spiral of marble with platinum handrails.

There was a huge fireplace at the back of the room that was large enough to fit a whole tree in at one time if it were cut properly. This was purely ornamental since magic was used to keep the entire palace at a constant comfortable temperature.

Joleen crossed the room quickly to the doors that were the main entrance into the palace. Their size was unmatched by any other doors in the palace.

They stood nearly two hundred feet high, and fifty men could have walked through it at once. They were made all of silver, gold, and an assortment of other precious metals. They had the faces of all the Valaseri family carved onto it.

Joleen never cared for these showy doors and privately thought that it MUST have been a man with "confidence" issues, which built those doors. She walked outside into the warm air of a late summer day and started down a path that would lead her to the gardens.

Narok "leading" her to the destination was most likely a way to mess with her but on the off chance that there was a slightly different meeting location or Meterove and Jolson wanted him there as well Joleen kept him with her.

These gardens were massive in size being at least a thousand acres. Spatial magic was employed here as well allowing for all this land to exist while taking up extraordinarily little space.

In these gardens there were every size, shape, and color of flower imaginable. Some areas even had spells that managed the climate keeping the area in optimal conditions so that plants could thrive even outside of their normal season. It was one of the few places in the world where one could find lilacs in bloom year-round.

Throughout these gardens there were many trees and winding paths that went through them. Joleen set out on a path that would take her to the family orchards. As she walked, she would occasionally pass someone tending to the plants, and she would acknowledge them even if it were not necessitated by courtesy.

It took her a quite a while to get through the paths to the orchard and from the edge another five minutes to reach the place that Jolson and Meterove were waiting for her. The orchard was not as massive as the gardens having some hundred acres of land but considering that it was all for the use of the palace it was a bit excessive. She walked through many trees and over a few hills and then at last she came to the section where the apples were.

The scent of the apple trees on the air brought memories back that, though she tried to suppress them, pushed their way to the surface mercilessly.

She had often come here with her mother and walked along the paths with her when she was a little girl. She could almost taste the apples now, though she had not eaten one since the day that she had walked here with her mother for the last time.

A tear rolled down her cheek. It was hard to believe that she had been gone for so long considering how raw the feeling of loss currently felt. She shook her head to clear it. Feeling slightly frustrated with herself.

Mom died just after Meterove was born. That was almost twenty years ago. Why does it still hurt like this?

She could see in the small clearing that was around her a large apple tree with two young men under it, her brothers. Meterove was younger by a three years and Jolson was her younger twin. Meterove, young though he might be, was already a legend in his own right.

He could handle a sword better than the best of the soldiers in the army. The speed with which he moved stunned most anyone that tried to fight him. His skill with offensive magic was also highly advanced, even more so than some of the best mages in the Empire.

He was blonde, though it was a darker hue than her own, with one bright green eye and a vividly blue one. This characteristic was highly uncommon and was said to herald potent magical powers. So far this seemed to be quite true. His face was like his brothers, though it felt almost as if he were a little wilder.

He had one other characteristic that was rare though this one he shared with Jolson and Joleen. As great events in his life unfolded, they would be etched into his skin in different colors, forming magical tattoos that acted as an illustrative story of his life and the choices he made.

This was called Soul Etching, though Meterove tended to refer to it as Soul Ink. Noting that Meterove seemed to have grown a little more in the last six months Joleen shook her head. That boy was always outshining them and now he just had to be taller too.

His body was well muscled due to his constant training during which he got many scars that he felt showed his status as a warrior. Though in Joleen's opinion it was hit or miss if the scars were representative of his skill at avoiding a worse injury or his recklessness for getting hurt in the first place.

All who knew him knew that pampering was not something that Meterove accepted. His clothes reflected this in that they were those of the common soldier instead of a prince, though admittedly he could replace them more often than many foot soldiers and the quality was certainly higher.

These were darker in color and were reinforced in any area an enemy might aim for. The sleeves of the shirt were shortened and had a light pair of leather pads that protected the shoulders, what appeared to be simple cloth pants, though Joleen knew that there was more to them.

In actuality, the pants and shirt were not cloth at all but chainmail links that had been magically shrunk down giving him the pros of metal armor and cloth clothing in one. He also had a pair of black leather boots.

Jolson was not nearly as muscular as Meterove, though he was well toned his constitution simply was not as hardy as Meterove's, thus his smaller build. He also spent far less time doing physical training.

This was due to the discovery of his precognition abilities. This rare gift had not been seen for many generations and though the abilities could not be used consciously, they were still well looked after so he did not train in combat much.

Jolson must want to talk to me about something that he had seen.

For the first few years that he was aware of his abilities, he had fretted that he might see something that he would not wish, and in his attempts to avoid it end up being the catalyst of some catastrophe. It had been a few years since something had bothered him enough that he wanted to have a quiet discussion about it. It worried her. He must have seen something truly horrible to make him send for her.

Though to be fair I do not actually know why he wants to speak with me. Maybe it's something else entirely?

While Narok stood a short distance away keeping watch Joleen went over to her brothers. Her misgivings must have shown through her face for as she drew near,

Jolson gestured for her to sit, smiling to reassure her. It did not help.

Based on how strained that it was Jolson was pretty stressed over whatever he wanted to talk about. She had barely lowered herself to the ground when he began his story without so much as waiting for her to ask a question.

"Joleen, I have much to discuss with you and some of it I have no idea what to make of myself."

This alarmed Joleen greatly. When Jolson could not piece together information what did he expect her to be able to do? But Jolson had continued talking so he put her confusion and panic in check.

"Last night I had a vision and while I can divine the meaning behind most of it Meterove and I would like to know what you think."

Joleen nodded, not reassured at all. **Why do they need my input?**

Jolson took a deep breath, "I am going to put myself into a trance and repeat the vision that I had."

Joleen looked at his face with some apprehension. She had never really gotten used to the look of her brother in an oracle trance. Creepy was DEFINITELY the word for it.

This was the limit of control that Jolson had over his powers. Once he had seen a vison, he was able to, at great cost, reproduce it so that others could also see. He sat cross-legged with his oracle vest showing the many tattoos that adorned his body.

The right half of his chest had many ancient runes in an emerald-green ink. The left side of his face had three tattoos of the gods that governed time: each jagged yet intricately drawn in green line work. His arms had similar runes going from shoulder to elbow and elbow to wrist, then at the base of each finger.

He raised his hands palms up until they were level with his chest and after a moment several things happened simultaneously: His body floated several inches off the ground, each rune on his body gave off a bright green light, his eyes opened but they no longer were human. Instead, they gave off the same green color as the runes on his body even where there should be the whites.

Jolson had two emeralds that went through the center of his palms that were altered with magic to allow him full use of his hands. These gems glowed with the same light, the cut of the gem sending rays of light all around them.

The orchard disappeared as the vision was transferred around them; or were they in the vision? Joleen never really understood how this worked. The only thing she knew was that it was unsettling.

The vision was of all the land charred and dead and a city in ruins. A disembodied chant of many people, both men and women; of those long dead or perhaps not yet born was around them. Jolson's mouth opened and a voice that was not his yet, in a way, was came out. It was as though he were speaking as many of himself instead of one.

"The foulness of discord has caused the world to decay for far too long. Soon all shall end. That which is the origin of discord has returned and shall be the one that causes the world to fall from creation. The Ashen Soul approaches.

All paths lead to this. Treachery, arrogance, righteousness and even valor shall invite the ashen soul to feast. AN end is coming but how many ends must happen may still change."

The green light subsided, and Jolson lowered to the ground. He held his gaze down for a moment, clearly tired from the strain, before looking Joleen in the eyes and asking, "What do you make of it?"

Thinking on what she had just heard from Jolson, Joleen wondered what terrible future might be in the making as they spoke. They had no way, at this moment, to know what to do. They did not know what actions would cause that outcome only that one or the other was looming ahead of them like a great mountain at the edge of the grasslands.

Finally speaking, Joleen said, "There really isn't anything that can be done one way or the other until we know more. Even then it is possible that this is unavoidable or that the "end" it speaks of may be metaphorical.

We have encountered both forms of visions from you. There is no reason to tell father yet for the same reason. There is every chance that this will happen well beyond our time. Now, looking from Jolson to Meterove, "I'm guessing that there is something else that you have to say else we would have met in a less secluded area."

Meterove sat for a moment, seemingly lost in his thoughts. "Jolson and I had already agreed that more information was needed before we could act on this in any way. There have been...rumors that have reached my ears that concern me and now Jolson has this vision."

Joleen cocked her head frowning, "Rumors?"

Meterove took a deep breath and again seemed to chew on his words before spitting each out.

"Just odd stories of something out there...something that haunts the night and when day comes it leaves butchered remains behind."

Joleen sighed, "Might this not just be a werewolf or other dark creature from the shadow territory Veiled Lands?"

"If I thought it that simple, I would have sent soldiers to the affected areas but that's just it. The attacks, for lack of a better word, happen in all corners of the empire from deep wilderness and mountain villages, to right in the heart of the cities."

Joleen contemplated this for a moment, "What makes you think they're connected?"

"Well," said Meterove with a twitch of his lip, an almost feral movement, "All the "attacks" have the same result and appearance...or at least rough appearance; horrifically mutilated. No signs of any kind of struggle."

"OK," said Joleen as she exhaled, "let's say that there is something, which at this point I agree that it needs to be investigated more thoroughly than a local guard unit can, but I hardly think it requires our personal attention.

I know that you love to get yourself into the middle of things but since this is most likely something that a special guard unit can handle..." Joleen trailed off realizing that Meterove had stopped listening to her about halfway in.

Meterove said, "I have a few ideas on that, but I'd rather test them before we start hypothesizing. That is why I am going to go to the Lost Temple of Swvyeon and attempt to recover the Oracles Idol."

Joleen raised an eyebrow, "What makes you think it's still there?"

"No one's been near that temple in centuries, so it may be a useless venture," Meterove consented, "but it is worth making the trip. Besides along the way I'll keep my ears open to any information that might shed some light on this mystery."

You just want an excuse to walk into somewhere that has a high chance of monsters to fight!

Joleen nodded in assent choosing to keep her thoughts about Meterove to herself, "and what are you doing Jolson?"

Jolson rolled his shoulders slightly then said in a tired voice, "I've decided to check the records of any prophecies and premonitions that could be related or even tie this together. Since those records are scarce, I also intend to search through historical accounts and even legends if necessary. I do not like NOT having any answers to this."

Looking more awake now he continued in a slightly stronger voice, "What we wanted to ask you Joleen is to stay by father's side and keep your ears open for anything suspicious that might have to do with this vision. That part at the end makes me a bit wary. I feel like its warning about something on a larger scale than what we are thinking."

Joleen nodded in agreement, and then said "In the meantime we should continue as though nothing is wrong? It would not do for someone to get hold of this information and start a panic or try to use it for political gain, yet I can't help but be a little worried now that I think on it." Jolson and Meterove nodded in agreement, Meterove said with a small smile.

"Don't worry I've mentioned this to a few choice men to keep an eye out. They don't know the details only that there's something that's concerning me and to be extra vigilant."

In the distance they could hear the bell in the city market sound, signaling the closing of the market for the day. They had been out here for quite some time. The other problem with Jolson showing his visions is that it appeared to affect the flow of time in that area.

Meterove's eyes suddenly lit as though a fire were within. It was a look Jolson and Joleen knew only too well. Every time he got that look it meant trouble for them, whether he meant it or not. Joleen and Jolson both waited, full of trepidation, for the inevitability that whatever insane idea that had crossed his mind would reach his mouth.

Finally, he drew back his hand, palm glowing, and said, "Jolson...I think a sparring session is called for. Whatever comes our way will require strength and we must be prepared. Besides, I've been dying to have another fight with you."

Jolson grinned back, "You are obsessive about this battle training. You do remember that I just forced myself to reproduce a vison, right?"

It was so typical of Meterove. He was getting restless and while some might try meditation to relax or even going for a simple run, Meterove wanted to blow something up and beat on his older brother.

Jolson could not deny that training was a good idea though. Whatever happened there was always going to be a time in the future where it would be useful if not outright necessary to be able to fight. Apart from that the occasional sessions that he had with Meterove were fun in and of themselves. He rarely had something that he could do that they both enjoyed.

He had been afraid of some ludicrous idea, like Meterove had suggested on other occasions. Jolson's favorite one had been when Meterove was twelve. He had tried to ride a dragon that had been an ambassador and had nearly lost his arm to the ancient creature. It had taken many apologies and gifts to placate the dragon so that he would not attempt to eat Meterove the next time he saw him.

Getting to his feet, Jolson took a deep breath and moved to the center of the clearing, enough space that it would give them plenty of room to maneuver. "I'll agree to this on the condition that its low output spells and no reinforcement spells used. I'm still quite fatigued." Then eyeing Meterove apprehensively for a moment he looked at Joleen.

Joleen nodded but stayed where she was. As far as offensive magic went, she was certainly not on the same level as Jolson, let alone Meterove. Besides like Jolson she was apprehensive about dueling Meterove...he was a little overenthusiastic to say the least. It had not escaped their notice that Meterove had remained silent on Jolson's requests.

Her job would be to heal one of them when they were injured which was inevitable and would likely keep her very busy. After a moment's hesitation she put a ward around them and catching Jolson's eye knew that he had been thinking the same thing; that would prevent them from accidentally destroying some of the trees or worse, and by them she meant Meterove. He was not known for subtlety either.

Meterove raised his hand and a bolt of lightning shot out at Jolson who batted it aside with his hand, leaving a charred area on the ground. "Hey, I said LOW OUTPUT!

He then sent out two fireballs that exploded right where Meterove was, but Meterove dodged to the side and sent out a glowing ball of green light that Jolson tried to block, but he wasn't quite strong enough to resist the whole blast, leaving a large burn on his left forearm.

Joleen sighed and shook her head. *Jolson you are not following your own rules. Way to go. You let him bait you again.*

Joleen started healing the wound on his arm and continued to watch.

Jolson kept up his attack and even intensified it by sending out a volley of yellow energy after Meterove, each blast exploding in midair and forcing him into a corner where he was forced to dodge left and right to escape the onslaught. Jolson did not want to let up but as he had said, his was heavily fatigued.

He had let Meterove draw him into another high-powered battle that he did not have the stamina for. This forced him to change tactics. He decreased the power of his attack, while increasing the speed greatly, the runes on his body began to glow green as he pulled some of the reserve energy that he had stored in his "Meterove is getting rowdy" stash, which he kept stored in a special rune that was on his chest.

Meterove managed to get a small ward up while he brought out more power. Leaping forward again he sent out a stream of fire with one palm, and with the other he created a ball of lightning that he hurled towards the ground, which hovered a few feet above the ground sending bolts towards the nearest target: Jolson. Using the time that this gained him, he managed to get behind Jolson who was busy with the two-sided attack.

Meterove launched another blast of fire which Jolson blocked by creating a vacuum with wind magic. This dance of light caused their movements to look even faster than they already were. This continued for quite some time.

Meterove knew that ordinarily Jolson would be able to take him out no problem in a battle of tactics, but since his brother was SO exhausted now was the time to pull out his new trick. A smirk touched his lips, and he muttered an incantation under his breath. Instantly his body surged with power. His whole body was covered in crackling flames of bright blue and then there was a small flash of white light.

Joleen's eyes widened and when Jolson saw the light behind him, he turned, and his mouth opened with shock. The light faded and Meterove could be seen again but he looked different.

His whole appearance was the same; his clothes, hair and eyes had all changed yet remained the same. After a moment Joleen realized that what was different was not how he looked but how light was interacting with him. It was more like light was coming from within him than emitting from his magic outside him.

Joleen had learned about this at the academy when she had been younger. Meterove had internalized a spell, allowing him to greatly increase his affinity towards magic, allowing for stronger spells and faster mental processing. In short Meterove had just become superhuman in every way. This had to be the real reason behind this duel. He just had to brag and show off his new trick. Joleen shook her head. ***Such a child.*** Of course, she ignored that she had been playing with a wooden sword earlier.

Jolson also knew exactly what it was that Meterove had pulled off and felt the same way Joleen did, albeit with a stronger feeling of jealousy. Jolson's magic was something that he prided himself on. He had never been as physically strong as his younger brother but his technical skill with magic had always been higher. He threw up his hands in exasperation declaring Meterove the winner.

When that happened Meterove let up. Meterove slowed his pace and came to a stop about a foot from Jolson. Meterove smiled and the color returned normal on his body leaving him looking like he had before. Joleen hurried over to check on Jolson and healed a few injuries on his body. She looked at Meterove with open awe. Jolson could not hide his feelings either.

Sitting down on the ground from exhaustion he said "That was incredible! When did you learn that?"

Meterove smiled at his siblings and said "It's a very recent acquisition of mine. I have been training myself to get to it for quite some time and finally I have managed to use it completely. Once I get back from my little trip, I will go more in depth about it."

Jolson smiled and said "No I think I already have a good idea as to how the process works and I must say that

I'm impressed. You have always been able to easily best me in a contest of strength and now you were finally able to best me in a contest of magic. It is a bit aggravating but do not think that I am leaving it like this. I will catch back up to you. If you can learn that skill so can I."

Bringing himself to a standing position, he waved his hand, a small pulse could be felt leaving him and the damaged clearing began restoring itself back to the way it had been. Joleen lowered the ward and the four of them left the clearing. It was now late in the evening and the stars were beginning to show. Those two always did get caught up in their little sibling rivalry.

Each was quiet, thinking about the tasks that they all had ahead of them. Back at the palace, Joleen bid good night to her brothers and went to her bedroom. As she lay in bed, her thoughts were still on the vision. Her last thought before she lay down to sleep was that she had forgotten something important. She shook her head trying to either dispel the feeling or coax out the thought when it hit her.

I NEVER MODIFIED NAROK'S MEMORY!

Now thanks to her embarrassment it was much later in the night when she was finally able to sleep.

CHAPTER 3
MADNESS

A man walked around his laboratory, robes billowing around him and a massive wall behind him was one large chalkboard on which formulas kept writing themselves out only to erase themselves moments later. The other walls around him were lined with large glass tanks with deformed bodies within.

While some were adults many of them were children and the ones nearest a door at the back of the lab held what appeared to be newborns. Some had limbs that had been magically modified so that they had scaley texture, or some had feathers. One looked to be as much shark as human in nature.

Just in front of the area where he paced was a large stone table on which a human child lay. The gender was impossible to determine but they could not have been more than six years old.

At present its eyes were wide with terror but it was unable to make any sound as its mouth had been magically removed so that no sound could come out. Hundreds of tubes came from another table full of a massive assortment of crystal vials and beakers and were being fed into the child's body intravenously.

The man who was clearly a mage continued to pace back and forth talking to himself and with each chant a different combination of liquids would transfer from the beakers and enter the child's body. Each time a look of agony appeared on the child's face. There was not even the faintest trace of remorse on the mage's face at all.

Finally, the chemical combination was finished, and the mage turned to look at the child and waited, his face completely cold, uncaring about the suffering. Only once a reaction started did even a hint of interest show itself.

Spines erupted from the child's body and his eyes and ears began to pour out blood. Quite suddenly there was a far greater change. The body split from neck to groin and from within a set of decayed wings and a twisted body rose out of what now resembled a sickening fang and blood-filled mouth. Even through all this the child was alive and stared in horror at what was coming out of his body. The creature turned and looked first at the child then the mage and reached one hand out.

The mage walked forward quickly... appearing eager. Had he finally done it? However even as he thought this the creature let out a piteous moan and fell forward lifeless; nearly face to face with the child who was yet alive.

Enraged the mage gave a wave of his hand and the child vanished from the table and reappeared inside one of the tanks along the wall.

"Another failure." He growled as behind him the child was attached to several tubes in the tank and was then preserved as a physical specimen, still aware. He walked over to the door at the back of this lab and entered the smaller room beyond.

Set in the center was a large machine that held a naked woman that had many tubes hooked up to her. Like the child she had no mouth though he had not stopped there. She was kept alive by the machine, so he had removed her nose as well and there was no need for her to see so her eyes had also gone.

A small apparatus that had several chilled vials of milky liquid attached to it was connected to the machine. Pressing a button on the machine caused one of the vials to lower slightly.

The fluid entered the machine then after a small glow of magic flowed down through a tube that entered her abdomen. Another surge of magic and her back arched and within seconds her abdomen had swollen many times larger and then just as quickly it began to recede.

Another tube larger than the rest came out from between her legs and led to a small tank at the front of the machine. Through this tube a small slightly red tinted baby flowed down to the tank.

Once it had made its way into the tank the fluid drained, the glass vanished leaving the newborn baby crying on the small metal table. With a wave of his hand energy wrapped itself around its mouth and it fused together.

He reached out and picked up baby and began walking over towards the door before stopping and turning back and saying. "Thank you, my dear wife, you are so kind to indulge my curiosities."

Walking back out to the laboratory he placed the newborn on the table and with a wave of his hand its body began a horrific growth spurt. The rapid growth was almost nauseating to watch.

The skin strained to keep up with the rapid growth of the bones and muscles. In mere moments where a newborn had been there now laid an exhausted and terrified young man.

His body was matured but yet his mind was still that of a newborn, so he registered nothing but pain and fear. There was nothing that he could do about it as his mouth was now missing and he was strapped down and hooked up to the tubes.

The process was repeated but this time only the mouth opened on the body. There was no sign of the wings or twisted frame. Snarling the mage sent a burst of fire that burned the child to ash.

Walking back over to the room with his wife he muttered under his breath, "Now for number fifteen for the day...dear, dear what am I to do if I don't start getting better results? It has already been six months of this. I might have to get a new egg source soon."

.   .   .

Orelion was vexed. Another day and another one hundred failures. He had left his lab being sure to lock the door behind him. The last time that he had forgotten to do that he ended up having to have several maids "quit" suddenly.

He was currently sitting at a small table sipping tea looking at the grounds through a window. A number of servants could be seen as well as his private security team. If there weren't a need for secrecy, he would gladly have used them as test subjects.

He took another sip of tea. His stomach was slightly off, and he was hoping this would help. He had been SO close he could feel it. The feeling of frustration was like a weight in the pit of his stomach.

Now that he sat here thinking about it, it was entirely plausible that the reason his experiments kept failing was because of his egg source. The maids that he had used before had yielded negative results, while some of the subjects from his egg source worked better than others.

Well obviously, my blood is superior so maybe I should attempt to create a purer source? I could always rapidly purify the egg sources blood out by replacing it with one of its offspring... Yes that could work. Any developmental issues would not matter since its purpose is incubation.

Orelion finished his tea, and a maid came by. "Would you like more Sir?"

Orelion looked at her and said, "No, I think I am done with tea for now."

As the maid walked off with his saucer and cup Orelion's eyes followed her. To anyone seeing this it might appear like he was planning on making her a mistress, a common feature among the nobles. The reality was that he had decided to try several new approaches simultaneously. It was time to be more aggressive. Maybe that would make this feeling in his stomach go away.

While he was in thought he momentarily thought he heard an organ being played. It was strange, almost like the sounds of the circus from his childhood. Shaking himself back to his senses, he no longer heard it. He couldn't afford to sit here daydreaming.

CHAPTER 4
MEETINGS

Meterove started the next day in what can only be explained as usual for him. Though rather than the intense physical workout that he would be doing early most mornings, today was lighter simply because he did not want to wear himself out. Once warmed up and feeling energized Meterove grabbed his gear that he had set out the night before and walked over to his personal balcony.

He looked out over a city being hit by the first rays of light from a rising sun. He shouldered his pack, which was far smaller than one would expect of someone going on a journey. The reason for its size was simple. In the second year at the magic academy all students were taught how to make a small personal dimensional pocket in which they could store whatever they liked. Most students made use of the spell by making a satchel, but Meterove thought that a pack where each pocket was its own separate storage dimension was far more practical.

Meterove was packed with enough provisions to last weeks, though if he could catch and eat wild game when he was traveling that was his preference. He also had his sword belted over his shoulder with a baldric right next to a short bow and quiver. There was also tiny shield that would expand to a larger size attached to his bracer.

He wore the type of cloak that was favored by adventures and explorers, which was intended to help camouflage him. While the quality of his gear was a little flashy it was not out of the ordinary for a higher ranked adventurer to have similar equipment so it should be fine. Meterove took a deep breath savoring the morning air and stepped off the balcony of his sixth-floor chamber.

Normally a person would panic seeing the ground approaching at the rate Meterove saw, but to him this was so normal now that he barely even got an adrenaline rush out of it anymore. After falling two-thirds of the distance he began to use a bit of magic to manipulate the wind and air density.

It only took a few seconds after he had stepped off his balcony before Meterove had landed on the ground. He started walking as though the previous step had been on the same level as the second.

His sudden arrival startled one of the patrols that was currently moving around the courtyard, though only briefly. "SIR!" The three-man patrol gave a nod and walking salute. They had all been through this so many times that they knew what Meterove expected of them.

Meterove gave the men a nod and walked over to the nearest palace wall and with a combination of his strength, agility and magic scaled the twenty-foot exterior wall and was off. He could have walked over to the gate but that would take longer.

Meterove made his way through the city keeping a moderate profile to avoid being unnecessarily delayed. Walking the streets and watching the people of the empire was one of Meterove's calmer pastimes.

All around him the people of the city began to stir. Shops began to open for the day while carts and stalls were setting up in any location hoping to catch a shopper on their way through and get them to buy on impulse. Meterove made a point to buy a sticky bun from one of the carts. The woman running it was the wife of one of his favorite guards.

The man, Gelson, had recently been out with an illness and Meterove used this chance to check in on him. After learning that he was feeling better and would be returning to his post tomorrow Meterove felt glad. He paid for his treat and Gelson's wife Sarah thanked him for his concern and waved him on his way with a smile.

Many of the buildings that Meterove passed were made of various types of stone. Often the type of stone reflected the nature of the business, with blacksmiths having stone with high heat retention or even refined metal in some cases, while an apparel store may have a softer smoother stone to reflect the nature of the clothing that they wished to sell.

Though he had never gone in there was even a dwarven jeweler who had taken the theme to a whole new level and had carved his shop out of one massive piece of amethyst.

The number of vehicles and pedestrians steadily increased on the streets as the sun rose higher. Most magic powered vehicles in the empire were for trade but in the larger cities, where there tended to be greater wealth, passenger vehicles were also common.

Large crystals that held several spells for maintaining stability and directional movement were imbedded on the underside of the frames and depending on the size there could be as few as two and as many as a hundred. These crystals needed to be regularly charged with power to maintain the spells.

Meterove pulled his hood a little lower over his face as the number of people around him increased, then laughed to himself, unsure why he bothered really. It was not like he was going to get into trouble if he was caught.

As far as their father was concerned Meterove was going off to explore some of the ruins to the north looking for nothing more than a good fight, which meant he was not at HOME looking for a fight.

This wasn't exactly off the mark either, because in the centuries since the forest had swallowed the temple, it was bound to have held the lesser creatures out, yet they would live nearby for shelter against the forest's magic.

Known to most as the Frozen Forest this vast wood was an elvish experiment that had gone wrong, or rather taken on a life of its own even after the elves had left.

Most people never ventured near the forest, much less in considering its bitter cold. Well, there was that as well as the fact that the forest went up against the border of the Vampire and Werewolf territories. Also, part of the forest went up against the mountains that contained the shadow territory of Veiled Lands.

As Meterove neared the edge of the city the buildings went from commercial to residential and the materials used began to vary now. Now there were times that brick, or clay were used to shape the buildings and sometimes even wood.

Regardless of the type of building they all used the same roofing material in the form of flat interlocking clay plates.

As he approached the edge the number of side streets began to dwindle, and a gate came into view. There were three main gates into the city and a fourth that was a special evacuation gate in the event of emergencies.

The main gate was quite large and was a gate only in name. There were twenty booths set up that individuals or trade wagons would stop at and submit to checks. If need be, a large magical barrier could spread across the gap in the wall sealing it closed.

The side gates were traditional gates, and these were the ones that Meterove preferred to use since there was usually much less traffic. Meterove walked up and took his place in the queue. After about fifteen minutes it was his turn and approaching the guards he asked, "Could you direct me to the Azure Mountain Inn from here?"

The guards all knew this phrase and acted accordingly. "Aye, just follow the main road and then head west at the third intersection."

The guards completed their "check" on him and let him through in just a few minutes. Walking along Meterove spent his time working out the rest of his route. He never really did plan much ahead. It made the trip so much more interesting if he was never sure where he was going.

Besides sometimes you found hidden treasures by picking your path at random. Why the greatest treasure he had ever found was when he stumbled upon The Golden

Oak, small wayside inn and ordered the house special of stew and their personally brewed ale!

At the same time, this trip could go in any number of directions and Meterove knew that, so it wasn't like he lacked preparation. He knew that the bitter winds and snow would slow him; far better to go out of his way slightly than to go for a straight path. He also had several contingency plan items in his storage.

He reached a fork in the road and now he could see several cargo transports in either direction, the first traders of the day. For the second time today, he was glad that he had chosen the long cloak with a hood or else he would have caused a scene.

He couldn't help but smile to himself, thinking of the time that he had effectively shut down a trade way when he got drawn into a card game and the traders piled around to watch.

Most nodded a friendly hello of acknowledgement as they passed but one cart in particular held his attention. An old man was standing next to the cart that was leaning heavily to one side. It was clear that one of the crystals that allowed it to hover off the ground had run out of power.

Meterove could tell by the state of general shabbiness that this cart was quite old, though it seemed as though it had been maintained meticulously well.

If this old man was the owner of the cart, then it was no wonder that the crystal had been exhausted. Everything about the man gave off the impression that he had never been particularly gifted at magic and now in his declining years filling the crystals was far from easy.

"Would you like a hand with that?"

The old man turned "No but thank you kindly. It'll take a bit, but I'll be able to get it going again in no- "and his voice trailed away as he looked into Meterove's face, his eyes locking onto Meterove's own. After a moment, his eyebrows raised a bit "You couldn't be...?"

Meterove held up a finger to silence the man. "Please I would rather not draw a lot of attention."

The old man nodded added "I don't wish to hold you up."

Meterove laughed, "You don't have much choice, if you don't get some help, you'll lose your day of trading. Not that the rest of these people are bad, but you know that they are going to prioritize the transportation of their own goods over helping you. Besides the amount of time that I'll spend here helping you will hardly add up to a significant delay."

And all of that aside, it is my duty to aide my people. Being kind and helpful is what any person should do.

Nodding the old man still seemed bothered but said, "I'm assuming that I don't really have a choice in this any longer. I will not be so rude as to refuse your aid if you insist. I'm Naldren and the reason for my trip today is more for their sakes than my own trading."

Naldren looked back at his cart and Meterove saw that two wide eyed children were sitting in the back along with an assortment of goods, both no more than six.

Naldren smiled, "Norn...Telna...now, now show some manners and thank the young man for his help." Norn glanced at his sister and then said, his voice strong for one so young, full of wonder, "You...you're an adventurer, aren't you?" then his voice became excited, "There's an adventurer helping grandpa and we got to talk to him.... WOW!"

Meterove could not help but grin...the boy reminded him much of himself and even Jolson a little when they were younger, and the girl showed more dignity and grace than Joleen had at that age. As this thought crossed his mind, she did a small curtsey then she gave him such a dazzling smile that for a moment he had to wonder to himself which of them was royalty.

Meterove began to channel his magic into the crystals charging them at a far quicker rate than Naldren had ever seen. The two children looked on with interested eyes as he charged not only the depleted crystal but the other three as well. When Meterove finished a few minutes later the boy, Norn looked at the crystal then back at Meterove's hands then at his own.

He began to concentrate and to Meterove's great surprise a small amount of magic power gathered there and stayed. No doubt about it that was the charging spell. He shouldn't be able to do that yet. He looked questioningly at Naldren.

Naldren shrugged and said, "I was going to take them to the academy to have them tested since they have shown some talent with magic. Not knowing much about magic beyond the charging spell I am not able to gauge them myself.

I had hoped to have them tested by one of the mages and then request for their enrollment...I finally saved the gold needed for tuition." He patted a small bag at his waist.

Meterove looked back at the children lost in thought, his eyes hiding the true feelings that he held on this matter. What that boy had just done was far beyond the normal for someone that was not level tested yet. No training yet and he technically just used a spell. His full potential was up for debate, but this was clearly worth more than just a casual glance.

My gut tells me that there is something more than just dumb luck on that boy's part going on here.

This was too delicate to be dealt with by one of the enrollment mages...he would have Joleen or Jolson get personally involved in the selection of the tester.

Otherwise, this might fall through the cracks.

Making up his mind Meterove turned to Naldren he said, "There will be a small change of plans for you. There is no reason why you need to visit an examiner." Naldren's face whitened. Noting this Meterove hurried on, "I want my sister or brother to personally be involved in the selection process of the tester."

Naldren's face underwent a number of expressions over the next few seconds that Meterove could practically see gears sticking and running inside. Ease, worry, excitement and worry again ending in puzzlement; it was like watching a comedy at one of the outdoor theaters.

He smiled but his face still showed worry, "Please excuse my audacity but is your sister not known for her short temper, especially when it comes to the academy?"

Meterove who had taken his canteen out for a drink almost choked on the water. Meanwhile both the children looked at Naldren, "Grandpa, do you know this man's sister?"

Naldren patted Telna on the head and said, "I'll explain later. For now, just sit quietly."

Meterove chuckled to himself. Not that he wanted to, but he could not refute that claim about Joleen being a bit testy and impatient when she thought that her time was being wasted.

"She has been known to show some "impatience" as she calls it, though it's more like a raging troll if you ask me.

I'll send her notice that she is to meet with a special examiner tomorrow at midday and I will also tell her to keep her temper in check."

Up in the car first Telna then Norn sat back down with Norn muttering, "Fine but if what he says about his sister is true maybe we should bring something sweet to calm her down if she gets mad. That's what I do with Telna"

Meterove who had taken another drink from his canteen actually DID choke a little on the water this time. He had just gotten a mental image of this boy throwing pieces of candy at an angry Joleen who caught them like a dog catching a treat.

That alone made stopping here worth it!

Meterove chuckled again after coughing a little to clear the water from his lungs and said, "I may have to try that sometime."

Meterove considered the wisdom of his next choice before deciding that this situation warranted it. He pulled off his signet ring and handed it to Naldren. "Hold out your hand please."

Meterove placed the ring on the open palm of Naldren's right hand and cast a fast spell. "I've bound that ring to you with a Lock Spell so it can't be removed except by someone that knows the Key Spell.

Show that to the guards and tell them that you met me on my way to the Azure Mountain Inn, then ask for Captain Narok. He will take the ring and ensure that I get it back. You will be housed in one of the academy dorms like other examinees, so you will not have to worry about food or lodging."

Naldren looked at Meterove a bit differently than before. Whereas he had been showing generic respect that was often shown to nobles out of necessity he was now looking at Meterove with true respect.

Meterove acted as though he had not noticed the change and used a bit of his power to initiate the spells and the cart hovered slightly off the ground. Meterove shook Naldren's hand and said, "The best of luck to you."

"And to you as well."

Meterove stepped back as Naldren climbed up into the driver's seat of the cart. Naldren raised his hand in farewell and Norn and Telna waved energetically from the back of the wagon. Quietly Naldren said, "So very like your father aren't you, Prince Meterove." Norn and Telna looked at each other and after a moment said with great excitement, "Wait! Grandpa! Are you saying...!"

Naldren put a finger to his lips. "Yes, now do not be so loud. He clearly does not want attention drawn to him, so let us respect the wishes of the young man who aided us."

The rest of that day passed without any further incident, though Meterove did ponder one thing above the rest about his encounter earlier. He had felt heat and a prickling sensation on his back earlier.

Why would those three be that intertwined with my fate?

Now however, he needed to concentrate on his task. There was no chance of their father remaining blind to the fact that he was acting on information from Jolson once he returned. However, he was going to cross that bridge when he came to it.

The whole reason that they had decided to not involve anyone other than the three of them was because they didn't wish to be dismissed strictly due to vague information and also Jolson's talent was still largely a state secret that could lead to tensions with some of the other nearby nations.

For now, he was going to enjoy some time out of the city, where there was less enforcing of laws and more living by them. He also used some time while he was walking to compose a message to Joleen about Naldren, Norn and Telna.

Joleen sat in her room reading a message from Meterove that had been sent barely an hour ago. The note was bold, somewhat insulting....and it made her smile, even though her hand was trembling with anger.

Joleen

I had the pleasure of meeting some extraordinary people today. More specifically it was a man bringing his two grandchildren to come get tested for entrance into the academy. Please do not go into rampaging troll mode or settling into an opinion at first sight and most importantly to test past the basics. So, in short, behave like someone with patience. I am sure right now you are doing your angry eye smile stare so stop it and relax.

Joleen stopped reading and realized that she was doing EXACTLY what Meterove had just said. ***That sassy little shit!*** Joleen took a deep breath and calmed herself a moment before she kept reading.

I sensed something in these children that leaves me to believe there is more than meets the eye. They should arrive later today so try and have them tested quickly, preferably tomorrow if you are able. Also make sure that it's someone more than just a standard admissions tester.

P.S. **xoxo**

She smiled again irritated at how he had walked her right along the path of reasoning that he wanted by knowing her reactions. Meterove knew full well that this note would irritate her and that was what made her smile even as she was annoyed.

She found it quite amusing, the "subtle" taunt in the postscript where he had written "xoxo" darker than any other word, did not escape her. He had been quite vague, knowing full well that her curiosity would lend itself to his desired outcome.

Regardless there was not any cause to think on it for the night since admissions to the academy would come tomorrow. She would see to these people tomorrow and then maybe the reason for Meterove's note would be explained.

Still, you would think that SHE was the younger one considering the tone of the note. Joleen almost swore out loud but caught herself. Her father would be FURIOUS if he learned that she had started using some of the common slang that Meterove had been using.

I'll punish that brat later!

.   .   .

Meterove had been traveling for several days along a gravel trade road, and had encountered many people going by, but none had given him a second glance. Thus far he had made do with what food he could gather from near the road or hunt just off into the trees or fields. It had mostly been rabbits and squirrels, though he had gotten one pheasant, which made that day particularly enjoyable.

He had saved some of the feathers from it to use for his arrows later. He also kept the pelts of the animals that he had killed and using magic quickly tanned them into some leather. He later came across a leather trader and bartered them for a small leather pouch, much to the delight of the man.

These several days of easy walking had spoiled Meterove a bit though and he knew it. When he had reached the predesignated point where he had to leave the established roads and headed west. For the first two days it was nothing but wilderness with the occasional trapper or hunting trail but before long, it gave way to a vast open plain.

Looking out over the waves of waist high brown grasses, Meterove could see across this wide plane the stark pure white mass that was his destination, The Frozen Forest.

Still crossing this plane was not as easy as it sounded. Meterove created a fist-sized ball in his hand and launched it at the distant mass. It returned several minutes later and Meterove caught it. "That's still over a week's walk to get there." Meterove looked at the sky and noted that while there was not a storm that he could currently see that did not mean one was not just outside of his sight.

Meterove sighed and began to make his way out across the fields. It was really quiet the scenic view and Meterove made sure to enjoy it as he walked.

A massive plane with occasional "islands" of tree scattered about to the north and west the vaguest hint of mountains could be seen, while to the south was nothing but grass all the way to the horizon and to the east was the forests that he had come out from.

When Meterove finally reached the forest, he paused for a moment noticing the total lack of leaves on many of the deciduous trees. There were many coniferous trees as well, but the sense of natural desolation was odd. Meterove took a deep breath and then stepped into the woods, curious just how cold it was and was assaulted by a bitter cold that nearly numbed him instantly.

Though he had been expecting it, he was so unaccustomed to this level of cold that it took his breath away and he stepped back out into the warmth. Meterove walked the perimeter of the forests heading north while pondering his next move.

He decided that despite the fact that it was midday, he would do best to rest the night on the edge of the forest and prep himself. He had no more decided on that when he came over the top of a hill to a stunning sight.

The hill declined steeply and there was a small river that had been hidden to his sight before that led into the forest. The water ran at a steady pace all the way to the edge of the forest where it instantly developed ice at the banks. There were a few rocks peeking out at the edge that seemed quite large, which meant that more than likely there were more scattered nearby on the forest floor, though buried deep in snow.

While he had been looking into the forest, what really had caught his attention though, was the storm that was bound by the magic of the forest. A great storm was rolling towards him and was he watched the wind whipping at the branches and the snow falling thick and fast, only to stop at the forest's edge.

Shaking his head Meterove walked around and tamped down some grass making himself a small camp. He spent the evening preparing his warmer clothes, mentally preparing himself for the next day and the unknown number of cold, miserable days ahead of him.

Waking the following morning he dressed and after a moment of hesitation stepped into the forest. The icy blast that met him the moment he entered pushed him partially back out into the clearing. Clearly the storm had cycles to it and was currently on the high end of its severity. Pushing forward, he made his way slowly into the forest. Already wishing he were out he kept at it for nearly an hour.

Thinking that he must have made good progress he looked back only to find that he was hardly a quarter mile in, he could barely see the edge of the forest and the warmth beyond. Time moved differently in here as he watched in the distance through a small break in the trees an outline of a deer was visible as it inched along each step seemed agonizingly slow. This intrigued him since he could have sworn that from the outside everything had been the same. Meterove continued pushing until it felt like it was midday.

Deciding to make a camp he thought he might as well rest for a while since there was little light, due to the storm, he would have to stop to check his direction and he would have to warm himself by a fire to ensure that he would not be freezing to death.

After a short meal and brief rest, he continued until it became almost pitch black and he knew that the sun must have finally set. Turning back was not an option so he moved towards a snow drift and using magic hollowed out the center and crawled inside for warmth.

Taking the shield from his pack he placed it tightly over the entrance.   Next, he used an arrow to punch a few small holes that would allow fresh air to enter and placed a small barrier that kept the cold out.

While he lay there, he listened to the howling outside, whether it was from the wind or wolf he knew not. As he dosed, he thought he heard sniffing from outside but was unable to tell for sure. Not willing to remove his shield from the entrance Meterove decided that a more complete barrier would be a good choice. There was something strange about this forest. His thoughts had felt slightly muddled since entering.

Next day as he emerged from his frozen tent he gasped as the cold hit him and throughout the day it only got worse. The cold was all consuming and there was nothing to distract him from it. The fog of his breath froze over his face causing him to stop frequently and clear it away. There was also a sense of venom around him, a hostile feeling that seemed at times to come from the forest itself.

This was only increased by the sight that he had found outside the opening of his shelter. The snow was churned up for several yards around the entrance and there was a trail that led to the cleared section. Meterove had spent some time examining the tracks but was at a loss as to what they were, partially due to the continuous snowfall.

He could only assume that whatever it was had gone back the way that it had come. The fact that the perpetual storm that hovered over his head made telling the time nearly impossible was also annoying. Meterove could only use the times that it became pitch black to tell that a day had ended.

He continued for the next several days stopping each night to sleep in a snow drift and each morning there was the same clearing around the entrance. His barriers seemed to be keeping whatever it was out, but that did not remove the anxiety of not knowing what was stalking him in the night. Perplexed as he was about this, as far as he could tell it was not a dangerous creature for it had not attempted to dig into the drift nor had he caught sight of it during the day.

Yet it nagged at him in the back of his mind. It was careless he knew to not investigate this, but he had other more pressing things on his mind, things like hypothermia and a nice mug of hot tea. Also, there was still that feeling like his mind was muddled.

Maybe it is just the cold getting to me? Afterall I am not exactly used to cold weather.

Every so often a span of time would come where it would just be overcast instead of a full-blown blizzard. These times were a blessing, as they allowed for a slight temperature increase and better visibility. Usually after a few hours though, another storm would circle the forest and the cold seemed to grow greatly in strength and it looked as though it were going to last for several days.

One such storm was currently on the rise and based on how those clouds looked it was going to be a big one. Since he was forced to take shelter Meterove decided that now might be a good time to see what exactly had been following him in the forest. It took three nights after the storm blew in for his nocturnal visitor to grow curious enough to appear when there was daylight.

Meterove had been dozing when he awoke to the same sniffing sound that he had heard several nights before. It stayed there near the entrance for a few minutes then went away, though he could still hear it moving around outside. He used magic to turn a small section of the drift transparent, though he immediately changed it back, his heart pounding.

The thing outside was no animal but a man. Yet he was unlike any man that he had ever seen before. He was on all fours and his ears were pointed but not the elegant point of an elf. They looked almost crescent shaped. His body was powerfully built with long black nails and his skin appeared to be nothing but a solid mass of scars, and he wore the tattered remains of a vest and what might have once been pants.

What had bothered him the most was the eyes, yellow outside and red pupils glowing brightly. And there had not been just one, he had seen several more of them further back, half hidden in shadow.

Clenching his sword Meterove tried to master the stab of fear that he was feeling. He had heard that there were werewolves in the forest but had thought them to be tales of bards and drunkards. If he had been able to seed the man's feet better, he could verify whether his hypothesis was correct.

That was easier said than done. His barrier kept them out simply because they were not actively attacking it. He did not specialize in barrier spells and thus his tended to be on the simpler side.

Quickly reviewing all that he knew of werewolves his heart sunk slightly. It took a powerful blow to kill one since their ability to regenerate would allow them to repair damage almost instantly. Completely immune to magic of any kind and worst of all, the powerful curse they carried in their fangs; to change you into one of them forever.

As much as I like dogs, I am not thrilled at the idea of becoming one.

Fitting an arrow, he used magic to make the snow transparent again and took aim. There were four of them and taking aim at the nearest werewolf he took a deep breath before he released his arrow.

It caught the one closest to him in the head, tearing a hole clean through the leaving a splattered mess on the ground and sticking high in the trees. Its body hit the ground with a thud and instantly the other werewolves knew that something was wrong. Stopping and though in human form looking for all the world like regular wolves scenting their prey.

Blood poured out from the fallen werewolf, yet it wasn't red but nearly jet black like liquid shadows. It looked more like liquid shadow. Tearing his eyes away from this Meterove looked over at the others. Their bodies had started convulsing as they underwent the terrible transformation from man into wolf.

Well shit...now things are getting interesting.

Even to Meterove, who had seen his fair share of repulsive sights it was, to say the least, shocking if not completely revolting. Theirs muscles writhed beneath their skin and pulsed outward as furry masses tore their way through the skin. Their faces elongated into the snout and the ears now had tufts of matted fur.

Standing over eight feet tall and weighing close to five hundred pounds they were far larger than they had previously been with matted gray hair and bulging muscles, in which veins were pulsing from the transformation.

While they had appeared somewhat unnerving in human form, they now had a lethality about them. Mouths full of fangs that were several inches long and serrated and each hand had claws that were at least five inches long, like obsidian daggers.

Now fully transformed they stood up on their hind legs and let out a loud howl and growling set about searching the area for him. The size of them alone would have been intimidating for most men. Their massive forms were barely visible as they stalked through the trees with terrifying speed and agility.

Loosing another arrow that hit another one in the neck, tearing a chunk out of its chest, exposing its collarbone, and tearing the head backwards, Meterove jumped up through the snow and onto a tree branch then jumped again and again getting high up in the branches. Taking hold of its trunk, Meterove began searching the ground for movement. At first, he saw nothing.

How can there be nothing? On top of the fact that I know that they had to have seen me come up here there is the matter of the one that I hit with the arrow just before I jumped... OH SHIT!

Meterove had just noticed, to his amazement, that two of them were already partially up the tree that he was in. The other two were nowhere to be seen. Pulling his dagger from his belt, he threw it at the nearer of the two, catching it in the throat.

Not wanting to waste his advantage he jumped from the tree trying not to think about the landing. With a crunch he hit the ground and rolled. Clambering to his feet he ran over to his shield and brought it up.

There was the deafening sound of something grinding across the metal face of his shield. Meterove gave a strong shove and jumped backwards to make some distance. There were two werewolves advancing on him, one jumped over him while the other tried getting under the shield.

Dropping down slightly he was able to use his shield to close the gap without giving up an opening up top, he swung his sword around behind him and was pleased to hear a howling scream, though he was unable to assess what damage he had caused since his full attention needed to be directed back to his shield at once. Giant claws had pierced the enchanted steel and were cutting though it was as though the metal were nothing but straw.

Well, THAT'S not good. I wonder if there is some magic involved or if they are simply just that sharp? That would be great if I can figure out the trick- OH SHIT! OH SHIT! I better focus!

Meterove felt a slight movement behind him and knew that he had little time and made his decision. He pushed forward turning to the side, hard. The werewolf in front of him gave a howl of pain as the shield bashed into its face. Meterove also gave a cry of pain as claws raked his side and the sharp twist caused them to tear further. Dropping the shield, he swung his sword high and severed the beast's head.

Turning around he saw the other werewolf with a large slash across its chest that was quickly healing and behind him the one that he had thrown the dagger at stirring on the ground. With a final writhing of its flesh the wound healed, and the werewolf ran at him in rage. Meterove ran forward and flipping up over its head brought his sword down and cleaved its head in two.

Turning on the spot Meterove felt uneasy, the last werewolf was not accounted for. Looking all around him Meterove's unease grew. It was a strangled growl that drew his attention. Turning to his right he realized his mistake at once but barely reacted in time. It had let out the growl as it had jumped and attacked from the opposite direction of the other two.

Meterove swung and missed, his blade deflected by the beast's paw. The werewolf landed and stood up and looked at him and Meterove looked back into its gaze. Its eyes burned with hate; with a bloodlust...it did not care anymore about pain or even its life. All that mattered to it was killing him. Additionally, the knife that had been in the throat of the one werewolf was now in its hand.

Oh great, I gave it another weapon.

The two other werewolves came at Meterove at the same time. Luckily, that proved to make them less of a threat as their attacks got in each other's way. This allowed Meterove to pull off some more elaborate swordplay and he managed to catch one on the side of his neck and mostly severed it, cutting down nearly to its armpit. The other jumped backwards but Meterove had been ready for that and with a backhanded slice caught it in the throat. It crumpled into a heap twenty feet away.

Looking back at the last werewolf Meterove watched as it gave a shudder and another strangled growl and Meterove realized that his dagger left some blood in the creature's throat, which was why it had not attacked yet.

Interesting that it hasn't tried to vomit the excess blood...wait never mind.   There it goes. That's gross...,

The beast shook its head and the remnants of the blood mixed with bile splattered around its feet. It then leapt forward, the last mistake it would ever make.

Meterove closed the distance between them so that they met when the velocity of the werewolf's jump was at its highest and severed its torso and kicked its upper body away from its lower. There was a burst of the same shadowy blood from both ends of the body with a long trail that connected the two. Even as he watched the liquid attempted to reconnect the severed body. Standing over the torso Meterove severed the creature's head, and its body was still.

At the same time a sharp pain appeared in his left shoulder. Looking down he found his own dagger lodged in the joint. Looking around him he let out a sigh of relief mixed with a groan of pain. All the werewolves were dead...

__WAIT this thing had been trying to regenerate its body! The OTHERS!__

Meterove turned to the two that he had not completely severed their heads to find them getting back on their feet their wounds healing. Meterove sprinted over and managed to sever the head of one before it got up. The other looked around at its fallen brethren before looking into Meterove's eyes with a different emotion. Sadness and confusion were the only way that it could be described.

Another howl came out, this time instead of bloodlust it was full of sadness and despair. It looked at him one more time, almost asking "why, why must it be us who suffer?" before running off into the forest.

Weary as he was Meterove was not going to spend the night this close to the bodies. He made his way west for about an hour then dug his way into another drift deciding that he would rest for next day then head out again. He knew that it was highly unlikely that this was the worst that he would encounter and wanted to be rested for it.

__Also, I need to treat these wounds. Damn beasts... or maybe not? Huh... The look in the eyes of that last one was unexpected. Looking back, I guess I would have felt the same way if our positions were reversed.__

.   .   .

Deep within the Frozen Forest was another lost marvel...an ancient keep not overly large but a keep none the less. Within this keep there was a divide, both figurative and literal. The grounds and upper floors belonged to werewolves while deep inside in the darker areas and dungeons were vampires. There was a peace between the two that was kept by four who ruled over all in the keep with brute force.

Titling themselves as Despair, Devastation, Chaos, and Blight they could be seen patrolling around and would slaughter all that dared break the peace, often by sucking the very essence out of the offenders leaving a shriveled corpse behind. On those occasions that they felt the need to go out into the forest they rode upon perversions of a pegasi that were more akin to demons than a horse.

Usually when they did this it was to hunt a larger creature when food was low, and fights seemed near. Last time they had brought back an Ice Wyvern and the vampires had drained blood from the still warm body while the werewolves had ravenously devoured its flesh. Today the leaders of both races were to have a meeting with their masters.

Striding powerfully forward across the courtyard the werewolf leader Mikhail, made his way towards the entrance hall that would take him to the large room where he would kneel before those that had recently made themselves their masters. As he entered the entrance hall and closed the door, he saw a chandelier was lit and from the shadows his vampire counterpart could be seen leaning against a pillar.

Perhaps now after months of gathering all the outcasts of the dark races, it was time to learn what reason there was behind working with the vampires?

The vampire leader, Reveka was tall for a woman, pale with fangs protruding ever so slightly from her mouth, which was currently sneering at Mikhail. While she appeared to be a young woman in her twenties those eyes said something else.

They were a deep inky black, and you could feel a sense of history from them. Additionally, the clothes that she wore showed she had once been a noble and he still held that air about her. She too was curious as to what this was about.

Maybe the reason they had to live with these filthy mongrels was to become apparent?

Eyeing each other with loathing the two walked side by side through the entrance hall over to the large set of doors that led to the main hall. While they may hate each other, it wasn't worth getting themselves killed. They both knew that they were far outclassed by their masters. As they approached, they noticed that there were several armored figures that stood guard outside the doors. From within the visor of the helms a vile blue glow emitted, and they held the stench of death.

Drawing level with these guards they stopped and after a moment the doors swung inwards. There had been no motion from these guards, but Mikhail felt uneasy and glancing sideways at Reveka he saw a similar expression on her face.

There is something more going on here than we've been told. I have a bad feeling about this.

Within the main hall was a runner made of black silk that was easily thirty feet in length. Torches were placed every ten feet and there was a large chandelier made of a jet-black crystal which had several magical fires burning where candles would have been. The wall was lined with columns and there were two that stood directly in the middle of the room.

These pillars had two large statues of what appeared to be near angelic beings locked in combat, each wielding a large sword, which crossed near the hilt. What they were made of was impossible to tell, only that it was some form of stone. On closer inspection one of the angelic figures seemed slightly off. Its wings seemed to be in a state of decay.

At the far end was a long table at which sat four figures each wearing armor though their helms were resting on the table in front of them. Drawing level with the statues the figure on the far right raised its hand and said in a deep voice that echoed slightly, "Come no further."

Feeling a trace of irritation Mikhail nodded and in his peripheral saw Reveka do the same. Clearing his throat the werewolf began, "I am Mik- "

But the figure cut across him, "You have no title werewolf neither do you vampire. You are here at our bidding. You have nothing. You are nothing."

Clenching his teeth, the werewolf began to transform slightly. "NOTHING! Then why are we here if we are NOTHING? I will not tolerate such words agai- "

A sound of air parting under pressure and a split second after the sound of gurgling; the middle figure had flicked a piece of ice in the direction of the werewolf and blown a hole through his throat.

After a moment, the hole sealed itself and the werewolf fell to its knees. He knew, though he loathed the thought, that he had not been spared but simply used, as a demonstration of the cost of insubordination.

HOW? How was this possible? Magic should have no effect on me. What is the meaning of this?

He, however, still had a grain of defiance in him. Standing back up he said loudly, "If nothing is what we are then what use have you for us? Who would bring the outcasts of our two kinds," He gestured at Reveka, whose face now looked fearful, "together and for what purpose?"

Half expecting to have another hole punched through him he swallowed nervously but the blow did not come. Instead, a deep ringing laugh came from the far left and was quickly echoed by the rest.

The figure on the far left stood and entered the fire light. With a gesture a wisp of magic left its body revealing that it had been using an illusion thus far. As the face was revealed Reveka let out a shout of surprise and she and the werewolf fell backwards its head low and eyes wide. Both said simultaneously, "We are nothing and shall do what is asked without question!" There was one thought between these two.

I should never have come here!

.   .   .

Meterove stood at the top of a hill stunned by what was in front of him. He had been walking for several hours that day when he had noticed that there was a break in the forest ahead. According to the records that he had read on the temple there was no way that he was there yet. After several hours of walking, he had at last pushed his way past a large bush causing the million tiny beads of ice on it to crackle as the branches moved and found himself in his current state.

Before him was a large frozen waterfall. Literally from top to bottom an enormous cascade of ice was frozen in place. Even the place where the water had once hit the lake below it there were frozen splash marks. Looking around he could see a multitude of small caves that lined the cliff from which the waterfall had once poured.

Quite suddenly he had the feeling that he was being watched and turning left then right rested his hand on his sword ready to draw it at a moment's notice. Walking forward slowly he continued to look around, even glancing behind him now and then. From his left there was a sudden soft crunch of snow, and he reacted instantly drawing his sword and swinging.

The blade came to earth quickly; he had barely avoided the young girl that was standing next to him looking up at him with eyes of a bright ice blue. A quick look told him that this was no human. Her skin was so white as to be nearly transparent and the hair a deep raven black. All she seemed to be wearing was a simple robe and looking down Meterove could see that she was barefoot. Looking back up he started and took a step backward.

Now there were more of them, some of them older others younger. All of them held the same characteristics though each looked lightly different. He knew what they were though he was having a hard time believing it. Tales of

Snow women were one of their father's favorite stories to tell them when they were younger. Yet was there anything else to explain this?

The cold that was all consuming around him was nothing to these women, a few of which wore nothing at all. Against his better judgment he sheathed his sword, while trying to recall what his father had told them. All that he could remember right now were the bits about appearances and that they were unaffected by cold. Also, that they were weak against heat.

Meterove had magic but also had a funny feeling that these women wouldn't be bothered by that fact. So Meterove took a deep breath and prayed that these women didn't freeze him where he stood. As though they had known his thoughts one of them spoke in a sweet voice which shocked him since he had been expecting an icy howl.

"What are you doing in this place mortal? Your kind does not belong here."

It was just as he had thought, she DEFINITELY had freezing him on her mind. As his mind raced looking for a way out of this another of the women spoke, "Perhaps we shouldn't send him away just yet...after all we haven't had any travelers for so long that have wandered willingly into our home."

She turned and spoke to Meterove, "Usually we need to grab men from the nearby towns in winter and use them for their seed. However, to have one walk so willingly into our midst..." her voice trailed off.

A third one spoke, "He looks and feels different than the men that we have seen before though."

Meterove was getting more tense the longer this conversation went on. The part about his seed didn't sound ALL bad but he was still nervous about the direction this was taking. The first girl that he had seen locked eyes with him. She couldn't have been more than twelve. Suddenly Meterove felt another presence in his mind.

You stopped your blade when it would have struck me. Also, I feel a mixture of emotions in you. While fear IS amongst them it is not the dominant one. I also feel impatience excitement curiosity and even anger amongst others. You are a strange being. I think that I Like you. I shall appeal for your safety.

Just as suddenly as her voice had been in his mind it was now gone. The little girl gave him a smirk and nod before turning and walking through the other women, clearly with some purpose.

Uhhhh, what happened to appealing for my safety? What is going on?

Meterove was just about to activate his magic and fight his way out when another voice came this one older than those that had spoken so far. "You will leave this man alone!" Turning his head to the right Meterove saw a beautiful woman walking across the snow. She appeared older than the others though still quite young in appearance by human standards.

"You are of the blood of Valaseri, yes?" she asked in a voice that held the same sweetness as the little girl yet was slightly deeper.

Meterove, even though he was in shock that she knew this simply by looking at him when he wore no insignia that would show his status, nodded. Now did not seem the time to argue with someone that didn't want to freeze him or steal his seed.

Again, the woman spoke and with his shock subsided a little Meterove noticed that all the other women seemed slightly afraid of her. "This man has come to these woods on an urgent errand that is of great importance. Leave us!"

Looking resentful but obeying nonetheless the group of women departed...all except the small child that had first appeared to him. She spoke to him, "I was always told that humans hated us...that you wanted us gone, yet you don't. I saw it in your mind you knew what I was even as you swung your sword, yet you didn't wish to hurt me." She cocked her head, "Why?"

Because you were just another adorable little girl.

The thought had barely formed in his brain when a smile broke on the girl's face. "You really think so? You are so kind!" She gave a little giggle then ran off leaving no trace in the snow.

Meterove now turned his attention to the woman who had saved him. She was eyeing him appraisingly to which he responded with an uncertain, "Yes?"

Looking at him for another moment the woman broke her silence, "Her name is Rakira, and she was truly pleased by your thoughts...as was I." She waved her right hand a small set of ice stairs formed at the base of the waterfall leading up it. "Continue on your way Meterove. Remain vigilant. There is no telling what you shall meet as your story continues to tell itself."

Just as suddenly as she had appeared, she vanished, fading into the snow. It was while making his way up the stairs that he was finally able to register that his back had grown hot during that encounter. Whatever had just happened, it was important enough that it had been Soul Inked.

CHAPTER 5
CONUNDRUMS

Joleen sat in a high-backed chair set up on a raised dais and was looking intently down at the two children that were in front of her. There was certainly something about them, Meterove had been right about that, but it appeared to her at least, that it was nothing more than having mastered their skills by chance. She had been testing them for the last several hours, their grandfather watching anxiously from his seat off to the side.

Meterove had been so adamant about them being tested by someone other than a standard mage that she had taken some of her own time to examine them herself. Sighing she said quietly to herself, "I'm not quite sure what my brother was expecting me to see but so far all I have seen is that they mastered some basic magic and have good observation skills." She noticed the old man had been watching her and saw him close his eyes and sigh; he had gotten his hopes up.

Standing he quietly sighed before saying, "Norn.... Telna...time to go." The boy stood where he was; defiant, the girl a little less so, though with more dignity. She motioned for one of the guards to escort them out of the academy, then prepared to leave. Turning her back on the children, she walked towards the exit when the girl spoke, "but the prince said_"

Joleen stopped but didn't turn around "My brother was clearly wrong. It happens from time to time."

Now the boy shouted, "HE SAID WE HAD TALENT!" In his anger tears were spilling down his face. His sister too had begun to cry. Several things happened now that made Joleen regret this last statement. There was a loud crack, a bolt of white lighting shot past Joleen hitting the door and melting it and the floor shook. She turned in time to see her guard grab the child in an attempt to restrain him only to be blown back ten feet. However, the children still kept her gaze.

Each had a golden aura about them, and gold light shown in their eyes. What was more interesting was what was happening in the five-foot gap between them. Time was moving backwards between them. She watched as students who had been in this very courtyard years ago walked by in the portal. With her understanding of magic what she saw was impossible yet here it was right in front of her...defying every known law of magic.

Momentarily speechless she stared at these two children trying to understand. Deciding that there was nothing more that she was going to be able to get out of this conversation she began to ponder her next step.

Why does that brat always have to be right? I can't even begin to guess who would have answers to what is happening right now and who I could trust with this information.

She spent a moment trying to find her voice before saying, "Hmmm... and speaking of being incorrect from time to time it seems that I have some apologizing to do. I was the one who was wrong, and it seems that my brother was, yet again, more observant than I was."

She waited for the two children to calm themselves. They seemed to understand that not only were they being allowed to stay but that they had just done something, though they were clearly wondering what. Calming themselves they sat cross legged on the ground and waited for her to continue, their eyes still puffy yet watery smiles now appearing on their faces.

Glancing at the guard who seemed to have suffered no serious injury, Joleen continued, "My brother was correct to ask for someone more specialized for testing. However, you will NOT be attending classes here, at least not at first."

At this the two children looked confused and a little angry, and expression that was mirrored on their grandfather's face.

"What I just saw requires special attention so you will have a private tutor working with you until you have gained some measure of control. Once that happens THEN you may begin attending classes."

Now Joleen looked to the left of the boy, "Guard, take them over to the dormitories and get them settled in."

Though the man still looked a little shaken, he acknowledged the order and after a brief pause said, "If you would follow me." The guard made a point to keep a good five feet between him and the children, not that Joleen blamed him.

Their grandfather made no move to follow, which Joleen had expected. The children glanced back at him, and he nodded as if to say, I'll follow shortly. As the door swung closed behind them Joleen started speaking to Naldren. "I don't know what happened with those two but whatever it was it wasn't normal magic."

Here fear began to etch its way onto his aged face as Naldren asked, "Then what is to be done with them?"

Joleen sighed, "Meterove sent you here to be examined by a more experienced examiner and I became interested enough that I chose to do it personally. I now think that I held too high of an opinion of myself, painful as that is to admit."

Taking a small steadying breath Joleen continued, "I'm assuming he had more reasons than he said in his message. Personally, I have no ideas as of now, but I will see if I can get some answers. Meterove often does things without thinking but not usually when it directly involves someone else, which says to me that HE knows or suspects something."

"At this moment he is likely the only one to know what to look for, however, I'll have the head of the theory department work with them for the time being and once he deems it appropriate, we'll integrate them into the academy. I'll also have my brother Jolson keep an eye on them. In the meantime, I ask that you say nothing on the matter to them."

Naldren nodded solemnly, "Yes my lady."

There was silence for a moment that was broken by the old man. "Then I guess that I shall be heading home then your highness." There was just a hint of remorse in his voice. He knew that once you entered the academy that you didn't leave for years. He had known that if they had been accepted that it was unlikely that he'd live to see them again.

Joleen felt a stab of pity for him. Making her choice fast she spoke, "Your grandchildren are something that this academy has never seen before and, in my opinion, the current system is ill structured to properly train them. Also, I think that some of our general practices need to be altered due to the unusual nature of this situation. I shall spend some time with our professors on the matter.

"There is much about this that is not clear, but one thing that IS clear to me is that they will need to be treated differently. To that end I am going to improve upon my brother's wishes and will allow you to visit as much as you wish, provided that it does not disrupt their studies."

She saw the old face whiten with shock and saw tears well up in his eyes. "Thank you.... THANK YOU...you dear...kind child...I-I mean my lady!" His face was suddenly fearful. Joleen merely smiled saying "It is only the two of us here and there is no shame or dishonor in what you said, only an honest and deeply felt compliment.

Besides, I can't tell you the last time that someone treated me as though I were in fact just another person. To be treated so plainly and honestly is a great gift that I would rarely be able to accept. Now, go rest, the room you are in will be held for your use whenever you should wish to visit your grandchildren."

Nodding one last time to the man whose eyes had welled up with yet more tears Joleen left the room. Making her way through the academy she hardly noticed her surroundings and so barely registered that Jolson was a little way down the hallway waiting for her. When she drew level, he spoke.

"So, what have you learned?"

Joleen was startled. While she had seen that someone was there, she hadn't really PROCESSED that

Jolson was the one there until he spoke. Also, she had been so deep in thought that upon hearing his voice she almost cursed before she shook her head and responded.

"The children have power...but it is beyond my knowledge to explain what and especially how they manifest it." Stopping where she was, she turned and looked into her brother's eyes. "They showed the past Jolson...they actually opened a rift that showed the past."

Jolson's eyes widened. "It's not unheard of to show something that happened in your own past..."

Joleen shook her head, "This wasn't their own past. It was the past of that specific area...years of it too." Joleen could not be sure, but she thought that she may have even seen a younger version of their mother briefly.

"I was under the impression that that was an impossibility." He said cautiously.

Joleen nodded, "We took the same classes. To the best of my knowledge, to the best of anyone's knowledge it is. I can't understand it. Maybe the elves will know of something that can explain it, but I certainly do not."

One thing for sure though, I'm not letting just anyone teach them.

"I'll look in with the Grand-Mage Leronsa and see if she would be willing to help instruct them. I will take some time as well and I hoped that you might be able to spend some time with them yourself. Of all of us you have the most experience with time.”

Jolson nodded, “If you would like I could spend as much as once a week with them. There is always a reason for things, and this will certainly be no exception. There is an aura about this matter; it almost feels like the work of some Greater Magic.

Joleen closed her eyes again. When they had agreed to split off in their own directions of research, she had thought that her end would be boring. Well fate and Meterove had decided otherwise and now that she had what she wanted, she wished for the quieter road.

After a moment Jolson broke the silence.

“Not the simple road after all and your path is about to get all the harder Joleen. Father will need you shortly. We have several ambassadors arriving today and we need to know all we can.”

Sighing Joleen opened her eyes and gave Jolson a sad smile. “Looks like you’re the one who lucked out Jolson. You still plan on looking through the academy’s library?”

“Yes.”

“Good I have a feeling that the past may have just as big a role as the present now in making the future,”

"Let's hope that there's something in there that will guide us. Now is not a good moment to be fumbling in the dark."

.   .   .

After her brief conversation with Jolson, Joleen hastened to her father's side, curious as to who had sent ambassadors. Upon entering the meeting room, she saw several of the ambassadors and her stomach lurched slightly. There were only three human nations in the world and neither of the other two were present, the rest were NOT human, though it was one PARTICULAR ambassador that made her uneasy.

Seated at a large oak table was her father wearing golden and teal robes and standing behind him was the captain of the guard Narok in full dwarven plate and an elvish lightning forged blade on his hip. Standing at attention along the walls were dozens of guards from many different nations. In addition to those guards each person had their guard captain standing just behind them, along with an aide.

Sitting at the table to her father's right was a dwarf in chain mail under blue robes and on his left was an elf, wearing a forest green cloak over light traveling clothes.

Joleen knew both of them for they had visited many times in the past. The dwarf was Khantrad, and the elf was Olethe. The others, however, she was far less familiar with.

One was clearly of the Acephali for he had no head, the face was part of the torso; the eyes higher up where a neck would begin on a human, with its nose and mouth following suit. The mouth was a ring of needle like teeth. It was wearing only a light pair of leggings and an oddly cut shirt to accommodate its strangely proportioned body.

To its left was one of the Leturai, creatures of magic like the elves, though where elves were exceptionally beautiful, the Leturai were a people that had long since tossed aside vanity. Their horns, which ended only a few inches above their foreheads also came out behind their ears and ended in a curl below their chin. Their heads were nearly twice the length of a human's. Their grayish blue skin, long fingers and dead wispy hair gave off a sickly image. It also wore robes, though they looked more like seaweed than anything else.

On the other side of the Acephali was what appeared to be a human at a glance but once she looked closer, she saw that it was in fact one of the Vlatari, their neighbors to the north. A race of shape shifters, they had long been feared and hated in their lands. They had originally rebelled and took a northern island province of Yxarion as their own.

Her grandfather, who had no desire to lose more men than he had already ordered the naval forces to destroy all ships in the island's harbor from a distance then granted them the whole island more land if they agreed to more peaceful negotiations. In the end her grandfather had been unable to reach an agreement with them and they became an isolationist country. It was not until her father had taken the throne that they had been able to make any progress in negotiations.

He was easy to pick out because while he was good at impersonating a human, the slight instabilities that happened when one transformed were evident. For one the glow of energy that came from its eyes was not of magic being used but of his actual form, pure energy.

As she entered the room her father glanced towards her and seeing who it was smiled. "Ahhh Joleen. Come to join us, have you? Ambassadors allow me to introduce my daughter and heir to the throne. At this point Joleen pulled at the hems of her dress in a curtsy. "I am Princess Joleen Erencia Valaseri. It is a pleasure to make your acquaintance."

This statement was treated with mixed emotions on the part of the ambassadors. The Acephali and the Leturai both looked disgusted while the Vlaadyri looked amused. Both Khantrad and Olethe nodded to her. They had known this information for years and as their races were also known to have female leaders had no complaints. The

Vlaadyri had no gender and thus did not have a concept of the issue. Also, her father's tone gave those that knew him confirmation that she was supposed to be joining in this meeting and that it had been delayed allowing for her attendance.

Taking a deep breath Joleen walked across the room and past Narok giving him a quick side eyed glance before looking straight again quickly. He glanced sideways at her and gripped the pommel of his sword. Joleen sighed inwardly; he was as uncomfortable as she was with the ambassadors was her first thought, before she remembered that she had not wiped his memory.

That realization almost made her freeze mid step. Now she wasn't so sure she wanted to know what the source of his tension was. Joleen took a seat beside her father who had waited until she was seated before he started talking again and she focused herself on the conversation trying to keep her cheeks from getting red. From what she heard there had been some sort of attack in the mines of the dwarven nation.

Khantrad took a drink from a mug in front of him. As Joleen watched him avoid getting both his braided mustache and beard in the mug, she wondered for the millionth time,

How does he avoid getting food in that?

Khantrad wiped his mouth with the back of his hand and resumed speaking, "It really has the king spooked Aphen. No idea at all what it might have been in there. The only thing that we know is that it was after the ore 'cause all the ore that we had mined and left in carts is missing. We lost nearly a hundred miners in there and some of our finest geologists and then there's the cost to retake those mines!"

Joleen could sympathize with the dwarves as that was a tragedy but couldn't understand for the life of her why it warranted bringing up to a neighboring nation at a meeting with other delegates. Khantrad wasn't done however and continued with his story.

"Over one-hundred and eighty soldiers were lost within those mines. Most of them we simply found scorched sections of rock with the outline of a dwarf. Those that we did find, their bodies...never seen anything like it before...parts of their bodies have resurfaced around the mines...all turning to dust when they were touched."

OK now that's weird! This didn't sound at all like anything that had been seen before. A mysterious new monster or something else in that same vein was DEFINITELY worth warning others about.

Khantrad shook his head sadly, "so many lives lost and not one clue as to what even happened. If we could at least have had one survivor that had seen something of use."

Aphen cocked his head in confusion "what do you mean of use?

Khantrad looked a little awkward and sad "There was one miner that we found huddled on the ground muttering to himself as he rocked back and forth hugging his knees. All we could get out of him as he slowly crumbled away were the words "Its eyes" over and over."

Well, that sounds even worse than knowing nothing if you ask me. Now all we have is a cryptic message from a likely insane dwarf, which may not even be a clue to what happened anyway.

Khantrad then leaned forward and asked the table, "Does anyone here have any thoughts on this matter? When it comes to magic and mystical creatures most others have better resources than us dwarves."

There were a few moments of silence as the rest of the table processed this story. The strangeness of it made the bloodless massacre seem even more gruesome. Joleen had a bad feeling that this was tied to what her brothers were looking into but held her tongue. As they had agreed speculation about a prophecy that they weren't sure about either, the accuracy or true nature of, was dangerous.

In the ensuing gap there was only the sound of breathing and a faint hum that Joleen assumed was coming from the Vlaadyri though she wasn't sure. Finally, Olethe leaned forward and cleared her throat. She like all of her kind looked perpetually young, though Joleen knew that she was nearly three hundred years old. Her light brown hair was kept out of her face with a simple copper leaf hair ornament. This meant that there was no reprieve from her piercing hazel eyes constantly reminding you that YOU were the child here.

That aside she was a generally pleasant person, for an elf. It was just harder to see eye to eye with someone who's culture views the eldest of your own as children by the number of years they live.

"Well that truly sounds horrible. My condolences for your losses." said Olethe, "To answer your question, we've seen some unusual phenomena in several places that we're not quite sure how to explain." she stared at Khantrad for a moment before, "One incident was similar to your attacks. Several weeks past a young tender from one of our groves on the outskirts of our forest near the Flowvx mountains stumbled into a small town talking senselessly."

The Acephalan seemed to sit up a bit straighter at this. True this was the opposite direction from their home, but there were now two accounts of something driving its victims to madness. The Leutari still kept an air of disinterest about the whole matter. What did the matters of the land dwellers matter to it? The Vlaadyri likewise appeared uninterested.

Olethe continued, "There were many burns on his body and upon closer inspection he had suffered injury from something similar in nature to a necromantic spell. We were unable to save him, and he died before he could say much. We sent scouts to investigate the grove and found it completely charred."

Here tears welled in her eyes. "Many of those trees had barely begun to grow...hardly half a century at their oldest...the loss- "

"YOU'RE MOURNING TREES AND ONE DEAD ELF!" roared Khantrad pounding his fist onto the table, upsetting the mug, which spilled onto the table. Cleaning magic erased the spill without a trace and one of Khantrad's men stepped forward and righted the mug looking both apologetic for the outburst and angry at Olethe's statement. "Over three hundred of my people are dead and you are comparing this to the death of ONE elf and some TREES!"

Olethe's features hardened at once, though tears still flowed down her face. "We are connected to the land. You KNOW this. As our forest dies, we die inside. Though I suppose a race that hides itself in the earth, gouging great holes in it, hiding themselves, has little understanding of such a thing!"

Here the Acephali spoke, its voice oddly musical. "While we all would love to continue to hear you argue..." A malicious "smile" contorted its lips, "We have more important matters to discuss. The attacks in my own lands for instance!"

Here Khantrad and Olethe stopped arguing and looked curiously at the Acephali. Joleen noticed that her father seemed slightly interested in what it had to say and gave it the go-ahead to speak, though it seemed more out of gratitude for stopping the argument. Joleen herself was very interested in this news.

What had attacked both the dwarves and elves and from the sound of it the Acephali as well?

"Several of our ships and ships of the Vlaadyri," the ambassador of the Vlaadyri nodded, "Have been attacked over the last several months! Four attacks and of those three ships lost and the last with no crew or cargo! Most of the deck was charred and useless! Whole crews gone! Massive shipments of invaluable supplies that were desperately needed lost!"

"And what of OUR problems ambassadors" said the Leturai coldly. "There have been mass disturbances in the magic of the world, and it is affecting our people quite adversely. Many of our cities have had to be evacuated because the barriers that have long kept back the sea were flooded before they could be reinforced by our mages. No deaths yet but many have been forced from their homes and we have no source yet for this disturbance."

Finally, an answer about why the Leturai were here when thus far they had been showing no interest in the conversation. As a race of highly magical beings, they cared little for things outside their own matters. However, when confronted by something that they didn't understand they became helpless and chose to "tolerate" the presence of other races to try and find answers. Still when it came to matters of primal magic and the wild magic of the oceans in particular, why come here?

Now everyone at the table was on their feet arguing on slightly raised voices. Her father Aphen was doing his best to calm the others but was having little success. So far all of the personal guards of each delegate were staying out of it, though they were ready to protect their charge at a moment's notice.

Joleen was having trouble remaining quiet. Why were they all fighting? Why couldn't they just sit down and rationally discuss what was going on? It was like every one of them thought that all the rest were responsible for their current problems. She was so preoccupied with her own thoughts that she hadn't noticed her father start talking.

"-there isn't much any of us know at this time. What we do know is that there is someone or something that has started attacking your nations. At this point nothing has attacked anything in Yxarion that I am currently aware of. Either we have bandits of a more bloodthirsty nature out there or the Vorthens have been a lot more active than usual."

At the mention of the Vorthens the tension in the room became very palpable. Even Olethe and the Leturai seemed slightly nervous at the mention of them.

Vorthain was one of two nations on the continent that were not currently in attendance. The other was Sorren. Sorren was another isolationist nation that none had been in contact within hundreds of years. They hid behind their massive border walls and barriers.

Vorthain, however, was the only hostile nation on the continent, though it was something of an isolationist because of their necromantic nature no nation was willing to work with them. The magic they practiced was viewed as evil as it went against nature in a way that every race here despised on principal. The origins of both that magic, and that country were lost to history.

The Acephali spoke first, "well that's not an idea with much merit since the closest nation to the elves' groves is the dwarves and the Leturai have several cities near where our ships went miss- "

"If you're suggesting that WE attacked the elves you headless-" shouted Khantrad

"HOW DARE YOU! WE steal from LESSER creatures! I- "

"Lesser creatures! You horned frea-" growled Khantrad

"The only way they're lesser is that they have less arrogance!" shouted Olethe

"Coming from an elf that means a lot!" snapped the Leturai.

Joleen was doing all that she could to not show her impatience with this mess. None of them were going to get anywhere. Her father's shouts for quiet went unheard and Joleen finally snapped someone needed to shut them up. Leaning forward she slammed her palm onto the table and activated a spell to create oscillations. This made not only the table but the air tremble in the most uncomfortable way. This was a Meterove special.

I can't believe that something he came up with to annoy me as a kid became useful in a summit!

Joleen let up on the spell after ten seconds and looked around the table, "Can I get your attention for a moment please." She had not meant it as a question and each of the ambassadors read the meaning well enough to stop bickering for the moment.

"Now if we could all just sit down and discuss this slowly and rationally, I think we can realize that all sides are suffering the same- "

The Acephali chortled nastily "Do you often let your children speak for you your highness?" He added a hint of sarcasm to the last word. Joleen's face reddened but she pressed on.

"What we need to do is_"

"What is NEEDED," said the Acephali "Is for the children to be silent and for those who understand these matters to discuss them."

Now Joleen's temper rose, and anger came to her aid. "Yes, because you are SO wise. You have already shown that you do NOT know the source, and therefore do NOT understand what is going on.

Is there room in there for logic of ANY kind? Think about it. Something attacked all of you and not only that but every race you have tried to blame has more reasons to AVOID antagonizing their neighbors than to attack them. So far all you have done is make a mockery of your own people in these negotiations. This is our hall, and you would do well to remember that. You think that we do not know how to deal with such situations! WE, who share a border with Veiled Lands!

The temperature of the room almost seemed to plummet at the name. Few talked of that place, out of the desire to forget that it was there; to forget the atrocities. Joleen gave one last glare around the room before closing her eyes and taking a deep breath to calm herself.

It was over an hour later that the meeting broke for a recess. Joleen left quickly and was sitting in the library when her father entered along with Olethe and Khantrad. All three were smiling. Her father raised his hand to forestall questions. "What you did in there earlier was tactless and very reckless. It might well have made all negotiations worthless.   Not all things can be solved with reasoned argument and certainly not with a short temper. Though this time…" Here he smiled again and Khantrad and Olethe laughed.

At Joleen's puzzled expression they explained that she had shamed the Acephali and Leturai enough in front of the rest that they had lost much ground and that negotiations had taken an interesting twist.

"Basically," her father said, "There is going to be a massive investigation into the matters and there is now none, save the Acephali, which seem to wish to continue to argue and stall investigations. Though there is still a long way to go."

Joleen listened to her father explain what else had happened in the meeting both before she had arrived and after she had left. From all that she heard she gathered the worst though she said nothing. The future was not hers to reveal, at least not yet.

.   .   .

Joleen hurried excitedly through the halls towards the passage that would take her to the academy. Once she reached the door, she pressed her palm against it and the door, rather than opening gave off an odd shimmer and she was able to walk through it. One the other side she was standing on a large balcony that led from the palace to the academy.

A large glass bridge lead from the balcony over to a spiraling tower made of Jade that was the administrative building. There were over a dozen other smaller towers surrounding it, also made of jade though each was made of a different gemstone, each with many bridges spanning between one another.

It was to the administrative building that she was heading, and she crossed the bridge she looked around and could see some of the students that were currently attending the academy glancing over the edge or down through the bridge with interest.

Joleen smiled to herself as she did the same thing. The view never did get old. Far below was the large outdoor area that was exclusive to students. The other part of the view that was always interesting was the floating islands on which one would often see a professor with a group of students.

Entering the administrative building Joleen walked over to the directory and finding the name of her destination pressed the glyph next to it and was instantly transported to the ninth floor. She walked down a hallway to a door with a plaque on it.

Professor Orthine

Head of Artifact Research
and Application

Joleen knocked and was told to enter. Inside was about as odd a collection of items displayed as you could find. The entire left side of the large room was lined with bookshelves and there was a large wooden desk with several chairs in front of it on the far wall in front of a window.

The right side of the room looked more like something you'd find at a blacksmith's workshop. Right in the middle of the room was an anvil and forge. Scattered around wherever there was an available space small crystal bobbles could be found.

Sitting behind the desk was a middle-aged woman with a monocle and navy-blue robes. Joleen walked over to the desk and took a seat in one of the chairs. Joleen's first thought was that Orthine looked tired. But then forging magic was one of the most intense and energy consuming of all magics.

"Well, Joleen I have completed the task that you had asked of me." Orthine was looking at her with a mixture of interest and worry, not a good combination. "Your soul has been analyzed and your Artifact has been identified and, should you wish it, can be forged."

While this was good news, exactly the news that Joleen had been hoping for, there was nevertheless, some trepidation. Artifacts were objects that, while they knew the HOW and the WHAT could be divined it was the WHY that was still unanswered. Simply put they were a person's soul manifested into a physical object that had great magical powers. No one knew exactly why mages were able to have the artifacts forged or what the end cost was to one's soul by forging the artifact.

Few mages had them since it was such a difficult art and the lack of knowledge on the subject only fueled the fear of the artifacts. In fact, besides Orthine there were only five other mages in the city that had one and less than twenty overall. Meterove had one, and that was one of the reasons Joleen wanted her own, though he had never shown her what his artifact was.

"I know you well enough to know that you have already made up your mind to at least hear WHAT your artifact is. Discovering your artifact is a life-changing experience and should not be taken lightly. Should you wish it forged we can do so."

Joleen nodded in response to Orthine, who understood that she was to proceed with her explanation. "Your artifact is...slightly unnerving to me. It appears to take the form of twin weapons."

Joleen was slightly taken aback at this revelation. On a list of people that gave off the aura of skilled combatant Joleen would have been near the bottom. It was not that she was unable to fight; she was simply more attuned to healing magic.

Why weapons? And TWIN weapons at that. It makes no sense.

Joleen took a steadying breath and said, "I understand, and I still wish to have an artifact."

Orthine said nothing but simply stood and walked over to the forge and anvil. As she approached the forge burst into life suddenly hot enough to have been in preparation for hours. They had been over this before, so Joleen stood and walked over to her designated location, just behind and to the left of Orthine.

Raising her right hand Orthine directed her hand to the forge and a set of tools made of energy began to work furiously over a lump of ore that had appeared there. Now Orthine's left hand came back about level with Joleen's face fingers pressed tightly together with an open palm.

Now Orthine was chanting under her breath and the tools began to work faster. Now Joleen felt a pinch that escalated into a stabbing pain in her chest, a sensation she had been expecting but found shocking none the less, due to the amount of pain that was coming from it.

For several hours this continued, until Joleen began to think bitterly to herself that she no longer cared for an artifact, that she would be happy to simply have the pain stop. These thoughts never touched her lips though. Orthine had been through this, as had Meterove. There was no reason that she could not hold out.

Soon that statement seemed to her to have been highly arrogant as the pain was quickly doubling. Looking down at the anvil in hopes that the artifact would appear nearly done Joleen felt despair. The ore that had been in the forge was barely more than a roughly shaped set of double ended daggers. There was far more left to be done.

Seconds turned to days, minutes to weeks and days to years as she stood unable to sit to fall to anything! She had reached a phase that Orthine had described to her. From this point on there WAS no turning back. Orthine was now using magic to hold her in place so that she did not move and potentially damage or destroy her soul.

At last, when Joleen thought that she might succumb to madness if she were in pain any longer the magic holding her was released and she was lowered backwards into a small leather armchair. She looked up at Orthine who she could see though it looked as though she was looking through a very dirty window. Distantly she heard her say, "Rest now Joleen. The forging is over.   All that remains is for me to temper the Artifact. I shall wake you when it is ready." Joleen walked over to one of the chairs and practically fell into it. Before she knew it, she had closed her eyes and fell into oblivion.

What felt like minutes later to Joleen she awoke feeling slightly uneasy. She was exhausted still yet she had felt a certain awareness that had caused her to awaken and looking around saw that Orthine was sitting in a chair next to her watching her anxiously. Seeing that she was awake Orthine smiled. If Joleen looked and felt exhausted, it was nothing to how Orthine looked. She looked as though she had aged years.

Sitting up slightly Joleen had opened her mouth but Orthine held up her hand forestalling the question saying, "I have a pretty good idea what you are going to ask so let me say this first so as to save you energy. The sensation that awoke you was you. That is to say that you sensed your soul which now resides outside your body, forged within this artifact. It takes some getting used to but eventually you will get used to the sensation."

Joleen nodded, she really wished that she could sink back into the chair and sleep for hours, days even, but she knew she needed to get back to the palace. Orthine handed her an ornate ash box about three feet long by two wide, engraved with her family's crest. "Here is your artifact. I must insist that you return to your chambers at once and rest before trying to explore your artifact."

She helped Joleen to her feet and once she was steady Joleen prepared to leave. Joleen stood there for a moment mentally preparing herself for the walk back. As she steeled herself to leave the room, she thanked Orthine once more then walked towards the door. Reaching it hand on the doorknob, she turned and looked back at Orthine about to say something, but as their eyes met something seemed to transfer from her to the older women through the gaze and Orthine said, "Don't worry I will."

Joleen smiled wearily and opened the door and made her way back to her chamber. She was exhausted so she followed Orthine's advice and stripping; she lay down in her bed and was instantly asleep.

When Joleen awoke, she looked out the window and thought that she had only slept a few hours. She walked across the room when she suddenly became aware that she was not alone. Taking a stance that Meterove had taught her she prepared herself to fight only to have the form drop from shock.

Sitting at the small desk she used for letter writing was Narok who, though he seemed unabashed to be there was still averting his eyes. Joleen was suddenly aware of her nakedness and her first thought was to cover herself.

As this thought passed another took its place. Why was Narok there, and why hadn't he said anything? Taking a deep breath in preparation to begin lecturing and interrogating him, Joleen found herself cut off. His voice was slow and deliberate, inflected to show that he was not going to mislead her.

"I can hardly wait for the tongue lashing that is sure to follow this part of the conversation but let me answer a few of those questions before they are shouted at me. First and foremost, I am here because your father asked me to watch over you while you recovered. There are any number of people out there that might be interested in taking advantage of you in that state. You having an Artifact made, without consulting him has caused his highness much worry."

Joleen's eyes widened a little at this.

How had he known?

Narok continued, "The next question that you must have now, is how I knew."

Don't read me so easily!

"When you had been unconscious for two days, he sent me to the academy to speak with Orthine. His guess was correct and, once that was confirmed, he ordered me to stay within this room and protect you."

TWO DAYS! How had she allowed herself to sleep for that long? She had work that needed her immediate attention, work she wanted to get caught up on immediately now that she knew of it. However, Narok had not finished talking yet.

"Now for that last part." Here he smirked slightly, and Joleen blushed. He was referring to her nakedness now. "I was in shock when you stood that is why I remained silent and as far as what I saw-" His voice trailed off a little, yet he continued a moment later, "Let us just say that I saw more than I should but that I averted my eyes once the shock subsided." He paused then added suddenly, "If you would like you may magically erase the memory."

This last part surprised Joleen. Throughout the entire statement Narok had kept his gaze off her which limited her embarrassment, yet this new offer nearly eliminated it. Erasing memories was not often done, since targeting memories was difficult at best. It would more than likely cost Narok more memories than just of this embarrassing encounter.

Also, that ass knows full well that I never got around to erasing the last time this happened. So, why is he offering to let me do it now?

Now that her own shock was fading some of her wit was coming to her aid so instead of anger, she decided to toy with him a little. Placing her hands on her hips and moving her right leg slightly forward and to the right Joleen rolled her shoulders a few times then paused to enjoy the effect.

Whereas Narok had been calm and cool a moment ago, albeit slightly uncomfortable, he now looked moderately uncomfortable. While it was hardly ladylike Joleen could resist pushing him a little further, so she walked over and stood slightly behind and to the left of him leaned forward and placed her hand on his shoulder saying, "Well I thank you for your concern and for keeping watch over me, but I see no reason to erase that memory. Now she leaned forward and whispered, "It can be our little secret. After all it's not like this is the first time."

Narok looked confused for a moment, then turned and looked her full in the face and now it was her turn to feel uncomfortable. He had looked at her again and this time there was no doubt that he had gotten a good look at her. Blushing deeply Joleen had to consent defeat. She walked over to her armoire and pulled out a set of forest green robes, which she put on noting that Narok was looking away again.

That was weird. I didn't erase his memory of the other day so what was with that look? It was too natural for it to have been an act. Someone else perhaps? No, we were the only ones there so no one would know to do it. Whatever I will think more about it later.

Once she was dressed Narok looked at her again this time slightly expectantly and Joleen after a moment glaring said, "Fine that was your win. I would like something to eat would you be so kind as to escort me?" Narok smiled they had played this side of the game many times before. "It is my duty to keep you safe until his highness sees fit to change my task."

Together they left Joleen's chambers. It had been this way since they were children. Narok's father had been Captain of the Royal Guard before him and was a good

friend of her fathers. They had often used excuses like this
so that Narok could spend time with her and her brothers.
Her father could not have cared less it was more to keep the
nobles that supported him happy that they used excuses like
guard duty to justify them spending time together.

True before the other day Narok had not seen her
naked since they were very small children and even then,
how much he remembered from back then was likely vague.
Him seeing her naked now was more than a little mortifying
yet he seemed to have let the matter die already for which
she was thankful. Though perhaps he was saving it for the
right occasion, keeping it in his back pocket for when he
needed something from her?

She noticed that Narok had brought the case with
them. He truly did take this matter seriously. Joleen sighed
inwardly if only they could be as carefree as when they had
been children.

***Eh, I guess that wouldn't make him a very effective
guard then, would it?***

Joleen made her way to a small seating area on a
balcony that she enjoyed asking a servant that she met along
the way to bring something for her to eat. The servant
wasn't gone for too long, likely, she had only had a few
words with one of the cooks before returning with a small
serving tray. Joleen had barely even had a chance to take her
seat when the maid brought her food. This balcony was a
small dining area that was set aside for the family.

Taking a seat at the table Narok laid the box containing her artifact atop the table. His back to a wall watching her, but also alert to any potential dangers. The box drew Joleen's eyes she wanted to see it, yet she was nervous. The thought of seeing her soul in front of her scared her slightly. Narok understood what was going on in her head and said, "It's not as bad as you think."

Joleen closed her eyes. That was right. Narok had an artifact as well. After Joleen had finished her meal and the maid had cleared the table she reached across the table.

Joleen opened the box and looked down. Within were twin rods that had a small section in the middle that was wire wrapped and large enough for her hands to fit comfortably around them. Taking hold of these objects she felt a burst of heat rush up her arms and the rounded sections changed. Now they held the appearance of double ended daggers that curved out at a very slight angle.

Placing them back into the case they returned to their former shape. Joleen somehow understood. It would be dangerous to carry them on her as they had been, so when she wasn't wielding them, they would revert to a less dangerous appearance. It was kind of like placing them in a sheath, only her willpower was the sheath.

Looking up at Narok who had been looking at the weapons with an appraising look, raised an eyebrow. Narok noticed her gaze and said simply, "It just surprises me that you got a weapon is all."

He looked as though he wanted to say more but now wasn't really the time. Closing the case Joleen made a mental note to investigate them more thoroughly at another time. For now, she just wanted to rest a bit more and looking up at Narok smiled, have some time where they were not Princess and Guard but nothing more than two old friends having pleasant informal conversation.

CHAPTER 5.5
CRACKS

It was truly fascinating to watch the story unfold around this tiny entity. He had always been so powerful, so far beyond reach of all the others that had been around him in terms of power that his ability to perceive what was dangerous to him seemed to have not developed.

He had met with several legendary existences on this journey, yet had no idea that it had even happened, of the significance of them. Well, that may not be entirely true. Afterall, he had to have felt the effects of his Story being etched into his back.

The others, again such a concept was odd, were also interesting to observe. The female was moving around and interacting with a great many others. The other male was minimizing his exposure to the Records of Time and was instead attempting to find the answers that he was searching for, in a slower, roundabout manner.

Interestingly there were a few other rather interesting beings that were on the edge of joining these three. These others needed just the smallest of pushes to become as interesting as the first three. One could become a leader, while the others would be followers, though the kind that needs a firm hand to keep in check. The sheer number of females that the one had joined with was already more than cause for concern.

.   .   .

What was that? Why did it feel as if "things" had just cut out, then were restored? This was not normal. Was there a period where things were lost, or did it just freeze? What had happened then if in fact there was a lost period? Observation was over for now. This new development needed to be investigated.

CHAPTER 6
INSIGHT

Jolson was alone...as usual, in his study. Very few people came to visit him anymore. Ever since it had become known that he had oracle abilities people had left him well alone, which he had found strange at first believing that people would be pestering him for information about their futures. Instead, he had been greeted with a quiet so complete that sometimes he thought that he might go mad from the lack of sound.

Today however, he did not regret his isolation from the world. He needed to concentrate as much as possible on his task. His time might be limited as likely as it was infinite so he might as well get done what he may when he could.

Reflecting somewhat ruefully that most people's minds did not work this way...that they worked in so much a simpler way with far less confusion, he wished for a simpler life or that people would understand his own. Of course, it didn't help that he was frequented by insights from the future and occasionally scenes of the past.

Right now, he was moving between two areas of study. He was putting himself into trances and pursuing all information that he could through books to find an answer, or at least more information that might explain his vision.

At the moment he was perusing ancient texts on the time of the creation of the Veiled Lands and The Veiled. There wasn't much of interest so far, as much that had been written was of their terrible power and the fear that they had inspired. Here and there though, Jolson was able to pull a fragment of information that helped him. Over time the fragments formed something of a whole that allowed him to understand what he was seeing.

And what he found was far from helpful. If anything, it only showed their situation as getting graver. Standalone observations that by themselves meant nothing were slowly drawing a picture in Jolson's mind. The race as a whole was of magic as had been suspected but there seemed to him that there was something more.

There had to be a source...an origin to this evil race, and not just them but to evil itself. There existed scrolls that predated the age when the The Veiled had been born that spoke of great evil and of a mighty upheaval of fire lightning before a long calm that ended with appearance of The Veiled.

It was believed that some of these evils may well still exist for there was nothing to suggest that they had all been destroyed. There were numerous examples of this in folklore scattered across the races. If legends were true, then the White Mountains to the south weren't mountains at all but the bones of one of the ancient evils that had been brought low by the gods.

Then there were the beliefs of the other races. Of those only the tales of the elves and dwarves were known to Jolson. The only thing known about the dwarves' religion was that it had something to do with gods and dwarves being brought into the world by being grown from stone much like a flower from the soil.

The elves on the other hand there was a fair amount known about, though little was understood of their religion. For the most part elves believed that the world was formed during an explosion of sorts and that over time life appeared.

There were no longer any gods only what they referred to as the "one that is four" that acted as guardian of the world and other "planes" that existed alongside the world they lived in. It had never made much sense to humans and dwarves considered it blasphemy to even hear the elves speak of it.

It was into these and many other areas that Jolson searched long and hard... looking for even a fragment that might help uncover more information that would light the way. Looking at the ceiling of his room which was a gigantic time piece he found that he had been at work for only a few hours and yet he was already drained. Sighing he prepared himself for a long day and buried himself among the books.

In the middle of a particularly dull passage in a scroll about a brief war between Yxarion and Vlander Jolson suddenly went rigid. He barely had time to register that he was going into a vision outside of his self-imposed trances before he was completely consumed.

Two teenagers stood in the ruins of a city wielding magic of a level he had never witnessed. The area through which they walked seemed familiar yet there was no place with ruins like that anywhere he had ever been. Then it blurred and went to a frozen landscape with a large black citadel in the distance and an evil blue glow from the top. Then all went black...so black that all was gone.

This confused him for he had never had a vision where he had been aware in blackness. Then it seemed to recede, and he saw a great black bird. He knew not what to call it...it was large with black flames...or what looked like flames...and it seemed to him that it emanated much evil and hate. So much hate that it was almost painful to just sense it. Around this black bird was a shell of purple energy. It was unable to move and as he watched, it tried to shatter the shell around it. Then his eyes opened...the vision was over.

This new turn of events interested him greatly. What had he just seen? He grabbed a roll of parchment and a quill and ink and went to work quickly writing all that he had just seen. He wasn't worried about not being able to remember it but hoped that maybe seeing it written might help him understand some part of it.

He closed his eyes and replayed his vision in his mind making sure that he had written every part of it down. Opening his eyes, he began to read what he had written down only to find that it made just as little sense as the vision had in his head. How the two teenagers in the ruins, the black citadel in the middle of a frozen land and a great bird encased in black flame and trapped within a shell of purple energy fit together was beyond him.

He was so curious about this new vision that he set aside his current task for a moment in hopes of finding more information on this matter. He left his study sure that if the information existed in their possession, then it would be in the Academy Library.

Just outside of his study there was a glyph that he placed his hand on. In a flash of green light, he vanished and reappeared inside the Academy Library. Walking over to large desk he sat and placed his palms onto two glyphs on the desk which brought up a touchable display of energy.

From here he could search the entire contents of the library to see if there was any reference to a black citadel or a bird of black fire. He was fairly certain that nothing would come up and was proven right on the bird. The closest reference was the dragons, which having seen a dragon before Jolson knew that his vision hadn't been that. However, a small notice had appeared.

Ancient historical archive. Must be viewed in person only.

Annoyed and intrigued in equal measures Jolson took down the location of the source and left to search for it. Only after standing and looking at the location did he realize where he was going. There was a tablet protected by many enchantments in the very bottom floor of the academy.

It was not viewed often for few could understand what was written upon it. Wondering what he might find after examining it he walked over and placed his hand on a glyph and appeared on the bottom floor staring at one of the few items in the room, the tablet.

Calling it a tablet had always seemed a stretch to Jolson since the stone was nearly fifty feet in length. Its sheer size and the fact that the writing was not large caused a certain foreboding in Jolson. Before him were many hours of tedious boring work that most likely did not have anything to do with what he was looking for.

Unsure as to what he was really reading only made his situation all the harder. He could read the archaic runes well enough but since the tablet was worn and was obviously only a fragment of a whole, his comprehension was by the very nature of the situation hampered and incomplete.

He sighed to himself letting his eyelids droop for a second in weariness and suddenly a vision flashed in front of his eyes. It was brief, only a handful of seconds, but it burned into his brain. The same black citadel but this time he could see a single line of runes inscribed in the courtyard.

Most of the runes were translatable but several made no sense, and one was completely foreign. Placing his hand over a small square area with a rune inscribed at the top Jolson muttered an incantation and brought up a display in front of him. Using his finger, he copied the runes and set the glyph about tracking it.

The system wasn't perfect since every time that it would chance on one of the runes it would leave it glowing but, in the end, nearly a third of the way into the tablet was a section with quite a lot singled out, selecting that section on his display a quill bound by enchantments to the glyph scratched fervently across a piece of parchment writing out the section he wanted.

When the quill had vanished from sight Jolson rolled up the parchment and made his way back to his study. Locking the door Jolson went back to his desk unrolled the parchment and began to read. While it was true that Jolson was hardly the most experienced when it came to these glyphs, he had seen some of these only rarely and as for the one that he found incomprehensible he was unable to find any other recorded use of the symbol.

This puzzled him since there wasn't any other symbol that was even remotely like it. Whatever it meant it was sure to be important. As for the rest of the glyphs, the translation was roughly; Darkness shed from the fire, the water, the sky, and the earth, fell into the world from{   } now until the end.

Jolson looked down at the parchment frowning. He was certain that he had translated it correctly, yet it made little sense. He was sure that the citadel he had seen was somewhere in Umakk, or Veiled Lands as many people called it. That made it highly interesting, though he wasn't sure as to what the correlation was yet.

The two teenagers walking through the ruins made no sense at all to him. They must be something either far in the past or future, thought Jolson. Still, what importance they had was hidden from him.

Shaking himself mentally, Jolson decided that there was nothing more that he could get out of the information and decided to set it aside for the time being. Looking around the room Jolson was trying to decide where he was going to look next to try and find more information, when it hit him again.

.   .   .

He came out of the vision shaking; his body wasn't used to such stress. Looking down at his hands the gems were glowing far brighter than he had ever seen before. His body began to spasm and again he was launched into the vision again.

He emerged coated in sweat, and barely able to unclench his body. His muscles were screaming in agony and there was blood leaking around the emeralds in his hands. What was going on? Why was this happening to him? He was starting to panic.

Barely able to control his body he lifted his hand and muttered an incantation and the parchment burst into flames. He lay where he was on the floor and after several minutes before he came to his senses and though it was beyond reason, he felt comforted now. The parchment had caused the visions he had no doubt at all as to the "what" it was the "why" that baffled him.

Pushing himself up Jolson wiped his chin for a small amount of foam had collected during his episodes. Heaving himself off the floor and into a chair, he picked up a quill and pulled parchment towards himself and began to record what had happened, sure that Joleen and Meterove would find it interesting, and also, he was certain now that it was intertwined with their own investigations.

When he finished, he sighed to himself looking out the window. It was going to be at least a week before Meterove returned and that gave him plenty of time to look into the matter some more, but for now he was going to rest.

.   .   .

Eternal twilight, the continuous embrace of darkness was all that the world seemed to hold at that moment in that place. There was nothing for any of her senses to perceive and now that she came to think of it nothing to remember either.

What was hearing and seeing? For that matter what was she and even more perplexing who? Suddenly, as though these musings had woken some part of her being a spotlight shown through the ink that was the surrounding her. For the first time she was able to see what was around her.

She was sitting on a carved high back chair with gargoyle heads on the armrests. This was sitting on top of a platform made out of some black wood that held the appearance of being slightly decrepit while seeming quite recently built. Perhaps it had been built to give that aura?

The spotlight shown down on her from a massive tower in the back of...what was this place? Looking around it seemed quite large yet the area where the spotlight shown from was far from the tallest area... the center...where she was at. Looking up she saw a faint dark line that as she followed it, she came to see that it connected two large polls.

Turning in her chair she could see many more objects in the background that were but faint outlines. A large box was sitting on the platform as well as a massive iron case that was roughly man shaped. In the distance there was something ...something large moving yet she couldn't make out what it looked like.

Turning back to the front she froze with terror.   A chair similar to the one that she currently sat on was now sitting some ten feet away from her and sitting in it was...the only word for it was a child. Yet no child had ever come into this world, or exited it for that matter, that looked like that.

It, for its gender was impossible to guess appeared to be around ten years old. It had shoulder length filthy matted black hair and every bone in its body could be seen on that emaciated frame. The skin was as inhuman as could be...a sick gray almost like ashes that in some areas appeared to be charred.

The eyes, however, were the worst. They were sunken, solid green except for a horizontal slit of red that were the pupils and leaking large quantities of black coagulated fluid out of them. However, it was the look of savage glee that was in them that rendered them truly horrifying.

As she watched it raised its right hand and snapped its fingers with the sound of charcoal rubbing together. To her left a man walked up to the stage and making his way onto it walked over to the great wooden box opened the lid and climbed in.

The child now spoke, and its voice made her blood run cold and her hair stand on end. The high pitch of a child yet with the gravelly sound of an old man; a true perversion of nature to be sure, "Stand and take up the blades."

She was unsure what it meant by this and was resolved to do nothing when against her will she felt her body stand and walk over to the box next to which a rack of swords now stood. She placed one then another and another through the box. On the eighth one she felt something different there was resistance and with horror she knew what it was, yet she was forced to push and from within the box came a scream of agony. She could feel herself reaching for another sword and tried with all her might to resist yet there was no stopping it. As she placed another sword through the box more screams of agony came forth accompanied by a gleeful peel of childish laughter from behind her.   Seven more times she did this until at last there were no more screams issuing from the box.

Now the child had stopped laughing and looked slightly crestfallen that it had gone silent. Then its expression brightened, and it snapped its fingers again and the box fell apart, the sides passing through the blades as though they didn't exist, revealing its contents. Wanting to scream, to vomit she could only stare down at the man in horror and grief. She knew him...she knew it. Unable to place it but certain all the same she recognized the figure contorted agony with the blades still sticking out of it.

Again, she heard it snap its fingers and another persona, a woman slightly younger than her get up and stand upon the stage. She walked over to the great iron box and opened it. Now the younger woman walked over and climbed within. Looking at the front part that she had just opened she felt a stab of renewed horror.

Large spikes were fixed to the front of the lid and again against her will she felt her arm reaching up to close

the lid. As it swung closed, and a single cry of agony filled
the darkness around them she was able to let out a single
sob. She had known her as well, though how she couldn't
remember at that moment. Turning back around she could
see the child rolling around in its chair, laughing.

What kind of horror was this? What creature could
take such joy in suffering? Thinking that this creature could
hardly do anything worse she now begged in her mind,
praying for death. It straightened up and suddenly there was
a low growl from over by the chair and yet again its snapped
its fingers and this time one of the swords spun in a circle
and with a large piece of the man's abdomen attached flew
across the room and the child caught it and after a brief vile
smile began to gorge itself.

Too busy eating to snap it merely waved its hand and
suddenly there were several cries of fear as from far above
her three children and an elderly couple plummeted from
the wire above them each leaving a bloody pile where it
landed. Suddenly understanding came to her. Her name
was Landra and...and...those people! That had been her
husband! Her parents! ...and her children!!!

Looking around again as tears filled her eyes, she
knew what she was in. It was a massive circus tent. Looking
in the distance she could see that the large creatures she had
seen earlier were elephants, emaciated like the child.
Looking around there was no people in the stands watching

apparently this show was just for the foul creature in front of her. She wanted to destroy it with all her might, yet she could do nothing more than stand there.

Suddenly she had a set of instructions come into her mind. She had asked for death, but it had not occurred to her that it might come in this fashion. The horror was overwhelming and as she walked over to the center of the platform it occurred to her that her family must have been every bit aware as she had been.

Suddenly she was placing her right leg over the back of her neck. Her left arm went underneath that. The creature sat enthralled in its chair as she forced her body into an imposable shape...one that tore her body apart, as she did it screaming in agony

The child stood and after a momentary pause walked over to Landra who was now bleeding from many areas where the skin had torn and many of the joints had separated. Seizing her right hand despite her whimpers the child pulled with superhuman strength and ripped her arm off. Landra let out a single scream before going into shock.

As it walked away from her, her own arm dangling over its shoulder, the world sped by beneath her. The whole room was now gone and the last thing she saw before the lights faded from her eyes was a large open field filled with black and ash gray silk tents and horrible skeletal animals.

.   .   .

Yuromea trotted his way up a trail at a leisurely pace. His paws were tired from the long trip, and he really wasn't in the mood to rush. Besides, it would be a total waste to not take in the beautiful scenery as he went by.

Hikoa had certainly done an excellent job landscaping the lands. On both sides of the trail were a number of Cherry Blossoms that were imbued with her energy to be in constant bloom, filling the air with their sweet scent. Every so often he would pass under a torii.

This meeting had to be of great importance to call so many together and to call them here, the birthplace of his kind. Turning a corner Yuromea was struck with awe at the view. There was a massive valley below filled with Cherry Blossoms and to the right of it the trail continued, and he knew from stories that just as many trees were to the right of this trail going up the hills.

In front of him he could see the temple shining red and gold, its clay tiles showing the emblem of the goddess in bright silver. Now Yuromea picked his pace up, his tails swishing in the wind behind him. After a few minutes he caught up to several more of his people. One he knew to be named Ychien and one other that he didn't recognize.

He wasn't going to slow down though. He simply kept up his speed. There was no way that he was going to be the late one now that he knew it was avoidable. Passing them at a fair pace so as to not invite a race, which sounded exhausting, Yuromea passed under the last torii and entered the temple.

Inside the main courtyard was a large garden. A pond in the middle with several large rocks placed so that each was equal distance from two of its brethren. Outside the main garden sacred stones were scattered in the grounds.

Clearly birds were a problem around here. At the edge of the pond a length of bamboo, cut to allow water to drip into its hollow body, clacked against a stone, emptied of water then tilled back up to a small trickle that came out of a small pile of rocks like some miniature waterfall.

A number of lotuses were painstakingly placed around the pond so that no matter what angle one looked you could always see a sacred stone framed between two of them. This place was clearly run by the traditionalists.

Yuromea understood their views but still felt that their fears were exaggerated.

It was because of the traditionalists that their people had stayed on the island for so long. This isolationist view had preserved their people and culture but had also slowed their progress. Many of the younger Spirit Foxes had never even seen a human for one thing. This amused him for they were able to take the form of humans if they so choose. Taking the form of something that you had never seen and based on the current laws would likely never see was, in his opinion, pointless.

Now that he was within the temple grounds he transformed into his human form. He had never cared about vanity, so his form was slightly more, wild, than some of the others. Long black hair fell past his shoulders, and he wore a simple robe.

Without wasting more time Yuromea entered the temple and chose a seat that was somewhat out of the way. They could require his attendance, but he was not going in to be the center of attention, at least at first. He sat properly and proceeded to look around a bored expression on his face.

A young man who, based on the power that Yuromea felt from him was only a three tail was pointing at him and whispering to several others that appeared to be of similar power. They laughed to each other and seated themselves legs spread apart.

While he was not a traditionalist even, he had to draw the line somewhere. If you could not sit properly at least sit with your legs crossed! "Show some dignity children!"

The one that had pointed at him snarled and said, "Who are you to tell me what to do!"

Yuromea was about to respond when a voice to their left cut him off. "His name is Yuromea-Sunn, and you should mind YOUR manners Koetsu! Now apologize to your elder!" said Ychien

Koetsu looked at Ychien defiantly for a moment then lowered his gaze and said, "Yes father." Turning to Yuromea he said, "I apologize for my rudeness Yuromea-Sunn."

It was hard for Yuromea to tell if the apology was actually sincere. On one hand the boy was definitely rebellious. However even though he may agree with his father he clearly had enough respect for his father that he was willing to listen. That or he was just unwilling to challenge his father who last that Yuromea knew was a five tail.

Regardless he chose to accept the apology, "It is of no consequence."

Ychien sat next to his son and like Yuromea sat formally. Turning to the younger Spirit Foxes he said "Sit like Yuromea and myself. This is not something to be taken lightly. Even non-traditionalists like Yuromea-Sunn will agree that this sort of occasion requires a bit of formal composure."

While they certainly didn't seem enthused to be sitting in the formal way, the boys obeyed him for he had spoken with no room for deviation from the request. However, the boy Koetsu did lean in and whisper to his father who whispered back. Koetsu's eyes went wide, and he looked back at Yuromea.

Yuromea chuckled to himself. Apparently Ychien had told his son about him. Poor kid had no idea who had been talking too. "Ychien-doma your son seems to be a curious young man."

Ychien smiled and Koetsu blinked once. Apparently, it surprised him that Yuromea held his father in such high esteem. "That he is Yuromea-Sunn."

Here their conversation came to a close for the room had filled and now the elder council had taken their seats at the front of the room.

Akira, Misa, and Chizuru were the oldest of the female Spirit Foxes. It had long been tradition to have the eldest living females rule over their people. Traditionalists existed in both genders though there was a growing number of those who thought that their ways were outdated and perhaps it was time for some change.

Akira was the first to speak, "We thank all of you for attending this meeting. It is good to see that even those whom we don't necessarily see eye to eye with were willing to attend." Her eyes flitted to Yuromea briefly before returning her attention to the room.

"We have called everyone here because there are events that are transpiring in the outside world that have come to our attention. Yuromea's attention sharpened at this. If the elder council were bringing up the outside world, then things must be bad.

"While these events have no immediate impact on our people, they will eventually reach us. Like a ripple in a pond the effects will start out small and become far reaching. War has broken out in the west."

At this muttering broke out among those assembled. Yuromea was greatly worried by this. War was never good, especially if it involved the humans. He was worried now about his old friends back in the west. He had aided the humans during the Necrotic War, fighting against the

Vorthains. He had seen far more death than he had ever wanted to.

The sound of his own name brought him back to his senses. "Yuromea-Sunn you are one of the few of our race that have been to the west in last hundred years. What can you tell us of this aura of darkness and war?" said Misa

Koetsu whispered "Sunn?" He looked between the elder council, who were all awaiting his response, and Yuromea. Who was this man? The elders were all seven tails and yet they spoke UP to this man! All his father had said was that he was of higher status, but this was something else. Yuromea remained silent and many of those assembled looked confused as well. Well at least he wasn't the only one that didn't know who this guy was.

Finally, Chizuru spoke, "Come Yuromea-Sunn, he of nine tails please speak to us what is on your mind." There was an audible gasp around the room. Koetsu's mind went numb. NINE tails! There was no higher status! No wonder his father had spoken so respectfully to him and the elder council too! But why did HE hold my father in such high esteem? Chizuru had waited for the whispering that had broken out to subside before continuing, "I know that you have something, or you would have already spoken up."

Yuromea spoke slowly "To be perfectly honest I was worrying about some old friends in the human world.

Remembering the part that Ychien and I played in ending the Necrotic War and something that I have never told any other Spirit Fox, save Ychien."

Koetsu looked up at his father's face. It had gone quite serious. He had never seen him that tense before. Then again, he had no idea that his father had ever been to the west either. Another thrilling thought occurred to him. His father was a war hero!

Ychien said, "You are worrying about her, aren't you?

Yuromea nodded. The elder council looked back and forth between the two expectantly but patiently. After a moment Yuromea spoke again. "When I was in the west, I met a woman named Corinne. We fell in love and had a child. That child grew up and fell in love with a man that came to be one of my closest friends. A man that not only was I willing to show my true nature too but even considered him my equal. Together with Ychien I fought beside him and several others as Captains against the necromancers of Vorthain."

A great deal of muttering broke out again. While it was not uncommon for Spirit Foxes to become friends and even lovers of humans in the past for this to happen under the current isolationist conditions was unheard of.

The Elder Council showed some disquiet at the close of his story but refrained from open judgment. Yuromea was sure that they feared what might come from pursuing such a topic such as this under the current conditions.

Misa spoke again, "You still haven't given your opinion on what reason there might be war brewing over their again."

Yuromea said, "That is because I have none. It is possible that Vorthain has done something to escalate tensions again but somehow, I doubt that. The fact that you were able to sense this from so far makes me think that it is something bigger. What I can tell you is that now that I have heard of this, I need to look into the matter myself."

The elder council looked at each other. This was it thought Yuromea. This was the breaking point. They had spoken of the outside world, solidified his status and opened the doors to fear.

Misa was the first to speak, "We will allow this as this matter seems to involve us now whether we like it or not. Let us know when you are ready to depart."

Yuromea bowed; a gesture that kept the elder council's anger in check. He may be a nine tail but the three of them combined could still easily overcome him, the

elders thought smugly. He closed his eyes and whispered,
"Be well old friend."

CHAPTER 7
TEMPLE

Shivering, numb, and with a headache that the gods would fear, Meterove came to the edge of the forest. He paused briefly after exiting marveling at the seamless change that the ancient Elven magic created between the frozen lands behind him and the near rainforest in front of him.

Stepping out of the forest Meterove felt the temperature change instantly. Dropping his pack to the ground he began to remove his warmer layers and proceeded to stow them in the pack. While he did so he took stock of his surroundings.

Dense plant life populated the forest floor while trees twenty paces across rose hundreds of feet into the air, the needles blotting out the sun except for occasional patches. Here and there a squirrel skittered across a trunk and the birds sang as if it were morning, though by his reckoning it should be late in the afternoon.

Shouldering his pack Meterove started on the difficult task of locating one of the ancient roads in the forest.   Walking into the forest a bit Meterove made small cuts into the trees so that he could find his way back.   After a few miles he found a section of the forest that was clearer and using it as a reference made a wide circle scouting for a road.

After two hours he returned to the clearing having found nothing except a large stone which he could use as a second reference point. Going back to the stone he repeated the process this time coming across a few cobblestones. Looking up he could see some light high up in the trees. It was getting late so he decided to make camp.

Laying his bedroll down and dropping his pack Meterove made a small cook fire. After he had eaten, he dug a small whole in the ground which he filled with water with a spell. With a wave of his hand the water suddenly took on a perfect replica of the night sky.

Examining it Meterove concluded that he needed to head east from his current location to reach the mountains and once there head north. Ending the spell Meterove went over to his blankets and slept.

It didn't take long the next day before he reached the mountains. From there heading north he arrived at the temple by midday. It was so corroded that it was impossible to tell what it might have looked like when it had been built. It was hard enough to discern it from the mountain itself.

Meterove had been about to enter the courtyard in front of the temple when something caught his eye. Half a dozen corpses littered the courtyard and by the make of their armor they appeared to be Vorthens. While it worried him that Vorthens had been here it wasn't exactly a surprise.

Meterove surveyed the courtyard but saw no signs of danger at the moment and so went to examine the bodies. He could tell well before he had drawn level to them that there was something odd about the corpses and once, he was standing next to them he saw exactly what.

The large amount of blood that surrounded them came not from wound but rather that there were no bones within the body. Armor, flesh, organs, and blood lay in a position of a dying man yet acting only as an outline. Bloody footsteps were next to each body. A crash ahead of him drew his attention and he crouched behind a low wall and watched as a man stumbled out of a side door.

Clearly unaware and moving in jerky motions the man walked halfway across the courtyard then started to mutter to himself.

"Escape...they not...see us... No eyes to see us. Cannot become one...do not want to live dead."

The man fell forward and began to convulse. Meterove half rose to go help the man but quickly lowered himself back down with a look of horror.

The bones of the man's left arm ripped free of the flesh and then the right arm followed. Both hands were placed on the ground as if to push him up but instead of lifting him his skull, shoulders and spine ripped out of his body. Finally pushing itself into a crouch, this tore the rest of the skeleton free of the body.

Standing it looked down briefly at the corpse from which it had come then walked back towards the temple entrance...the eerie sound of bone scraping on stone as it walked.

Behind the wall Meterove was doing his best to master himself. He had seen his share of blood and had even dealt killing blows to man and beast alike, yet this sickened him.

That man hadn't died in battle; he had been turned by some foul magic into an undead monstrosity. Yet it was an undead unlike anything he had ever heard of. Everyone had heard the tales of necromancers that raised the corpses of their enemies to fight for them, but it had always been a body that retained its appearance of humanity.

This was magic of a kind that these men had clearly not expected which meant one of two things. Either a necromancer that had come with them had used them for some kind of experiment or there was something here that they hadn't had the power to defeat.

The sound of more movement made Meterove look back over the wall. Five of the creatures were walking over towards him with weapons and shields. Apparently, he hadn't gone unnoticed. More noise came from the temple entrance as a large number came running out towards him.

Until that moment he had known that something was wrong about the situation but had been unable to pin it down. Now it hit him full force. These creatures were able to walk on holy ground without turning to ash. Something had corrupted the temple itself.

Standing up Meterove raised his hand palm out and sent a volley of magic at the attacking skeletons blowing many of them apart. Up close he noticed that the eye sockets had a nimbus black energy that somehow emitted a glow. He now drew his sword.

He sparred with two of the creatures for a minute before catching them with a single strike with his sword severing their bodies. Four more had reached him by this point and he noticed that the ones that he had blown apart earlier were piecing themselves back together again.

He parried attack after attack and even broke a few bones on the skeletons, yet they persisted. He was about to deliver a powerful stroke and sever another spine when pain shot through his ankle. Looking down he saw the upper half of one his earlier kills attached to his ankle it closed its hand tightly like a vice crushing bone.

Without thought Meterove drove his blade down through the skull of the creature and after a scream and small flash of black energy it moved no more. Understanding now how he had to kill them Meterove fought with the remaining skeletons careful to let momentum carry his blade through one swing so as to be planted in the skull of the other creature.

Calling on magic again Meterove fired another volley at the creatures this time aiming for the heads. Many fell but those that hadn't been hit had learned from their fallen comrades to dodge the volleys that Meterove sent at them as he fought with the four nearest him.

Catching the blade of one on his cross guard he drew his dagger and thrust it upwards into the skull, yanked it free then threw it at another. One more swing managed to remove the heads of the two remaining and a quick volley cleaned up the courtyard.

Meterove let his breath out in a burst as he leaned against the wall and tried to regain his breath. After a few minutes he made his way cautiously towards the door.

Looking inside he saw at once that there was no more undead and proceeded inside. In the center of the room was a large hole that went into the depths of the temple.

Off to the left was a passage the lead down to the next level. Following it carefully Meterove made his way ever deeper inside. The smell of rotting flesh was heavy in the air and much of the temple was crushed and as he entered the main chamber of the temple he saw why.

Curled catlike in the center of the large chamber in front of him was a dragon. Meterove had seen several adult dragons in his life but this one was far larger than any other he had ever seen. As he watched, its wing shifted and what he saw made him step backwards with a curse.

Now that he could see properly, he noticed that the noxious odor was coming from the rotting flesh of the dragon. Here and there were great gouges and in some cases a hole that went clear through its body. Its wings had holes in the delicate membrane and its tail was nothing but bone.

Fear, true fear was pounding through Meterove at this point. What kind of evil magic would be strong enough to turn a dragon? Killing a dragon in itself was no easy feat and their bodies usually had enough magic left in them to protect them from undead influence once they had died.

He could draw only one conclusion...this had something to do with the Veiled. The very thought that such an evil might be this close to his home worried Meterove but more than that...the Veiled had not been seen in so long that many believed them to be nothing more than a myth and that the lands across the mountains, which were said to be theirs, were simply home to monstrous creatures like giants and not the land of the walking dead.

He had been brought up to believe that they were deadly beyond any human warrior and that sheer numbers were the only known way to defeat them. However, he was no regular warrior. Looking around the cavernous room for something that might help him his eyes fell onto the stalactites above him and the dragon.

Unlike many things in the room, they were left almost exactly as they had been formed. The only difference was holy glyphs that would normally spread holy magic throughout the room.

A grin spread across his face. He had an idea now and not a moment too soon. From the sound of things, the dragon had awoken, perhaps it had heard or smelled him, though regardless of the reason it was awake and scanning the room.

Then it spoke but in a language that Meterove had never heard before. The very sound of it made him go cold. It was an evil sound that was for sure; nothing at all like the voice of a dragon. The dragon roared and Meterove made his move.

He jumped out and charged the dragon at full speed, his sword raised. The whole time he ran his mind was slowly regaining focus, though fear was still there. The only thought going through his head was how crazy this was... one man charging a dragon...and an undead dragon besides.

The whole time the dragon did not move, but merely continued to stare at Meterove as he charged. It seemed to be assessing the threat of this small creature, and then when it apparently decided that he warranted response got to its feet. Taking in a massive breath its eyes gave off an even stronger nimbus of black energy until its capacity was reached and it sent its torrent outwards.

Meterove was ready for this and leapt to the side and behind a large statue. His initial confidence in his safety vanished when he noticed that the statue was in fact becoming molten. Behind him he saw that part of this section was being used to store some of the dragon's horde. Apparently, it had not lost all of who it was.

Catching sight of a tower shield, Meterove grabbed it and brought it to bare in time. The fire hit the front of the shield and persisted for a few more seconds before it ceased. The dragon roared again and Meterove casting the shield away charged again. The dragon reared and prepared to buffet him with its wings but in a blink of an eye Meterove had gone.

Appearing at the joint of the right wing Meterove swung downwards in the hope of severing the wing. The blow wasn't strong enough and the dragon reared again throwing Meterove into the air. He landed halfway down its back and was forced to grab one of its spines in order to stay on.

Sheathing his sword Meterove pulled out his dagger and using a combination of that and the spines made his way up the dragon's body. With every stab of the dagger into its flesh the dragon roared in anger. He had it angry and disoriented...it was now or never.

Firing a volley of magic at the ceiling he caused several of the stalactites to fall two of them puncturing the body of the dragon; one in its left wing and one in its right flank.

It hit the ground with a loud crash and a terrible keening moan. It was far from done though it whipped its tail around and though he saw it Meterove was too slow to react. It hit him full in the chest and he was thrown across the room.

Colliding with another statue before hitting the floor he was dazed he knew that he had at least a few broken ribs and after coughing up blood knew that he was bleeding internally. He needed to finish this soon or he was going to risk bleeding to death.

The holy symbols seemed to be doing the trick though. The dragon was unable to break free and it seemed to know this for it was trying desperately to remove them and finding it impossible turned its eyes towards where Meterove had been but was gone again.

In no condition to charge head on Meterove had decided to try and sneak as close to the dragon as he could. Peering around a corner he saw that the dragon was once again trying to free itself. Jumping forward with his swords held ready he thrust the sword into the dragon's neck. It snapped its head back towards him and he took advantage and planted his sword in the center of its left eye.

There was another scream similar to the one that the skeletons above had given yet different and far louder. The nimbus left the eyes but unlike the skeletons some of the reanimation magic remained and the dragon spoke again and this time Meterove was able to understand.

"I thank you human for freeing me..."

And before Meterove could say anything the magic escaped, and it was finally able to rest.

Who had this dragon been? And more importantly who had reanimated it and why?

A sharp pain in his chest brought him back to reality and after a few spells he knew that the bleeding had been stopped but he was still going to need to check in with a healer to make sure everything had been done right.

Wrenching his sword from the dragon's skull he walked back over to where it had been lying to begin with. On a pedestal not ten feet away was what he had been looking for.

It was a small idol that was used by the ancient oracles to search for answers by giving them the ability to partially guide their visions. It was made of black stone with emeralds set into the palms of the figure. Jolson had warned him not to touch it if he could help it, so he used a small piece of cloth to hold the idol while he placed it in his pack.

After one more glance at the corpse he made his way back up the stairs noting that the unnatural feeling was gone...that indeed the holy feeling of the temple was returning.

It was as he was ascending the stairs that Meterove noticed the doorway off to the side of the chamber. Curiosity getting the better of him he walked back into the chamber and over to this side chamber. It seemed odd to him that there was something else here. By the look of the stonework, it had been done after the temple had been built in the first place.

Pushing open the door Meterove walked inside. Once he had cleared the door it slammed shut behind him and a barrier went up. "Well, THAT'S not good." Turning to look over his shoulder he saw the barrier...arcane based with what appeared to be holy reinforcement. Tough to break, but not impossible however, Meterove's attention had already shifted to another matter. Why such high security measures? What was in here?

Scanning the room, he saw that there were three doors off this room, each with runes above them. While

Meterove was hardly an expert when it came to runes the meaning behind these were very clear. Meterove let out a slight snort of laughter. Life, Love and Wisdom, were over the doors from left to right. Of course, there were more words but those were incomprehensible to him. This was so cliché it was sad. Here he was in an ancient temple and had found the paths to those three goals. Ha!

More than likely this was some sort of training area for priests for the temple. Shaking his head Meterove decided that he might as well take a good look around those rooms anyway. Deciding to start on the left and head right Meterove opened the door and walked through it. Maybe this WASN'T as cliché as he had thought.

He was standing in a massive oasis, great palm trees and ferns all around him. He distinctly heard the cry of birds that were NOT like any that he had ever encountered. Turning back to the door he saw a large stone archway with a door hanging open on it that led back into the chamber he had just left. This was weird and needed to be looked into.

Suddenly the ground shook beneath him and looking around Meterove took a step back. A massive reptile-like creature was walking past not even twenty feet away. It most closely resembled a dragon, though it had no wings, had much longer legs that ended in round feet and a small domed head on the end of a long slender neck. It was chewing on some of the palm leaves.

As much as he wanted to look around, he was in no shape to start exploring an unfamiliar jungle-like area when there were creatures like that around. Meterove knew from experience that when there was something that ate plants around there tended to be another that was capable of eating it and had no desire to meet it in his present state.

He stepped back through the door and closed it behind him and with some trepidation opened the second one. Given how literally the last room had taken the word life he could only imagine what Love was going to be. Stepping inside he entered a strange room. There was some creaking and sunlight streamed through spaces on the wall.

Looking closer Meterove saw that it was the gaps between planks of wood. There was also the slap of water. Guessing that he was over some water Meterove let go of the door and it, like the one earlier, slammed shut behind him. Walking forward Meterove could see more of the room now. In the middle of this place was a large section of open water that looked as though the light outside reached far into its depths.

Floating in the middle of this water was on oddly shaped object that looked like a blade of red metal that had an extra blade that protruded at a slight angle from the base and side of the main blade. Each had an oddly shaped blood groove. And the bellies of the blades were pure white.

Stepping forward Meterove peered over the edge into water. Under the water there was a second shape that appeared to be the same as the floating blade. There was odd feeling of malice that seemed tied with that shape and as he looked at it again, he noticed that it was very far below him. Looking around he saw that there was a staircase that climbed upwards and looking up saw that it went far into the hundreds of steps.

Looking back at the blade he thought. He was clearly supposed to take the blade for some purpose but what exactly he was unsure of. Using magic, he pulled the blade over and as it met his hand, a deep echoing roar came from the water. Looking down Meterove's heart skipped a beat.

The thing that had been in the water was getting larger and at an alarming rate. Meterove sprinted for the stairs and hit the first landing as it broke the surface. He had seen whales smaller than that thing and its body was oddly disproportionate. It looked like a whale that had no fins except a massive dorsal fin. Its body it seemed was flexible like a snake and its head was like a whale's, yet it was full of serrated teeth.

Now was not the time to be making notations of its appearance and Meterove continued to sprint up the stairs. The creature had hit the area where he had entered and destroyed the floor and even tore part of the wall away. Still heading up Meterove saw that part of the stairs had come down where the wall had been damaged by the creature.

Luckily, it wasn't more than he could jump. After taking the leap Meterove looked down and panic returned, and he began to run. The creature was making a second attempt to get to him and this time it was moving faster.

There was a huge roar and water sprayed past him and the stairs behind him were crushed under its bulk and briefly Meterove looked into an eye that held no life yet looked at him with immeasurable hate. It hit the water and swam deeper than before then turning around and attacked again.

Again and again, it thundered to the surface in an attempt to crush him. Twice it nearly succeeded and Meterove was forced to use magic and even jump onto the creature as he jumped to safety. Just as Meterove was giving up hope of getting out of there he saw it. A landing was coming closer with a door. Reaching it he tried to wrench it open, but it refused to open.

The creature roared again and Meterove blasted the door in desperation. Nothing happened. A loud crash pulled his attention downward. The creature's fin had torn open the wall the landing was on and there was nothing there, just open sea.

Not sure what getting though the door would even do Meterove continued trying to open it. Thinking of the blade he had picked up earlier he looked for some way of using it as a key but there was no place that a key could even go. As the creature hit the landing Meterove jumped and caught hold of the ring on the door. He had nowhere to go now and as he dangled here the blade slipped from his belt and he grabbed it.

At that moment, the door gave a small click and a brief mental picture of a young beautiful woman flashed across his mind then was gone. Pushing off the wall the door swung open and after rocking back and forth for a moment Meterove managed to get himself through the entrance as the wooden tower collapsed behind him. Looking out the door he saw nothing but water as far as the eyes could see and nothing that could have supported the tower.

Not wanting to have anything more to do with that place Meterove shut the door and looked around. He was back in the chamber where he had started. What that whole ordeal had to do with love was beyond him, but he wasn't that concerned at the moment. He sat down on the floor to catch his breath and noted that the barrier was still up.

After what he had just been through his confidence that this barrier could be blasted aside with ease was gone. He had to complete his trials here to leave. Once his breathing had returned to normal Meterove got up and examined the last door warily. Life had an oasis, Love had an experience that made him want to kill a whale or two, now what in the gods' names was Wisdom going to be?

That answer was not what he had assumed. There was no monster waiting to attack no traps. In the middle of a small stone room was a pedestal and on that pedestal was a game board. It was an old strategy game and on one side of the board was someone Meterove had not seen since he was a child.

His grandfather looked up at him and gave him a smile and gesture for him to come over. Drawing level to the game board Meterove eyes were on his grandfather that had been dead for over ten years.

"Before you even ask," he said, "I am a manifestation of your memories."

Meterove looked into that aged face and said sadly. "Then you're not real." At this his grandfather looked stern. "Are you saying that your memories are false? That I never was?"

Meterove was slightly taken aback at this. It certainly was an odd way of thinking, yet not untrue. His grandfather seemed to know what had gone through his head because he said, "That's better, now let us have a game like we used to."

Meterove smiled and gave a small nod. He picked up a black piece and placed it on the board. His grandfather took a white one and placed it on the board. Back and forth they went trying to block each other's intersections. The game went quickly with Meterove losing in the end. He never had been able to win whenever he played this. In his youth that had gotten him so angry.

Now however, he accepted it and even enjoyed it slightly. What fun was there in always being the best? What was left to strive for? In fact, the more he thought about it the more it made sense. Wasn't there always supposed to be someone better or cleverer than yourself? At this his grandfather laughed. His body faded away and the last words he spoke came in an echo.

"You have grown Meterove. Continue to make me proud."

The door behind him opened again and turning to leave thought to himself that it was quite odd that the room in which he had lost was the one where he had gained the most. Exiting the room, he saw that the barrier was still there. Resigning himself to the fact that he had to enter the first room again and complete its challenge Meterove walked over to the first door and went through it.

Back in the oasis Meterove wandered around for a bit before coming across what was an all too convenient situation to be coincidental. A much smaller version of the creature he had seen earlier was trapped in a mud pit and was desperately trying to escape a panicked bugling roar coming from it.

Noting that the creature was unlikely to survive if he left it Meterove went to lift it out with magic only to find that it wouldn't work. Puzzled Meterove looked around and saw a number of stones that were engraved with runes. Magic

canceling auras were the last thing Meterove needed at the
moment. He was already sore as it was.

Meterove looked at the creature. It wasn't much
bigger than him. If he went in there, he, with his boots and
hands would have an easier time getting traction. Resigning
himself to getting bruised and very muddy he dropped his
gear by the side of the pit and climbed down into it. He got
behind the creature, which now that he was right up on it
had a slight purple color with large black spots began to push
it up and out of the pit.

As soon as he touched it the creature panicked again
and swiped its tail knocking Meterove down into the mud
and then brought it down hard on his chest. Well, he had
expected that, so he got up and tried again with the same
results. Trying a third time he managed to get behind it as it
made a lunge for the edge of the pit and with a huge shove
pushed the creature up and its front feet found the edge.

Now it pulled itself out and ran into the foliage
crashing through the brush. Meterove climbed out of the
mud and lay down at the edge of the pit. After a moment he
got up and hoisted his gear up and onto his back, then made
his way back to the door. He wanted to leave now. Exiting
the doorway, he saw to his relief that the barrier had
dropped. Running to the door he wrenched it open and
almost ran back to the stairway, which he followed up to the
courtyard

Moving across the courtyard and over to the edge of the forest he stopped and lowered his pack. Little though he wanted to, he put his warm clothes back on and after a moment's hesitation cursed and then stepped back into the icy darkness.

.　　　　　.　　　　　.

Jolson walked around his study in careful movements and measured steps. His episodes two days ago had exhausted him and, as he had found out after he awoke the following day, left him with very stiff and very sore muscles. Reaching across his desk for a book Jolson gave a slight flinch and groan.

"That was a bad life choice" Jolson grumbled. There had been a lot of those over the last two days. Many of the movements that were natural were now quite painful at the moment. This wasn't a new situation to him but was inconvenient all the same.

Shifting the position of his shoulder slightly to take the pressure off a particular muscle, he brought the book closer. Jolson paused to roll his shoulders and stretch his neck a little before bending back over his research.

Boring, tedious and with an aura of hopelessness about it this path had, without a doubt, been the slowest progressing one he had yet taken. Looking into the little information that there was on the disappearances and grisly deaths that were taking place had given him almost nothing of credit. What he had found was hardly something that was hardly fit for a tangible investigation.

The facts if you could call them that were simple. All the victims seemed to die in their homes with no explanation as to how no one in the neighboring homes had heard anything. The state of many of the bodies, the looks of agony for one thing, could leave little doubt that they had not been taken by surprise.

In addition to that there was the variation and types of wounds that were just plain baffling. Bodies crushed, severed, torn, and burned, as well as being in impossible positions were just the beginning. The worst were those bodies that appeared to have been gnawed upon.

Jolson leaned back and flinched again, "Bad life choice," he mumbled. He looked up into the clock, it was getting late, and this was certainly not getting him anywhere. All that he had found was that, based on the condition of the bodies and the area around them the only possibility was that some form of transformation or illusionary magic had been used.

That did almost nothing when it came down to finding the one who did it. The killer or killers could use magic, now were they a domestic or external magic user? Were they even human? Jolson shook his head; there were too many unanswered questions about this at this point. What he did know was that it was time he went to bed and maybe he'd investigate his vision tomorrow since this avenue was leading him nowhere.

CHAPTER 8
KNOWLEDGE

"Magic. It is the most powerful force in the known world and at the same time it is the most fragile and the most divided. There are many different types or schools of magic and there is no one thing that more than one school can accomplish."

Jolson was sitting in a corner of one of the lectures being given at the academy. He well remembered the last time he had heard this particular lecture. He had been nearly seven at the time; the same age as the children in the room at present. In fact, he had had the same instructor and to this day had the speech memorized.

"While the four 'modern magics' are the ones that are the most well-known it is prudent for ones beginning their instruction to be aware of a fifth school that carries a large number of sub-schools within it. This school is called primal magic. It is dubbed so because it is the most basic and most powerful of all magic.”

How he ever sat through this once was a mystery to Jolson and he was cursing Joleen for making him do it again. She had clearly looked ahead to find out when this lecture was going to take place and made sure that he was free and that she was occupied.

“At present we know of five sub schools, and it is presumed that there are at least another five if not more left to be determined. These five sub schools are: Life, Death, Soul, Elemental and Inscription. Now the reasons for their names are as follows.”

Gods above, below, and everywhere else! Why am I here? Looking over at some of the students he saw that his suffering was not only mimicked on their part but had been noticed to their amusement. How lovely that the students that would be in his class later would be able to discuss their instructor’s appearance of acting as though tortured by another lecturer’s lesson.

“Life magic is somewhat of an oxymoron since it gives the impression of purity. The fact is that it has this name because it requires life to fuel the spell. Unfortunately, the life used is ultimately lost. For this reason, it has been dubbed a demonic magic and is not tolerated.

Death magic on the other hand may be practiced in extreme circumstances as long as you remain within the guidelines given. The reason is that instead of killing someone or something, as the name might imply, it requires something to already be dead to use a spell. There are few circumstances during which this magic is considered acceptable, however. One such time is on a battlefield and even then, it is limited.

The last of this trio is Soul magic, possibly the most devious type. This magic uses the soul of whom or whatever is around as fuel. This can backfire on a mage if say there was nothing around alive and a spell were intoned then the magic would consume the soul of the caster.

A branch of Soul Magic, called Forging Magic, is tolerated but only under close supervision and should not be attempted by anyone other than an expert on the subject as it takes the soul out of the body and places it within an object that is preordained.

An obscure but useful type is Inscription magic. This type of magic is rather straight forward and had little negative features. Any glyph that has magical properties from those that are used for transportation to those that store information to those that exist in temples to ward off evil are inscription magic.

The most well-known of the primal magics is elemental. One who can command the elements is a powerful adversary or ally and should never be approached carelessly. Such mages can call fire, ice, and lightning down upon their enemies; cause the earth to split apart or cause a great tidal wave. A true master might even be able to create a maelstrom or form a volcano on a whim.”

Around the room the children had perked up at this last mention. Jolson smirked to himself. He well remembered the excitement he had felt when that wonderful possibility had first been revealed.

“Of course, there is no record of any mage ever attempting such feats and some who tried certain lesser feats have often died in the process.

Now that you have a basic understanding of primal magic we can focus on modern magical theory and methodology. There are few sources of magic in the world and of those only one can be explained.

This source is a connection that certain people have to the veil. Being attached to the world of the dead allows a person to manipulate the world around them as they see fit. Now the first step is to...”

There was nothing else in this lecture that could even remotely interest a person. Deciding that the best way that he could spend the remaining time of the lecture was to search for any news of Meterove’s return, he stood up and walked briskly to the door.

As he closed the door behind him, he saw that all the eyes of the class were on him, so he took a theatrical breath and rolled his eyes, much to their amusement and closed the door grinning. He was already going to be a joke with them so he might as well be part of it; much the best way to shorten its life. His own private lecture on the history of their Empire was coming up next.

He had gleaned very little about the two newest arrivals in that lecture. Originally the plan had been to separate them from the other students, but Jolson had opposed that plan, so a hybrid lesson plan had been devised. It just did not sit right with him to treat them like they were infectious.

They had acted like any of the other children and yet there was deep power there. Stopping only to grab something from the kitchen, Jolson set off for his chambers. He had work to do; first was searching through the quagmire of visions and prophecies to find a current location of his brother.

The second task was to prepare a few scrolls in Soul Script for Joleen. She wanted some information readily available during meetings that no one else could read.

Soul Script was one of the few forms of inscription magic that was still known. The magic was simple yet potent and highly effective. You wrote anything that you liked onto a piece of parchment that you prepared beforehand with an enchantment that was bound to the soul of the person that was intended to read it. In doing this the scroll was only readable by a single person.

The downside was that if it was used in war time and the information was vital and the person that the message was intended for was killed the note was unreadable. Thus, this magic was used only when the person was expected not to be in the battle or if information was too sensitive to be readable by anyone.

Jolson sighed to himself. He wished sometimes that he hadn't been born into this, that he had been allowed to deal with common life where his cares were harvesting the land.

Before he knew it there was a gentle knock on his door. "Enter"

The two children, Norn and Telna entered. They looked a little nervous. Telna spoke first, "Good day your highness." Norn looked even more awkward than his sister but repeated her greeting.

Jolson smiled to put them at ease. "Good day to you as well. Take a seat and we will get started."

"Once they were ready Jolson started his lecture. "The empire as we know it has only been around for four hundred and thirty years. However, the original empire is far older. The old empire would later annex various territories through various means including conquest. That's not to say there were no peaceful negotiations, but those times were turbulent.

The exact year of the original empire's founding is unknown, though it is believed to have been over a thousand years ago. Records indicate that the original archives were destroyed in a siege.

As far as our origins are concerned, humans are not originally from this land. Scattered relics along with records kept by other races from their early encounters with humans confirm this.

It is unknown exactly what kind of cataclysmic event occurred on our home continent, but all our kind appeared to have abandoned it. These travelers founded countless kingdoms and city-states. Most of these would eventually become the empire. The few remaining would create the nation of Vorthain as well as..."

.   .   .

Knowledge is Power. That was engraved over the entrance to the mage city of Al'faeren. This ancient city was built on a pillar of stone that rose from the center of a bottomless chasm that surrounded it like an eternal moat.

The only way across was either a rune that allowed entrance only to those who were able to use magic or to have a mage do so and have the Gatekeepers lower a drawbridge. The Gatekeepers were the guardians of the city and the enforcers of the law. Great golems composed of steel; they were all but immune to magic and conventional weapons. It could take a dozen men, mages, or warriors, to take one down.

Having just used the rune to cross over into the entrance of the city Joleen was "greeted" by one that reminded her that she must obey the laws of the city or face punishment."

Joleen happened to agree with this city in a lot of ways. For one she liked that the Gatekeepers would not, could not, discriminate based on the person's station. Nobles and commoners were punished equally here. She also happened to agree with the statement that was over the entrance.

Knowledge was indeed power and if any place was proof of that it was here. There were maybe two places in the world that had a better claim to that, and none were human.

The dragons and the elves probably had the greatest trove of knowledge in the world but were unwilling to part with it. Few outsiders were ever allowed to read or, in the case of the dragons, hear what secrets they held.

Looking around Joleen couldn't help but smile. No matter how many times she visited this place it would always impress her; the sheer amount of magic was blatantly obvious.

Most of the buildings were towers in varying heights. Some were only twenty or so feet high and very narrow while others were many hundreds of feet high. The different races that converged here and brought knowledge were part of the reason for the varying sizes.

There were a few dwarves that lived here, and one might on occasion see an Acephali but the rarest was elves. There was only one elf tower in the city and only two elves lived there. Two of the very oldest of the mage council that ruled this city.

She walked through the city looking left and right as she went. There was always so much to see. Magical vendors selling figures that resembled some of the better liked creatures in the world that had animation magic in them allowing them to walk around.

There were also people selling tomes, calling out news of new experiments or the results of others or stores selling components for experiments. Weaving her way through crowds Joleen soon found herself nearing the city's heart.

As she walked the buildings became still older and far more impressive. Some of the towers were built out of solid gold or seemed to have been crafted out of a single piece of marble. The most impressive to Joleen, though, was the elven tower.

Just ahead was a giant redwood tree; easily a hundred feet across and far higher than she cared to guess at. This tree was grown, sustained, and protected by some of the most powerful magic in the world.

Joleen, however, did not stop but continued on until she came to the largest tower of them all. Directly in the center the oldest building in the city, originally built by the dragons it had been modified slightly inside to accommodate humans, but its proportions were staggering.

Stretching over a mile into the sky and nearly two-hundred yards across the Hall of Knowledge was the library of the mages as well as the meeting place of the council and where they met with visitors of note.

Joleen clutched the scrolls that Jolson had prepared for her. They would be invaluable in this meeting. They contained important information that could potentially be damaging if it fell into the wrong hands and information that would allow her to have access to information about those she was meeting with.

Joleen stopped before the entrance of the tower that was guarded by two Gatekeepers.

This was so pointless, this visit and yet it was also very important. The only reason she was here was that her father disliked the mage council and so sent her in his place. Taking a deep breath, Joleen prepared herself mentally for the relays that were ahead and walked up the stairs.

Inside she was greeted cordially enough but knew better than to think of it as them being happy to see her. This was business nothing more and with a client that wasn't high on the favorable list. Most of the business that her father supplied was in the form of the military. The mages of this city didn't look upon force as the way to go about things, believing in calm discussion.

They weren't foolish enough to believe all would follow their ways though. When threatened they could quickly mobilize a force that had the potential to hold off an entire army for weeks in a matter of hours. What she was bringing with her was unlikely to make them happy.

Her greeter led her to a chamber with a long table with around twenty chairs around it. Having taken a seat and sipping the tea that the woman had offered her she waited. She didn't have to wait long. Soon an elderly mage entered, and Joleen choked a little over her tea. She had not expected this. The head of the council had come to speak with her.

A kind face with golden yellow eyes and a slight limp he had gotten in a war some fifty years ago he was perhaps the mage that was the most receptive of her. Today he wore the sky-blue robes of the council trimmed in white. He stepped forward and clasped her hand between his own.

"It is good to see you again young lady. Have you been well? It has been far too long and from what I can tell you have done much. Tell me, how long have you had your artifact?"

Joleen smiled she wasn't surprised in the least that he knew she had an artifact and as far as his speech, how did you lecture someone that was an old teacher? "I have been well Korinth and as for my artifact it has been several weeks now. I have begun to understand it now."

Korinth nodded, he too had an artifact and knew full well how the process went. "I always knew that you were strong enough and that at some point you would become seduced by it and succumb to its lure."

It was a bit embarrassing having him phrase it like that. So, Joleen moved the topic along. "Yes, though its form is not what I was expecting. It took a combat form."

At this Korinth's eyes widened slightly, "Is that so? That is quite interesting."

Sighing slightly Korinth said, "and now to the matter for which you are here. What is it that your father would ask of us now?"

Joleen reached into her satchel and pulled out the scrolls and after verifying the information looked back into those sun yellow eyes. "Basically, my father wants a replacement for the Colossus."

If Korinth looked surprised before it was nothing to now. His skin momentarily lost some of its wrinkle his eyes had become so wide. "What does your father need to replace Colossus for?" It is ancient true but there is still nothing that can match it and the magic that was placed upon it can never be undone so don't try and tell me that it has malfunctioned!"

Here Joleen paused wondering how much she should say but decided on the whole truth anyway. "The keystone has gone missing, and we have no leads as to where it has gone or who has it."

Now understanding came to Korinth. "Your father doesn't want something that can just replace Colossus. He wants to be able to destroy it does he not?"

Joleen nodded; again, it made the most sense to speak the truth. Korinth stood and paced the length of the table several times over. When he finally spoke, it was in a strained voice. "He believes that there is a chance the thief is among my mages. That is why he sent you here. Your father is a shrewd man, not wanting to insult he made sure to ask only for a replacement."

Here Joleen felt the need to add to this thought before it spiraled into something ugly. "We are also investigating every mage within the Academy. Rest assured that we are not strictly targeting your mages."

While this did little to calm Korinth he seemed slightly less angry. "What else does he have to say?"

Now Jolson's scrolls would show their true worth. Straitening in her chair Joleen said, "The only other information we have is that the room that the key was kept showed signs of transformation or illusionary magic." This last part was not known to her father but had come from reading some of Jolson's research and from his observations. Joleen was banking on Korinth being distant from her father to pull what information she could from him.

At this Korinth seemed troubled. "Transformation magic you say? Are you sure?"

Joleen looked solemnly at her hands "As sure as we can be. We know it was one or the other. We have also had a number of incidents throughout Yxarion that have shown the same magical nature."

"What kind of incidents are these?" asked Korinth

Still looking at her hands Joleen said, "A number of grisly murders. From what has been found at the scenes the bodies weren't moved from where they were killed but had sustained damage from circumstances that could not all have happened in the area, they were found in. We suspect transformation magic because of the wide distances between the killings."

Korinth was silent for a long while apparently lost in thought. Finally, he seemed to come to himself and said, "Let your father know that all his requests will be attended to and that I am taking a personal interest in this matter.

Should I find anything I'll contact you personally. I'll walk you out"

Joleen nodded. She had not expected even Korinth to oblige her stay for very long. As she left the tower she thought back over her meeting. It had gone far smoother than she had expected. That worried her slightly. One thing that she had learned from dealing with the politics of the world it was that smooth meetings meant ulterior agendas.

However, if there was something that she needed to be worried about here there was nothing that her being here by herself with a small party of guards out at the gate could manage. For now, she'd act as though she had got all that she expected and that she felt all was right. After all it was possible that she was over analyzing things.

Making her way across the bridge again her guard was already standing ready to be off. That was good, she had much to discuss with Jolson.

.   .   .

Meterove mounted a hill and looked out over the view. This was what I like, he thought, freedom. He could see the city across the open plains nestled against the mountains with scattered buildings on its outskirts.

He was reluctant to return to the city. He much prepared being far away from the drama and tension that was his life. Sighing to himself he made his way down the hill and followed a simple dirt road that would join up with the Royal Highway.

Though he normally didn't mind being noticed by commoners he decided that it was more important that he not be delayed in getting back to the city. So, as he walked, he pulled his cloak tight around him and pulled his hood low over his eyes. Now to anyone but the soldiers he was nothing more than a traveler. The soldiers he could show his signet ring.

He walked along quietly, and people walked past him in the opposite direction nodding in greeting. As he reached the gates, he rotated the ring so that it would show the seal if he held his hand open towards the guards.

As he came up to the city a group of guards were checking people as they entered and left the city. One of the guards beckoned to him and Meterove walked over.

"Welcome. What business do you have in the city?" asked the guard in voice that was both strained and polite.

In response Meterove lifted his hand so that the signet showed to the guard. The man's eyes widened slightly and Meterove made to step around him, but the guard said quickly "Apologies kind Sir, but may I see your face?" with a slight emphasis on sir.

Meterove stopped and his first impulse was to have the guard whipped for stopping him but after a moment of thought he realized that the guard was nearly certain that the ring was authentic but thought it derelict in his duties if he didn't make sure.

Meterove didn't lower his hood but lifted it enough to show his face to the guard who upon seeing his face caught his eye and nodded. One of the other guards called over, "Something wrong Dras?"

"No, just making sure he wasn't one of our wanted men. You may proceed."

Meterove nodded back and after pulling his hood lower over his head continued on his way. He would have to mention this man to his father or take actions himself. He was a capable man that would be better suited in a higher station.

His return was the same as any other time. His father made him tell his tale over a small banquet like dinner to which a few choice people outside the family were invited...in this case the ambassadors had yet to leave and in an attempt to seem both gracious and have a chance to show off they were invited.

He told them of the werewolves in the forest the undead and the temple without much interest on the part of the listeners. When he came to the dragon however his listeners became far more interested; the Acephali choked slightly on his wine and his father swore.

"What force could reanimate a dragon? Their bodies are too magical for a necromancer to overpower!"

Meterove took a sip of his wine before continuing,

"I haven't an idea as to how it was done but personally, I'm more interested in the who than the how."

This statement sent anther shiver of tension down the table. After a moment, his father spoke again, "You said something about Vorthen soldiers?"

"Yes, there were several bodies scattered around and the one man that I saw alive briefly. They may have had something to do with what happened or they may have simply sensed the dark power that was there and went there hoping for some way to harness it."

"We will have to look into this matter. Given the circumstances I think it best if we retire early so, we can give this matter our full attention in the morning. Besides I'm sure that you are tired after your journey and would like a chance to rest."

With that their father stood and bade goodnight to the rest of the room and left for his chambers. Joleen and

Jolson caught his eyes and he nodded and stood with them and after bidding their guests good night on their way out the door they sealed the doors and returned to the table.

Joleen was the first to speak, her voice full of trepidation and interest in equal measures, "So did you get it?!"

Jolson who had appeared tired all through dinner now seemed wide awake. Meterove smiled and reaching into his pack he pulled out the small, wrapped bundle that was the idol and handed it over to Jolson.

While Jolson unwrapped the idol with trembling fingers Meterove said, "There's something about that thing that's just not right. I felt it when I touched it even through the cloth."

"That's the idol trying to force visions on you but not being an oracle, it only caused discomfort," murmured Jolson who had nearly finished unwrapping the idol.

Once the last fold fell off the idol Jolson placed his hands on the idol and immediately went rigid and fell sideways, lost in his vision.

Dark swirls everywhere. So little that could be discerned. He felt pain and yet he was pain, and it couldn't hurt. Time had no hold at the moment either; a thousand thoughts and images in the span of one heartbeat. Suddenly everything cleared and time suddenly became unrealistically rapid.

He was standing atop one of the towers of the city looking out over a huge army...the mustered forces of his people. Then he saw a dark mass of swirling shadow and death. Behind it was a lone figure standing with its sword in hand. Its clothes were tattered and its frame nothing but bone and the fastener of the cloak...the Valaseri coat of arms.

Another symbol flashed across this vision so fast that he barely caught it and wasn't sure but thought he had seen it before. Next, he saw something that turned his blood cold. A great black creature encased in a great purple shell of energy strained and with great effort made a small crack.

Then he saw a group of people head for the crack in the shell. He counted eight of them and as another burst came and widened the crack, they entered this shell. Time sped forward and the shell shattered completely and for the first time he noticed something more.

There was the feeling of many entities that all had very similar auras. They had been holding this thing within this shell and now it was free, and they were powerless to stop it.

The group of people was still there and now was engulfed in a shell but this one was white and as he watched they vanished traveling faster than he could follow through the very fabric of magic. They emerged outside the city of Yxarion.

Here his heart nearly failed him. The city was in ruin and monstrous shadows walked through its decaying corpse. Then he noticed that there were many bodies scattered around the city and realized that the people that he had followed back had returned to a battle.

As he looked around one of the seven people stepped forward and from the shadows stepped the same figure he had seen earlier, sword held tightly in his boney grip. Then they started to duel, and the fight quickly escalated and soon there were small sections of the city falling around them.

It wasn't long before the person was defeated and just when the final blow was about to be dealt another blow landed on the creature and it turned to see a new figure attack. Now the tide of battle had turned in favor of the newcomer.

.   .   .

Jolson gradually regained consciousness though getting his thoughts to form in any coherent way was far more strenuous. He could not get his senses straight at first. He appeared to see what he should hear, and he heard what he should have smelled. After a moment, things began to move back in rhythm.

He began to understand his surroundings and realized that his eyes were closed. Understanding this he opened them and saw two people moving around him. Looking around slightly he recognized his surroundings as well as his siblings.

"How long was I out?"

There was a moment of silence while the other two looked at each other then Joleen responded. "Several hours...you've never been that bad before...we...I was so scared. You looked to be in such pain."

"Nothing to worry about though what I saw may be of concern. I'm not sure exactly what I saw but I'm pretty sure it's a very bad omen."

Meterove walked over slightly and looking down into his brother's eyes said, "What exactly did you see?"

Jolson stared in his eyes, so alike his own, yet with depths of sorrow and wrath that were not. He knew some of what he was going to tell him, that much he knew. How and when he could have learned it were beyond his understanding.

"Jolson...What Did You See. Time is not on our side here...if there is something that I need to know about then tell me now."

"We need to prepare for war...brother. That is all I can say, at the moment. I need to rest more and let the images come back to me. Time may be our greatest adversary." He stared at his brother then turned his eyes to Joleen and locked eyes briefly before they rolled back, and he passed out again.

.   .   .

Discussion with their father the next day did not go at all well. Regardless of their insistence that there was danger ahead he insisted on meeting the Vorthens in the capital and even agreed to meet them in person in the open.

Disheartened with his reaction and disconcerted by the lack of intelligence that was coming in on the Vorthen envoy they did the only thing that they could...prepare for what their father wasn't.

Meterove woke early the next day because he had some extra tasks to handle. There was the matter of the academy, since he wanted to check up on the two children he had sent there.

In addition to that he wanted to review the defenses and have a chat with Narok. Then there was the matter of the guard that had caught his attention upon entering the city.

Since visiting the children and speaking with the guard weren't high priority Meterove spent most of his day going over the guard and keep defenses. After lunch he paid a brief visit to the academy where he learned that the children were doing well and had managed to not only catch up with some older students in material but had surpassed a few.

From the academy he made his way to the city guard barracks where he had learned he could find the guard Dras Bradok. A few words were all that were needed and after a moment a slightly nervous man was brought to him.

"Is there something that I can help you with my lord?"

Meterove smiled, "its ok you needn't be worried. I came to thank you for the manner you handled my arrival at the city entrance yesterday."

"Sir?"

Meterove's smile became more pronounced and Dras seemed to relax a bit more. "You showed quick wits and from what Narok has said you have been a commendable member of the guard, but I think I have a better use for you. That is if you are willing. I would never dream of forcing you to do anything."

Meterove looked at the man in front of him. He was definitely a strong man, in both character and physique. It only took a moment before he responded.

"Whatever you need me to do my lord I will gladly help."

Meterove nodded he had hoped that the man would say as much. "I'm going to move you from guarding the gate to bolstering the royal guard for a coming envoy. After which, should you work well there, you will remain a part of the royal guard. Your move will be effective immediately."

Dras' eyes watered slightly then he blinked once and said, "I can never thank you enough my lord. May I go home and tell my wife?"

Meterove nodded "You have a family then?"

"Yes, my lord a wife and son."

"Certainly, my friend you may. In fact, take the rest of today off. I want you well rested for tomorrow. I'll leave your instructions with Narok so seek him out tomorrow at sunrise."

Dras saluted, "thank you again my lord." Then he hurried off through the streets. Meterove laughed lightly...it had been a good day all around and as for this man, Meterove felt that he had made a very good decision. At the very least a fateful one for his back had burned yet again.

CHAPTER 8.5
SPLIT

Well...this was new... The mortal...no...it had earned the right to be called as the name that he was given. Meterove had done something that was unforeseen, but how? To encounter an Ice Apparition at all was exceedingly rare as those beings weren't even native to that particular world. For some reason they had crossed over and chose to interact with Meterove early. This point should not have been reached yet. What was going on? This isn't right. "We concur." Wait...we? When was it we?

CHAPTER 9
ATTACK

Meterove was nervous. Word had come of the arrival of the Vorthain envoy. They had been sighted south of the city and would be entering the courtyard in less than ten minutes.

That was little more that he could do, of course, but he still felt as though more preparation was needed. Looking around him he saw that his men were stationed at every post in double numbers. The new guard Dras was just visible standing slightly behind Jolson.

Meterove wasn't particularly sure why, but he felt slightly more secure with Dras here. The man hadn't even proven himself in battle and yet...there was just something about him.

Well, he might be wrong maybe the guards weren't a necessity. Maybe the Vorthains really were here with intentions of peace. Maybe the sun was black.

A horn sounded in the city and Meterove was awoken from his musings to see people running back up the street in clear terror. His hand gripped the pommel of his sword a second ahead of the guards.

The reason for the peoples fright was apparent a moment later. Through the archway slithered a giant venom green snake-like creature with great leathery bat-like wings and a head that was somewhere between a human's and a snake's, its eyes a vivid yellow.

Meterove had seen such a creature before. It was called a Shenrow and was the result of necromantic experimentation. The Vorthains used them in battle and apparently as transport for this one had a great saddle atop its back like the kind used on the elephants to the south. In it sat two men.

One was clearly the ambassador and the other looked to be a high-ranking military leader, likely a captain of the Vorthan's forces.

That was not all either. A procession of what were clearly soldiers in armor that looked too flamboyant to be anything but for show followed them.

As the envoy moved closer Meterove glanced sideways at his family. Joleen and Jolson both appeared tense and Narok was so still and tense he might have been in rigor.

What really surprised him was that his father was not only tense but had his hand resting on an actual sword not the decorative one that was usually used to meet envoys. So, he wasn't being overly trusting in the white flag...interesting.

The envoy came to a halt and the two men dismounted and one motioned for the guards to follow. Meterove studied them as they walked up the stairs to meet them.

The man on the left who was clearly the ambassador was garbed richly in what looked like a silk robe, yet the texture wasn't quite right. His skin had the deep sickly yellow color that came from practicing necromancy.

His eyes were what disturbed Meterove the most though. Where it should have been white it was black with a vibrant blue for the rest. Reminded him of the undead and dragon that he had seen at the temple.

The soldier was even worse. The same skin and eye color yet unlike the ambassador who looked well fed this man looked starved his skin pulled tight over his skull.

They reached the top of the stairs and after a brief glance around gave a short, almost mocking bow to his father before bowing to the others and then speaking in what sounded like a death rattle.

"Well met all of you. I am ambassador Yurek of Vorthain, and this is Kirandal our most decorated warrior. Do not worry he's along solely as my bodyguard."

Meterove's jaw gave a slight twitch, but his father spoke before he could say anything.

"Worry? We were not worried in the slightest and have no reason to be."

The ambassadors eyes seemed to glint with malice as he said, "Oh but you would if he were leading an attack...he has unmatched skill in both mêlée and the arcane arts."

He felt his jaw spasm again, but he held himself back. The bastard was actually trying to bait him into attacking.

He looked from the ambassador to the soldier and saw that while he appeared relaxed his stance said that he was ready to draw his blade at any second.

His father spoke again, and his attention returned to the conversation.

"So, is there any relevance to this talk or are you simply trying to intimidate us?"

Yurek smiled in a way that intensified his aura of evil and cruelty. "It was part of our peace offering that is all."

"You call that a peace offering?"

"But of course, you surrender to Vorthain and there will be peace. We have no desire for war so please let diplomacy do its work. Surrender."

"I will do no such thing. If you hadn't come in under the banner of truce, I would have you killed where you stand. Now take your people and leave this city!"

Yurek laughed softly, "I was "afraid" you would say that. Well time to die for your people Emperor Valaseri."

Yurek raised his right hand, and a blue glow effused him as well as the rest of the men with him, including the Shenrow. The guards closed in but in a split second all hell broke loose.

The armor fell off the soldiers who collapsed began to twitch and then the skeletons tore their way free of the flesh and stood back up grabbing spare weapons from their armor which reassembled itself over the flesh that remained and stood back up.

The Shenrow gave out a cry of agony before it split open and dozens of The Veiled poured out of it.

The two men raised their blades and attacked. Kirandal went after Meterove while Yurek began fighting his father. Kirandal's blade whistled through the air and Meterove was barely able to block it.

Meterove returned the favor with a powerful stroke that was deflected then rained another four down before

Kirandal was able to attack again. There was no question the man was an exceptional warrior, nearly as good as Meterove. Meterove was still better...at least he hoped so.

As they dueled Meterove blocked out most of what was happening around him but at times he could help but notice as a man fell screaming, or a skeleton fell apart near him. Twice he was able to see Jolson spinning his double ended blade slicing his way through skeletons and Joleen blocking blows with magic or healing wounds.

It was when his muscles began to ache that he decided the time had come to augment this fight with magic. He knocked Kirandal backwards and while he was off balance infused his body with magic increasing strength and stamina.

Renewed and confident that his new strength would end the fight quickly Meterove struck. Kirandal was barely able to dodge but he was able to bash him with his pommel then jumped back increasing their distance apart.

His eyes were full of rapture and an evil grin crossed his face, blue light emitted from his body and then he struck with the same speed and ferocity as Meterove. The battle raged on with each blow sending small shockwaves out.

Across the courtyard his father continued to duel with Yurek. Yurek snarled, "You fall today Valaseri, and your people will fuel our armies. None can resist the might of Vorthain especially now that Veiled Lands has gifted us its secrets!"

The emperor faltered a moment staring at Yurek in horror. "Why...why would you betray the living...your own people! Veiled Lands is nothing but death...there is no fighting with them, only for them!"

"Not true! They fight for us! We are supreme! All bow to us or will fall before us!"

The emperor's eye widened but it wasn't Yurek he was looking at.

A voice of power with a slightly ghostly essence spoke from behind the ambassador "Is that so Yurek?

Yurek turned around and looked up into the shrouded form of what could have been death himself.

Standing nearly seven feet tall and wearing a cape of black mist and wielding a sword of black metal was a Living Shadow, a Veiled Commander.

"I think our "partnership" is at an end Yurek but don't worry your people will serve us well."

Yurek had time to register shock before the blade pierced his chest and erupted from his back. He convulsed once then was still.

The commander tossed the body aside and walked slowly towards the king.

"Now as MY master commands...you die!"

And they began to duel but the Living Shadow was already augmented with magic...it was only a matter of time.

On the other side of the courtyard several buildings were on the verge of collapse from the intensity of their duel yet neither Kirandal nor Meterove was willing to give ground. Numerous craters from impact and magical explosions littered the area.

Each man was covered in numerous small injuries and several more serious wounds, but they continued to clash. Glancing across to where his father was Meterove watched as Yurek was killed and then tossed aside. Panic flooded his mind...father!

He paid for his momentary lapse when he felt a blade cleave through the mail on his right shoulder and blood poured down his arm. Enraged and panicking Meterove pushed further into his powers than he had ever done before.

Kirandal's eyes showed shock...he had clearly never seen anything like it and that was his last mistake.

A quick slice from his swords and a blast of energy from the palm of his wounded arms and Kirandal was split in two and his top half was blown into ash.

Meterove turned to where his father was in time to see him forced to one knee and as the killing blow was about to be delivered Dras came out of nowhere and took the blow to his shoulder which severed his left arm.

Meterove sped off across the courtyard but even Dras' sacrifice wasn't enough. Halfway across the courtyard it happened.

The Living Shadow stood over the emperor's injured body and thrust its black blade into his chest. IT didn't have time to ensure death though because Meterove plowed into the commander a moment later.

Rage and increased flow of power allowed Meterove to override the complaints of his flesh. Nothing mattered except to obliterate this monster.

The air itself seemed to crackle with power as they fought. When their blades met with enough force that it began to shatter pillars around them Meterove knew he needed to end this now.

Pouring all the power he dared into his muscles at once he struck at where the commander's heart should have been. Once the blade was logged within, he concentrated and used the most potent holy magic he could think of.

A beam of white light poured through the blade and began erupting out of every orifice...even forcing new ones in its attempt to escape the dark body it was being forced into.

The commander gave one last scream of agony then the body fell to the ground and withered returning back to shadow then fading entirely leaving only the blade and what looked to be a shriveled brain.

Meterove didn't stay to ponder this but ran to his father. Jolson and Joleen were already there, Joleen cradling his head. At first Meterove thought him dead but then saw shallow breaths and then saw the blood and knew that he wasn't long for this world.

Anger and sorrow mixed in equal measures rose and fell within him. His father's eyes locked onto him, and he spoke, blood dripping down his chin. "I know you will not fail me Meterove. None of you Jolson...Joleen...you will not fail me. I know this so I can accept death. I beg you...accept my blessings and love one last time."

Meterove nodded at the same time as Jolson. Joleen mopped her eyes and nodded.

"Live well my children and know I love you..."

Then the light of life faded from him, and he was gone. Joleen sobbed cradling his head and even Jolson shed a tear. Meterove wanted to but knew this was not the time. Looking around the courtyard he saw men helping wounded over to where they could get aid and moving the dead away from the monsters they had fallen to.

A groan nearby caught Meterove's attention, and he looked to his left a few feet to see Narok holding Dras and helping him to his feet. While he had failed it hadn't been his fault and the man had truly given his all in the defense of his father, so Meterove walked over.

Narok looked slightly worse for wear, but it was Dras that Meterove wanted to speak to.

"Meterove, I know that look and I must protest. This man needs rest."

Meterove held up his hand forestalling any more advice. "I'm not here to state that you failed your duty Dras...you already know that my father is dead. I don't believe you failed completely because you gave your all against a foe that was beyond you. Know that I bear you no ill will and in fact I may even consider you a friend now. You will get all the aid that we can give you. Now go rest and recover but know that I am going to come see you soon."

Looking over at Jolson he nodded and received one in return. They both knew what they had to steel themselves to do now.

They both looked at Joleen who continued to sob but seemed to sense them looking at her. She looked up into Jolson's face and then over at Meterove and she understood what they were thinking. But, no she couldn't, not yet. She stood and ran from the screen tears streaming down her face. She didn't want to think, to feel to know, just to run for maybe she could outdistance her pain.

Joleen ran through the halls refusing to stop until she reached her room. She threw open the door and slammed it behind her then collapsed onto her bed sobbing.

In the blink of an eye all had fallen to pieces. Joleen could not bear to look at her surroundings. To do so would be to accept all that treachery had done to her. For the first time in her life, she wished she could just fall away into nothing...to vanish and not feel.

But it had happened. The world had been turned upside down and its foundations shaken leaving her life shattered. She knew that her brothers were taking care of matters as far as security and transporting her father to where a ceremony could be performed. What need was there for her?

There was the almost inaudible creak of a door opening and the sound of plate boots on the floor. While she should have been at least wary of who was approaching her she couldn't muster the energy to care. Besides, she knew that stride so well that it didn't matter.

There was a clink of metal and then a hand rested on her shoulder gently yet firmly, giving the auras of comfort and safety with one motion. Joleen couldn't help herself through her tears and pain a small smile touched her lips., "Thank You Narok..."

"Yes, your majesty..."

The formality mixed with the familiarity was almost as bad as the fact that it reminded her that she was now queen and that her father truly was dead. While there was nothing that could be done about her father, she was not going to let a friendship die along with him. She turned and looked Narok right in the eyes seeing some of her own pain mirror in them.

If I must make this an order, I will, but I'd rather ASK this of you as a boon. Can you not talk to me as you always have? While you are my captain you are first and foremost my friend."

Narok opened his mouth then hesitated a moment before saying "If that is what you wish."

Joleen smiled and said, "I'd not have it any other way."

Narok nodded and looking slightly nervous said "I know that you are grieving but there are some matters that need to be addressed immediately. I would not be so impatient, but Meterove asked that I bring you to him immediately even if I have to carry you over my shoulder."

Now Joleen actually laughed. That was Meterove's own words for sure...so brusque. Wiping her eyes on her sleeve she then straightened her robes and nodded to Narok who turned on his heels and led the way to the throne room.

Joleen knew what was coming and dread and sorrow filled her heart.

When she entered, she saw that a table that regularly sat next to the throne had a crystal ball resting on the stone likeness of two dragon's forepaws. It was there to transmit her image to all corners of the kingdom into anywhere a subject might be. Beside the throne Meterove and Jolson stood stone faced.

She knew why. Both of them had far more experience with loss than she did having served as a captain and seeing visions. She walked forward and stood next to the throne for a moment staring at it but then a measure of strength built up within her. She gave one brief glance at her brothers and Narok before sitting down on the throne and placing her hand on the crystal ball.

The effect was immediate she could almost see all the different places she was speaking from within her mind's eye. Steeling herself she began to speak.

"People of Yxarion...today is a dark day for we have been betrayed under the banner of truce.

The Vorthains came to us speaking of peace and changing their ways but instead they attacked us and now my father, the emperor, lies dead. What's more is that it appears that they have gone even deeper in their betrayal as they also forged an alliance with someone or something from the

Veiled Lands. We are currently at war and are now in the process of mustering all troops. May Sweveryon guide us."

After she had addressed the people Joleen had set herself to the task of gathering allies, planning recruitments and battle plans for both offensive and defensive scenarios. She wasn't going to kid herself that she had a lot of useful input on most of those topics but then that was what Meterove was for.

In the three days since their father had been killed Meterove had worked tirelessly to create strategies as well as work with Narok to ensure her safety.

Today was going to be a long day yet with many hours of nothing while waiting for the different envoys to arrive. She had already met with several ambassadors from the Acephali, Leturai and Vlaadyri. Of them only the Vlaadyri were willing to do anything more than fight the war on their own fronts. The Vlaadyri had offered little in the way of soldiers but a vast number of resources and craftsmen.

Looking out of the window of her study Joleen noted that there was at least four hours before the Khantrad arrived to discuss what the dwarves would do for her, and it wouldn't be until evening that Olethe would arrive with support from the elves.

Deciding that the best thing that she could do at the moment was to take a nap Joleen stood and left the room heading for her bedroom. She was still in a daze, but she did notice, however vaguely, that six guards followed her from her study to her bedroom door, quickly checked inside then allowed her to enter. How strange her life had become in such a short span of time.

.   .   .

Meterove yawned loudly. He had been sleeping little the last few days, preferring to spend the time making, checking, and rechecking battle strategies.

He had not forgotten his promise to Dras though and now that he had some free time, he figured it might be time to make good on his word and check in on him.

So Meterove set out with one of the senior instructors at the academy in tow to the home of Dras Bradok. The walk took him through the heart of the city into a poorer but decent neighborhood. The homes around him were simple but well-kept and there were no beggars here.

Meterove knocked on the door lightly and after a moment it opened inward and there stood a young woman with brown hair and a common yet elegant beauty. Her face, which was initially puzzled, now shown shock and then slight anger towards Meterove.

He could not blame her. If Dras had been left guarding the gate, he would never have been injured. What she didn't know is that he was here to reverse her fortunes.

"Good day Madam Bradok. I am here to check up on your husband and perhaps give some aid."

Her jaw twitched but she nodded and stepped back letting Meterove and the instructor enter.

The inside of the house was simple yet cozy. It looked like quite a nice life thought Meterove. Sitting at a small table was Dras who upon seeing who had come to see him began to stand but Meterove motioned for him to stay seated.

"No please my friend, stay seated. I would not have you exert more energy than is necessary."

"Please your highness come sit...we don't have much but I could have some tea made?"

"No thank you and please call me Meterove. After what you did for my family, I owe you that at the very least."

Dras smiled and nodded solemnly "We are actually here to see what we can do for you Dras" said Meterove.

Dras' face shown with some curiosity, "What do you mean my lor...I mean...Meterove?"

Meterove smiled and nodded at the instructor. "This is Kylarin one of our senior instructors at the academy he thinks that he can create an arm out of magic that would replace the one that you lost. It would be composed entirely of energy so it wouldn't feel quite the same, but you would be able to do everything you used to and more."

Dras looked pensive for a moment then tried finding words.

"While that does sound tempting...you'll forgive me for asking, but what might happen if I allow you to do this?"

Kylarin smiled and said in a calming tone, "There is nothing that I know of that would be a drawback...unless you count that it won't be the same color as your skin and won't feel the same to touch."

Dras seemed pensive again then nodded. "As long as I can continue to serve and provide for my wife then I agree."

Kylarin stepped over next to Dras and began to chant under his breath. As he did the air around the room seemed to tingle with power. A small beacon of light appeared at his shoulder. It spread down forming the likeness of an arm all the while rapidly changing colors as though it were filtered through a prism. After a moment, the light seemed to solidify and gave one last change of color before settling on a deep blue. Kylarin stopped chanting and the air seemed to settle down.

Dras lifted his new arm testing the movement then picking up a cup from the table lifting it to his lips and drinking, tears running down his face as he did so. He looked into Kylarin and Meterove's eyes and whispered, "Thank you." His wife too was in tears, all she could do was to echo her husband's words.

Meterove stood nodding in acknowledgement. "This is just the beginning Dras.   It seems to me that our fates are intertwined and there is likely even more hardship ahead. I'll expect you to come when I have need of you. Until then rest and recover."

Yuromea closed the door to his home and began his journey to the small port that existed on the western shore. Along with his pack he also brought a set of three blades. First was his naginata that was nearly as long as his whole body. The other two were his katana and wakizashi. Instead of his kimono he now wore a set of leather armor that he had hoped dearly he would need again.

As he reached the end of the trail that led to the road to the harbor, he noticed a few people ahead. As he neared the pair, he realized that it was Ychien and his son Koetsu. Coming to a halt in front of them he noticed that Ychien seemed slightly tense.

Ychien seemed completely relaxed however when he spoke, "So you're heading out old friend?"

Yuromea nodded, "Yes things are moving apace, and it is possible that my aid might be needed. The time for Spirit Fox and man to fight side by side has come once more." Seeing a pack on the ground and seeing a very familiar set of weapons next to it he asked, "Are you intending to join me?"

Ychien sighed and said, "No not me. The time to fight may come however I am no longer suited for war. My son will accompany you if you are so willing. He has never known the world outside of our island. I would like him to learn of it the same way I did with you leading the way."

Yuromea looked at Koetsu and reevaluated the young man. Now that he looked the boy looked nervous but determined. It was his eyes that sealed it though. The last time that he had seen eyes like that it had been his father. This boy had steel in him.

Yuromea looked back at Ychien and said, "If that is your wish then I will take him with me Ychien-doma."

Ychien tried to smile but couldn't quite manage it. Yuromea understood. Part of him had hoped that he would refuse his request. Ychien took a knee and placed his hands on Koetsu's shoulders. "Follow his every order Koetsu. Trust him and he will not let you down."

Koetsu said "I will father. Do not worry about me. I will make you proud."

Ychien smiled, "Then you should be off my son."

The three said their last goodbyes then Koetsu shouldered his pack and took up his father's swords. Whether he would be able to use them with any kind of skill was yet to be seen but that didn't worry Yuromea. After all he had taught Ychien how to fight and if needed could do the same with his son.

They had barely started on the road when Yuromea felt the boy's eyes on him. "I can practically feel your desire to ask questions Koetsu. Don't be shy ask what is in your heart."

Koetsu looked down at the ground hurriedly but after a moment said, "Well Yuromea-Sunn- "

Yuromea cut across him, "There is no need to be formal. Soon our lives will end up being in each other's hands."

Koetsu paused then after a moment his voice shaking slightly said, "Well Yuromea I was wondering. Are you really a nine tails? I've heard of them before but as far as anyone I've ever met knows they were just a story."

Yuromea chuckled, "As far as most of our race are concerned yes that is just a legend. Not many of our race ever get to eight tails and it takes something beyond just getting older to progress to nine. However, to fully satisfy that curiosity of yours-" Here he transformed in his fox form.

His entire body was a beautiful vibrant orange except for the tips of his tails which were black and just as he had said there were nine of them. Yuromea transformed back into his human form and couldn't help laughing a little. "You know, your father had the same expression when he first saw my fox form."

Koetsu just continued to look at Yuromea in awe. That's amazing! How do you get your ninth tail? I know you get one every five years and after your third, it becomes every twenty years, but you said that you do something to get the ninth. So? What do you do?"

Yuromea looked down at the boy and smiled. "I'll give you a hint nothing more. It is something that in order to truly work you must find it on your own. That hint is simple think to yourself, 'what am I willing to sacrifice?'"

Koetsu looked puzzled. "That's the whole clue?"

Yuromea said, "Yes now devote a great deal of time and thought to that answer and maybe if you are lucky the correct answer will come to you."

Koetsu said, "Alright I will."

Yuromea said, "Hmmm...on a related topic you should know that you were only partially correct when you said tails grow every five and twenty years. That is just the natural growth of energy with our kind. However, with intense training we should be able to speed that up greatly."

Koetsu looked shocked. "What do you mean speed up? By how much?"

Yuromea chuckled, "Oh I'd say if you stick to my training, you'll be equal to your father by the time we reach the west."

Koetsu was speechless. How could that be possible? Or was this man messing with him? No, his father had said to trust him. Besides what he had heard about this man so far had turned out to be true.

Yuromea said, "Another thing that you don't know is that you can also lose tails. This actually happened to your father. At the height of the war, he had attained his seventh tail. However, our forces were cornered and outnumbered during a battle. I have never seen such an incredible display of heroics and self-sacrifice as that day. We managed to hold off a far larger force but at the cost of four of his tails.

He was never quite the same after that, but his sacrifice may well have won the war."

Now Koetsu understood why Yuromea respected his father so much. So many things that he had never knew or understood about his father. It was strange to think of his father as a war hero, a man that a nine tails respected, and nearly a martyr.

Koetsu said, "So do you think that I have what it takes to be like my father?"

Yuromea chuckled again, "You're too young to see for yourself but you already are very much like him. You have that same inquisitive nature, that analytical and decisive personality."

Koetsu looked very happy at these words and continued now with a bit more spring in his step. Yuromea smiled to himself. Yes, this child would do just as well as his father had. He was sure of it.

CHAPTER 9.5
MANIFESTATION

Now some sense of the situation was coming together. This was most likely caused by the discord. Somehow the discord had affected more than was originally believed, which was worrying considering the levels it had clearly reached already.

Being split into multiple selves was certainly an uncomfortable experience to say the least. While the division of power was inconvenient and having "physical forms" was going to take some getting used to, in the long run this might be beneficial. Double edged though they may be these new abilities that came with being many in number would likely make taking action easier.

The only problem now lay in the Fragment that was like the others, yet unlike them. So far it was not acting with the same intent as the others. Odd...never would have guessed that a side like that existed until now.

CHAPTER 10
GATE

Joleen sat at her father's desk...her desk, going over the intelligence that she had on the Vorthains, the forces of The Veiled that seemed to be growing in power far to the north in the frozen wastelands of the Veiled Lands, as well as her own assets and those of her allies. So far according to reports there had been a swarm of undead coming down from the north. Joleen had requested that the dwarves build a massive gate which she had sent Meterove with four thousand men to guard.

Between her soldiers and those that the dwarves had posted there she was confident that their position was secure for the moment. In the meantime, she had other worries. She had not forgotten the odd murders and powerful magics that had been plaguing the people. Jolson had mentioned a suspicion to her and was currently looking into it. If his theory panned out, then she would have one headache removed and another far more serious one would step forward to replace it.

That left her other allies to cover their own borders with little to no assistance from the forces of Yxarion. Some like the elves had no qualms about this and were more than willing to send some of their own forces to the gate to help while defending their own border from any incursion. The rest were not so generous; threatening to pull all their troops to hold their own lands and nothing more.

Supply lines were long, and Joleen was thankful that this was, at least for the moment, a defensive war. Once, as it inevitably would, became desperate enough that they needed to go on the offensive the security of supply lines would become another arduous task.

"So four thousand of my own men, another two thousand from the dwarves once all is built and another fifteen hundred Elven archers at the gate...need to make sure that I don't put too many men on the gate at once though...can't have forces wiped out if they get overwhelmed....so much that needs to be addressed."

Joleen had fallen into the habit of speaking her plans aloud. It helped her to organize her thoughts and allowed her to catch bad ideas and flawed lines of thinking before it could become an issue that cost lives.

She leaned back in her chair and went over in her mind the numbers in her head of her total armies...some hundred thousand total if she conscripted... fifty thousand if she didn't and nearly a quarter of a million if she took every able-bodied adult and gave them a blade. Well hopefully it would never come to that. For now, she'd leave her forces spread out enough that all couldn't be wiped out in one battle but near enough that aid could be received. She hoped...

.   .   .

Meterove sat on the ground outside of his tent running a whetstone down the edge of his blade. The fire next to him danced and reflected in the cold steel of his blade and armor and gave little warmth. Around him the soldiers rested fitfully they knew that the enemy would be upon them in days and that the gate would not be completed in time. All the hopes of their people rested on whether they could hold the enemy off long enough for the dwarves to finish building.

At Meterove's request the elves had remained behind at the gate so that in the event that he and his men failed there was still someone to fight back the undead at the gate. To ensure that his own men didn't fall only to rise as an enemy the elves had cast a powerful cleansing magic over them so that they couldn't be tainted by any common undead. In addition, the ground that they were currently camped on had been blessed so as to cause instant death to any undead that crossed it...as long as the charm could hold.

Meterove hoped to use that as a trap weakening the undead before they reached them. From what he understood the ground around the gate had been similarly blessed. Meterove checked the edge of his blade and satisfied sheathed it. Putting away his gear Meterove decided that the best thing that he could do was to get some rest.

.   .   .

It seemed as though he had barely closed his eyes when Meterove was awoken the next day by one of the scouts who reported that the enemy force was less than a day away. Instantly Meterove was fully awake. "Well done soldier. Get some rest then take word back to the gate and remain there."

The scout saluted "sir"

Meterove donned his armor then he left the tent and went to the tents of his lieutenants and had them rouse the men. Once roused he had them run back and forth behind the camp. Meterove wanted them warmed up in order to ensure that they were at their best.

The sun was at its peak before all the men had formed up behind the camp Meterove had them do some basic training exercises to wake them up. Looking into the distance beyond the camp a dark mass could be seen.

Meterove guessed them to be no more than twenty minutes march from them at the rate they seemed to be traveling. Turning to his men he spoke loudly...confidently, "The enemy approaches. We cannot let them get any closer to the gate. For all that we love and all that we cherish fight!"

There was a roaring cheer from his soldiers. They weren't going to fail him; they'd come back from death itself to ensure that.

After what seemed like an eternity the undead reached the edge of their camp and the charm activated. There was a massive flare of magic, and it looked as though the world itself was fighting to cleanse the taint of undeath. Gigantic roots erupted out of the ground and ripped through ranks upon ranks of skeleton soldiers like the tentacle of a leviathan, their shattered remains falling to the ground to be covered in fresh growth of plant life.

From what Meterove could see it wasn't just skeletal soldiers in the ranks. Vile creatures such as vampires, ghouls walking corpses and monstrosities that he couldn't even describe walked in the ranks as well or in the case of the vampires flew somewhat like a bat overhead their skin like that of one embalmed over large, pointed ears longer than an elf's and fangs that stuck from under their lips halfway through their jaws and demonic blood red eyes.

They had made it over halfway through camp now and while the damage that had been done was massive it didn't break the advance and they kept pressing as though those that had fallen meant nothing, which Meterove reflected were probably true from their perspective. An army for which morale didn't matter could be useful but only under certain circumstances.

Now the enemy had cleared the camp and Meterove drew his sword, behind him he heard others preparing themselves. Raising his blade he shouted, "ARCHERS!" He hesitated a second then dropped his sword and a volley of arrows flew overhead. Each arrow was elven made and thus had small blessings upon them allowing each hit to cleanse the body that it hit.

"FIRE AT WILL"

A continuous swarm of arrows flew overhead and continued to drop ranks of undead. One of the larger targets a ghoul that was nearly thirty feet tall took ten arrows to cleanse before it fell backwards crushing some of the smaller ones behind it.

Meterove steadied his blade and shouted a third time, "READY! CHARGE!" As one force charged forward and met the undead head on. It became apparent immediately what the blessing that elves had put on his soldiers did and its effect was staggering. Upon death their bodies were covered in new growth preventing corruption, but it was the fact that it also sanctified a five-foot circle around their corpse that erupted in smaller version of the roots and held enemies helpless eventually completely overpowering them.

Meterove's blade whistled through the air as it cut down one foe after another. He would never remember how long he fought...nothing but action, reaction, dodge parry and overall, the splatter of gore...clotted and decaying. He could tell that things weren't going as well as he had hoped though. Cutting his way through a group of walking corpses and beheading a vampire that appeared to his right in a whirl of shadow Meterove jumped up and thrust his blade into the side of a ghoul's skull.

Standing atop its shoulder Meterove shouted, "TO ME MY BROTHERS! RALLY BACK TO ME!"

His voice bolstered the moral of his men and as they fought their way back to him, he saw that while they had lost nearly a quarter of their men the undead had lost far more.

The elves' enchantments had wreaked havoc upon their forces. Suddenly a deafening shriek tore through the air causing Meterove to cover his ears. Looking around for its source he felt his heart sink.

A wyrm was crawling over the ground heading their way and even from here Meterove could see that parts of its body were rotting...an undead Wyrm. Unlike their cousins the dragons, Wyrms had extremely long snake-like bodies, no wings, and an assortment of vibrantly colored scales. Their breath was even more of an inferno than a dragon's though. Not wanting to give it a chance to slaughter his men Meterove focused his weary mind and sent a volley of magic at the monster to attract its attention.

The blast hit the wyrm full in the side, causing it to lose its balance. Correcting itself it turned its head towards Meterove searching for the source. Meterove sent another volley which it ducked and stepped forward over a hill crushing a ghoul under its foot. It let out another ear slitting shriek, its eyes alive with the same vile blue glow he had seen in the dragons at the temple.

Now wasn't the time to hold back so Meterove put all the power he had into a single blast as it charged him. It hit full in its chest and a shriek of agony followed. Meterove wished almost immediately that he hadn't angered it for it too had a trick; it took a massive breath and released a jet of blue flames that engulfed hundreds of his men, burning them to ash. Anger overpowered any exhaustion now. Meterove readied himself to charge the monster.

Just as he was about to attack the wyrm reared again and sent a torrent towards him causing him to take cover. As he hit the ground, he noticed the face of the corpse next to him; one of his lieutenants. At least half his army was without direction then.

Another shriek cut through the air and Meterove was surprised to hear the note of pain in it. Raising his head up he could see one of his soldiers had managed to get onto the creatures back using daggers to serve as climbing aids. The soldier now at the base of the creature's skull let go of one dagger and drew his sword. The wyrm reared again trying to throw him from its body but the man held fast, as it landed back on its front legs the soldier used the momentum to help drive the blade into the creature's brain.

It reared and rolled backwards in agony and the soldier let go of his dagger and fell to the ground. It hit the ground with a massive earth-shaking crash. Looking around Meterove could see that his men had taken the field. There were only a few pockets of undead left that were far outnumbered. The battle was won.

Meterove made his way over to where the soldier had landed. The man was badly wounded. His armor was ripped open in several places and blood seeped from his abdomen. Yet in spite of that, or perhaps because of it, the man laughed with joy. He had just done the impossible, few men had ever slain a wyrm and none were known to have done so without the aid of powerful magic.

Meterove knelt down at the man's side and he seemed dimly aware that someone was there. "You have done a great thing here today soldier now you must hold on a little while longer. We'll see you healed and have you sent back to Yxarion as a hero." The man sputtered and choked.

Death seemed to be near. Meterove stood and yelled, "I need a healer over here now!"

Kneeling back down he placed his hand on the man's shoulder. The man seemed to come to himself a bit for he attempted a salute. A healer came over along with his other lieutenant. The healer went straight to work while his lieutenant beckoned him off to the side.

"My lord we have suffered great losses. Half of our force is gone, and the better parts of the survivors are wounded. What are your orders?"

There was no question now. "We have to fall back to the gate. I'll send word to my sister of the outcome of this battle and of our need to be reinforced."

The man closed his eyes briefly and sighed. Opening them he looked over at the soldier he said, "Incredible what he did isn't it?"

"Indeed, He will be sent back to Yxarion to recuperate if he survives."

The healer stood up, "He will survive but he won't be waking up any time soon. I definitely agree that rest away from battles is in order. He should also be watched less he caught the taint of undeath and returns a hero only to spread it. If you'll excuse me, I have a long night ahead of me yet."

Meterove nodded and the healer walked off to a group of wounded men. But turned back and said, "Oh and my lord?" Meterove turned and looked inquiringly at the healer, who spoke again, "His name is Vlad."

.   .   .

Joleen sat on the throne deep in thought. The men that Meterove had sent back from the front had just left and she was so emotionally drained that she had a hard time deciding whether to be happy about a victory or deeply saddened by such a great loss of life.

According to the men there was little time to get reinforcements to the front as scouts had reported another army of undead making their way towards the gate, which according to the letter that Meterove had sent would be completed in time to shield them from the onslaught this time making losses much smaller.

Also in the missive was the report of the man called Vlad's heroics with recommendation that he be returned to the front when able and promoted to his new lieutenant. In addition, he had sent back one of the claws from the wyrm to be crafted into a new sword for the man.

Joleen whole heartedly believed that man deserved both honors. The crafting process would take a great deal of time and she would have none but the finest smiths and the headmaster of the academy himself work on it.

There was much that needed to be done in the meantime. Joleen stood and left the throne room with Narok and Dras close behind. The new guard Dras had earned a great deal of respect for his valor and loyalty during the battle with the Vorthains.

He and Narok had become friends in just a few short weeks, close enough that he had entrusted the second royal guard position to him. A good choice in Meterove's absence, Joleen thought. The man had a keen mind and, more importantly, spoke his mind now that he was more familiar with her and Narok.

His candor had earned him some disgusted looks from nobles, but Joleen enjoyed it. It was nice to have someone that spoke the same way as Meterove around her. Just the other day he outright disagreed with a troop movement plan and when a noble called him out saying it was his place to be seen not heard he simply replied with "I'm to protect her highness regardless of the danger, even if it is only from a fat, arrogant noble that's never seen a battle."

Joleen still smiled about that one. The man had gone blustery and then mumbled some insult about Dras being a peasant, to whom Dras had simply raised his arm and removing the glove showed his hand. The deep blue light had terrified the noble, who got up and yelling something about evil magics, left the hall.

Joleen hadn't cared as the noble in question had little following and almost no power of his own. It had proven a valuable point to everyone, so from that point on she included Narok and Dras in her meetings as advisors as well as guards. The gate would be reinforced, and Vlad would be sent back.

.   .   .

The battle at the gate had been constant for several weeks now. The undead kept coming and the elves took every opportunity to refresh their spells upon the ground around the gate. Thus far there had been nothing larger than ghouls attacking the gate, which was a blessing, though the constant fear that another wyrm might be on its way was nagging at them. All in all, things were holding quite well.

More good news came in the form of a missive stating that Vlad would be returning soon. His presence would bolster morale, which had taken a dive with the prolonged assault on the gate. He would be wielding his newly forged blade and with luck help turn the tide of this battle which looked to overwhelm their spirits and crush them. Meterove sighed to himself, "That can't come soon enough."

When Vlad reached the front, he was greeted with rousing cheers from the soldiers. With the gate now completed the tents had taken on a more permanent look. Near the front of the camp closest to the gate was the command tent. His hands began to shake from nerves, so he gripped his sword to steady them.

The blade blazed with power, and it unnerved him slightly wielding it. He had never been able to use magic so he was unsure how it would react. Unbreakable, with a perfect balance and edge, the deep, cold grey felt as though it were its own entity.

He was near the front now and was getting unusually nervous. He had been a soldier for years but until now had never been in a position of command. He reached the front, dismounted, and was led into the command tent.

Meterove was sitting at a large table with many chairs around it. It was easily the largest thing in the tent. The remainder of the interior was taken up by a single cot, an armor stands and a small bookcase. He knelt as Meterove looked up, "My lord."

Meterove smiled back at him, "Stand."

Vlad stood back up and looked at Meterove. The prince was somewhat ragged. He was certainly weary and unshaven. He was living up to his reputation; he had no luxuries that his men didn't. Vlad liked this man more and more.

"As you know you have been promoted to my new lieutenant here at the gate. You will be in command of the Third cavalry as well as the Eighth through Fourteenth infantries. In addition, you will have the night command every other week. Understood?"

"Yes sir."

Meterove smiled again, "Good then I'll update you-"

A loud roar echoed in the distance causing both Meterove and Vlad to look around and instantly both were heading for the entrance. Outside the soldiers were looking into the sky with expressions of fear. Looking up as well they saw the source.

A deep gold dragon was descending on the camp. Meterove drew his sword just as it landed and was about to launch himself at the creature when it roared at him.

"WAIT!"

The force of the shout knocked Meterove back a step.

"I am tainted but am thus far not controlled. You must kill me, but first listen to my words and carry them to your leaders." The dragon convulsed, its eyes rolling in agony, flames erupting from its nostrils and mouth. "It is taking control of me. I can't hold it back much longer. You must seek out the wisdom of our lord." His eyes flashed blue then back to gold. "The elves know where." The dragon roared again. "KILL ME NOW...I WANT TO DIE AS A DRAGON!"

Meterove didn't hesitate...he stepped forward thrust his blade to the hilt into the dragon's skull. The eyes went back to gold and Meterove saw a brief look of gratitude before the eyes went blank. Meterove yanked his sword free of the skull, wiped it off and then sheathed it. He turned to Vlad, "It seems I have important matters to deal with our allies. I'll be leaving for Yxarion immediately you and Æthran will take command here."

Vlad saluted "Yes, my lord." Inside his mind was a whirlwind of fear and doubt with a bit of pride thrown in. His greatest emotion was his fear...could he do this...command in the prince's absence?

.   .   .

Jolson had been going through records nonstop since he had received word that the battle had begun at the gate. Lucky for him his artifact was like him and had multiple abilities.

It was able to aid in his search by giving him minor foresight allowing him to see what books and scrolls would contain useful information. Of course, every now and then he wanted to turn it into its weapon form and cut through the books that he was reading due to the information being so cryptic.

On top of that there was another matter that was concerning to him. There were a growing number of complaints about disturbances that seem to come from the home of a reclusive mage. People had been complaining about magical disturbances for the last several days.

While magical disturbances from the homes of mages generally were nothing quite common it was the fact that a number of people without magical talent were able to feel the magic. This meant that a surprising amount of power was being released.

His first instinct was that something was very wrong here and that he should wait for Meterove to return before telling Joleen. The main reason was that she would insist on checking into it immediately; something that Jolson was very uneasy about. He wanted someone that was more experienced in magic to look into it and someone that could take care of themselves if things got ugly.

It wasn't going to be too much longer then Meterove would be back. Word had been sent from that gate that he was returning with urgent information; something else that worried him.

Jolson worked for several more hours before a familiar step caught his attention. "Good you're back I have some things to tell you and I can only imagine what you have to tell me."

Meterove paused a moment before saying, "The attacks are continuing without pause. It's as if there is an endless army of undead that can just pour forever against us. On top of that this corruption was strong enough to ensnare not one but two dragons as well as a wyrm. I don't know much about dragons but I'm pretty sure that this one wasn't a young one either."

Jolson looked up concern evident on his face, "Indeed that is something that we should be concerned with. It's only logical to think that if these three fell that more have and even more will. The endless supply of undead is terrible as well, however given how long it's been since that last war and considering how they slaughter the Vorthains it's not surprise that they have these kinds of numbers."

Meterove said, "It's still not something that we should take lightly."

Jolson said, "I never said that. I was simply saying that it really shouldn't be all that unexpected.

Meterove said, "True enough. As for the dragons what do you think we should do?"

Jolson said, "what can we do, really?"

Meterove said, "also true. Though the dragon that I killed at the gate said to find their lord and to ask the elves where he was."

Jolson looked puzzled, "that's odd. I've never heard anything about any of this before. A Dragon lord huh?"

Meterove said, "well that's what he said, now what did you have to tell me?"

Jolson shook his head too clear it then said, "Ah yes, actually I have something that I want your opinion on." He looked around the table a moment and pulled a piece of parchment from under a stack of books, then handed it to Meterove. Meterove read it through quickly then looked over the top of it at Jolson. "This certainly doesn't sound like the effects of any of the sectioned experiments in the city. Whatever is going on there, if this information is accurate, needs to be investigated."

Jolson said, "My thoughts exactly. I was kind of hoping that you would think differently though. More trouble is the last thing that we need right now."

Meterove said, "Isn't that the truth. I'm barely back from the battle and now I've got to investigate this mess. I'm assuming that you were waiting for me to return because you have a bad feeling about this?"

Jolson smiled, "You caught me. Yes, I have a very bad feeling. I haven't had any visions dealing with this but all the same. It feels like this is somehow tied to our larger crisis."

Meterove said, "well I guess that we should go talk to Joleen."

Jolson agreed and the two left the library. Ten minutes later the two stood in front of the throne and relayed all that they had heard, all that they knew and a little of what they guessed.

Joleen wanted to scream, to cry, to simply let go of decorum and vent her frustrations and worries. Meterove had returned from battle with bad news. Despite the victory they were never going to get anywhere this way and furthermore the discussion that Meterove and Jolson had discussed with her was not one that improved her mood.

He had all but confirmed his suspicions which, to Joleen, meant that she had something just as serious as the attack on her borders to worry about. At the moment he was insisting on going out and investigating this matter at once and by himself, thus her frustrations and the current argument.

Joleen said, "I don't care how minor of a situation you have just returned from the gate and haven't even had a chance to rest yet.

Meterove said, "That kind of fatigue takes days or weeks to wear off. By the time I'm fully rested this could have turned into something greater."

Joleen said, "the fact that this could evolve into something greater is the very reason that you should rest and let me send in some of the guard."

Standing at Joleen's shoulders Narok and Dras shared an uneasy look. Meterove could tell that they didn't like the idea of some of their men going to investigate this place. Valuing their opinion Meterove said, "I share your unease Dras, Narok. Tell me what your opinions on this matter are."

Joleen looked over her shoulder at Narok and the guard seemed slightly nervous at being brought into the conversation so suddenly. While they had known each other since they were children Narok had never been good at speaking his mind unless he had ample planning. Dras though was different and yet again Meterove felt pleased with the man.

Dras said, "I'm sure that Captain Narok agrees with me when I say that most of the guard is ill prepared to handle the situation. While they are trained for magical combat, the more subtle art of investigation is not one of our specialties."

Meterove said, "Agreed that is most certainly true. If the men don't know what to look for, how to look for it and above all what to do with it if they find it, then things could end quite badly for them"

Jolson said, "not to mention out of all of the guards only a handful are capable of detecting and using magic."

Joleen almost shouted, "All right! All right!" She rubbed her temple, "I see your points. However, considering that it's you there's no way in hell that I'm sending you in there alone. That would be reckless to the point of foolishness."

Meterove said, "So what do you propose?"

Joleen thought about it a moment then asked, "Dras would you be willing to accompany my brother when he investigates this?"

Dras looked momentarily surprised but said, "If you want me to then yes, I have no problem with accompanying Meterove while he investigates this manor."

Meterove grinned, "I'll also agree to that." Dras was a good man and Meterove had full confidence that he wouldn't get in his way. Besides, it would be nice to see what the man was capable of now that he had recovered.

Joleen said, "very well the matter is settled. Head out as soon as you are ready."

Meterove looked at Dras and gestured for the door. Dras followed and the two left. Joleen should have known better. Of course, he was going to go right away. At least she had gotten him to take along Dras. Though, the two of them were so similar that it scared her a little.

Joleen said, "Jolson not that I doubt that those two can handle the matter..."

Jolson nodded, "I'll come up with a contingency plan."

Joleen rubbed her temples again. This was a huge headache. Meterove, you had better resolve this matter quickly.

CHAPTER II
MANOR

Meterove and Dras stood in the shadows across the street from a large manor house in the mage district. Through the wrought iron fence, you could see long flower beds and hedges that were meticulously cared for.

A number of gargoyle statues dotted the grounds and a large fountain with a large harpy in the middle, sprayed water into the air. The manor was home to a mage named Orelion. It had caught Jolson's attention earlier after a large burst of magic that had even been seen by citizens that would normally be unable to sense the power, caused some anomalies in the surrounding areas

It had now been several months since the last time that he had been seen outside of his manor grounds. While Orelion had a reputation of being a hermit, it was unusual to have seen nothing of him for this length of time. Now that he looked at the wrought iron gates in front of him, he got shivers. In general, mages tended to be a rather eccentric lot, but the gargoyles that he had forged into the gate went a little past that.

Hand on his sword Meterove turned to Dras. "What do you think?"

Dras didn't take his eyes off the gate and paused for a moment. "I don't know. I'm still getting used to using this hand. Being able to detect and alter magic is an odd sensation so my feelings may be off. However, based on what I feel and the tone of your voice it is probably what you feel as well...something is definitely amiss inside that place."

Meterove sighed, "Yeah there is something inside there I'm just not sure what it is. It might be-"

Here Meterove paused, his hand tightening on the hilt of his sword, and waited with bated breath. A moment later he released it, glanced at Dras, and knew from his expression that he had felt it too and then continued. "I'm not sure what is going on in there, but the aura is growing and feels almost...demonic. I had been intending on getting some reinforcements but based on what we just felt we need to get in there now. I'm just glad that Jolson didn't send any of the guard in there without us."

With a half glance at Dras, Meterove stared over to the gates with his hand resting on his blade ready to draw it at a moment's notice. As they reached the gate a glyph

appeared on the face of one of the gargoyles. As Meterove
placed his left hand on the glyph he felt a stiff resistance that
quickly yielded. That was the last bit of proof that he
needed that this wasn't some accident...someone wanted to
keep others from snooping.

The gate swung inwards, and they stepped through.
As they crossed the threshold, they had the sensation of
walking through a sheet of water and once on the other side
the world warped and seemed to tear itself apart. Patches of
the ground ripped itself away from the ground and floated in
midair while other sections turned into a massive pillar of
earth with the tree, statue, or flower bed upside down and
the sky where the ground had been.

What had appeared to be gargoyle statues from the
outside were now revealed to be angelic statues, yet
grotesque with sections of the body resembling rot and some
places, including the face, it was burned and black, in some
cases revealing bone. The fountain that had been spraying
water now floated upside-down, its spray now a gelatinous
black substance.

The worst of it though, was hanging in front of the
statues. Human children, all appearing roughly ten years of
age were shackled to the base, each with a monstrous winged
abomination sprouting from their abdomens. Seeing this
Meterove was suddenly very aware of the rancid odor that
permeated the grounds. The odor was quickly forgotten as

Meterove realized that both the children and the things sprouting from them were still alive!

Suddenly feeling vulnerable Meterove quickly assessed their surroundings and quickly spotted the source of his unease. Walking towards him were two adults, their movements had a horribly familiar jerky motion to them. Just as Meterove was about to attack they fell forward. Jumping back Meterove drew his words and yelled to Dras, "Undead! As soon as they are fully spawned destroy them before they can spread their curse."

In front of them the two had begun convulsing and suddenly there was that horrible sound of flesh tearing as the bones tore their way free of the flesh, spraying blood in all directions. Unlike last time though it wasn't just the bones that stood up, but the flesh seemed to absorb some of the evil in the air and using that as a frame on which to stand. Meanwhile the blood that had sprayed congealed into several blobs that formed themselves into four skulls that floated around the shambling flesh.

Meterove looked with shock at the now unfavorable odds, "Well...that's new."

A grunt from his left told him that Dras was slightly behind him. "That's just...repulsive."

Despite the seriousness of the situation Meterove couldn't help smiling. Well here seemed like a challenge so- Why not?! Jumping forward he slashed the skeleton at its skull intending to put it off balance so that he could use it as a shield after it was destroyed. The maneuver worked perfectly and as he swung around behind it; he slammed his dagger into its skull disrupting the magic. The shambling flesh aimed a backhand blow at him and Meterove put the body of the skeleton between himself and the strike.

It barely missed him as the arm bent around the bones that were in front of him. Jumping back Meterove swore and threw the femur at the flesh. He should have anticipated that it would be flexible since it didn't have any bones to keep it rigid. It dodged the bone and came at him with surprising speed and as he swung his sword at its neck.

The blade suddenly stopped, one of the Blood Skulls had flown in and caught it in its teeth.

Meterove aimed a trike with his dagger, but the blade sliced through the skull only for blood to seal back around the cut. As he wrenched on his sword to wrest it from the Blood Skull the shambling Flesh caught him with a powerful blow that sent him back several feet. Flipping back onto his feet Meterove could see Dras fighting with the other Shambling Flesh.

Holding his blade straight out Meterove forced a bolt of power out of the tip intending to blow the Blood Skull away. Just as it was about to hit the Skull gave out a horrible cackle and swallowed the blast. The energy caused the blood to multiply and turned into a full blood skeleton. Once fully formed it came at him while the other Blood

Skull hovered around the Shambling Flesh, as it moved towards him. The two combined rained a score of blows on him none of which were a clean hit but still kept him from attacking.

Parrying attack after attack demanded most of his concentration but not quite all. Meterove jumped back and took a new defensive stance. The whole time thinking to himself, what can I do to fight this thing? Well regular attacks won't affect the Blood and energy blasts are a BAD idea. Another strike almost hit him in the throat and Meterove swore.

I have to hurry this up. That blood, it's like water I can't cut it-.

Meterove stooped and slammed his palm to his face, "Can't believe I didn't think of this in the first place." Raising his sword, a small blue nimbus appeared at its tip and suddenly the blood began to crystallize. Within seconds the Blood Skeleton and the Blood Skull fell to the ground and shattered. A second blast of energy destroyed the remaining magic. A shadow to his left told him that the Shambling Flesh was right next to him. Turning Meterove raised his sword to strike.

The creature let out a sound that was somehow gurgling and rasping and it was lifted off the ground...a glowing blue hand had grabbed it by the back of the neck. With a single squeeze combined with a mental command

Dras caused the magic reanimating it to disperse and the flesh to fall to the ground lifeless.

"Thanks" Grunted Meterove.

"Well, I just got promoted and it might look bad if I let you die so easily" said Dras with a small smirk while he held out a hand. Taking it Meterove got to his feet "that it would, though if I were just a little maimed it wouldn't be so bad" Meterove grinned and finished "or at least no one would be surprised."

Meterove motioned towards the main entrance of the mansion, "Shall we?"

"Let's hurry; I'd sooner be done with this place, but it looks like we're needed here" said Dras.

Again, Meterove took the lead as the two of them made their way over to the main door. Now on the inside and looking closely Meterove realized he had been unable to tell what style the building had been from the outside.

Berating himself for not noticing this dead giveaway of concealing magic earlier. AS they walked Meterove noticed that the children and the creatures that were hanging out of their bodies had all died. If possible, it made the creatures even more grotesque.

Dras noticed his gaze and said, "What kinds of vile magic are being used in this place?"

Meterove spoke quietly, his words weighed with sorrow and a touch of nausea, "As for what was done to those children, I have never seen the like of it. Not even the necromancy of the Vorthains was that profane. As for the distortion of this place it's not really magic but the side effect of the magic that's causing these alterations to reality. I'm not even sure what is actually real in this place. Just remember that from here on out that the words real and possible are both relative."

Dras nodded and kept walking. There was nothing else that had to be said. This was truly a nightmare. Meterove grasped the handle of the door barely registering that it was shaped like a dragon's head. Stepping across the threshold Meterove and Dras both instantly felt that they would have rather stayed outside.

The entryway looked as though a massacre had taken place. Blood, parts of bodies and organs were strewn across the floor. Some of the blood spatter was nearly to the ceiling. Looking up Dras cursed under his breath...it DID reach the ceiling, or was that soaking through from the level above?

There was also some kind of corruption that seemed to spread tentacle like across the walls, twitching writhing and wrapping its way across the floor, walls and ceiling, its color impossible to tell. Besides the horror the inside was definitely interesting to say the least. The hallways were lit with oil lamps while the ceilings here were quite high with murals painted across them, all of a dark and twisted nature.

Black seemed to be the primary color choice of any kind of fabric or leather. Furniture when visible through the corruption was also dark in color. Just what the hell was going on here?

.   .   .

Joleen paced her study. The more that she had thought about it the more she disliked that idea of sending only Dras with her brother. Sure, he was capable and Meterove was even more so, but she still had this terrible feeling. This feeling was only heightened by news that the manor had recently sent out a massive burst of energy.

Continuing to pace across the room Joleen was so lost in her thoughts and worries that she missed the door opened and jumped when a voice said," Joleen I have news."

It was Jolson and judging by the look on his face She was not going to like what she heard. "Proceed."

Jolson spoke without further preamble. "The energy burst that was felt earlier was prior to Meterove and Dras entering the manor however they did enter shortly after it had subsided and from what we can tell they have completely vanished from the manor itself."

Joleen closed her eyes; it was even worse than she had feared.

Jolson continued "I have no reason to think that either of them are dead however further intelligence that has been gathered shows that the manor has been heavily disguised."

Joleen stopped in mid step, "Disguised how?"

"Well," said Jolson "From what we can tell heavy wards have been placed on the building that helps to prevent anyone from entering. In addition to that the appearance of the building itself seems to be altered to those viewing it from the outside." Between this and the aura that has been sensed it is obvious that this mage, Orelion, has been doing far more than he's been reporting and that this isn't just some isolated incident."

Joleen placed her left hand over her eyes, "What have you two gotten yourselves into?"

.   .   .

"Move it Dras! Find a room that we can barricade and get into it!"

Meterove's shouts followed Dras as the two sprinted through the twisting hallways of the manor. Behind them a pack of undead Cerberi were chasing them as well as a set of massive tentacles that kept bursting through the floor and walls. In front of them a horde of skeletons had been emerging to block their path every chance they could.

"You just had to mess with that damn mirror didn't you Meterove!" shouted Dras turning the corner. "Is NOW really the time to assign blame?" Meterove shouted back. "Just keep moving!"

Another massive tentacle over a foot thick at the tip burst through the floor, massive claws inside the suckers on the underside of it. It took a swipe at Meterove who parried it and severed the top three feet of the tentacle. Severing the tentacle seemed to have made whatever was at its source angry. The entire building shuddered as it roared back in the room with the mirror.

"What the hell did you let out of its cage?" panted Dras.

"I have no idea, most of the runes on the bottom were worn away all I could read was the last few which said '...death may die.' shouted Meterove as he jumped onto a long side table to escape the jaws of a Cerberus.

"And you somehow thought that after reading that it might be a good idea to touch that thing!" responded Dras as he did a spin catching one of the Cerberus with his blade, severing one of its three heads. Completing his spin, he saw that the injured Cerberus stopped and began to eat its own severed head.

"Well... THAT'S revolting." said Dras as he picked his speed up to catch up to Meterove who had pulled slightly ahead. Turning another corner Dras and Meterove noticed a massive marble archway halfway down the hall. There was the most unpleasant aura of darkness seeping from it.

Passing it at full speed it took them a moment to realize that there was a slight change in the feel of the air. Turning they saw the cerberi skid to a halt then turn and run away yelping. The tentacles stopped in midair over the arch before quivering and retreating with greater haste than they had shown during the chase.

Dras raised an eyebrow at Meterove. In response Meterove said, "Yeah...that really doesn't bode well does it." Walking back cautiously to the arch they took a closer look. The pillars were that same twisted angelic figure that they had seen in the manor grounds. Furthermore, it looked as though it was far older than the manor itself which seemed to have been built around it. The wall seemed to have been torn away from where it was leaving a slight indentation.

Meterove frowned, "It almost looks like the mage found something right here in his home, doesn't it?"

"Without a doubt" said Dras.

There were so many questions now thought Meterove. What had happened in this place? What was the significance of this angelic figure? It certainly was nothing that he had ever seen or heard of before. What was the tie to the undead energy that they had been encountering? Was this tied to the grisly murders that they had been looking into?

Without a word Meterove stepped forward and looked through the arch. Now that he was close, he realized that there was not another side to the arch but that it was a portal to another place. The amount of magic that could be stored in an object of that size was quite limited which meant that the distance that it could send someone wasn't very far, likely just to a chamber under the building they were in.

Glancing at Dras for an instant Meterove stepped into the portal. A second later he was standing in darkness. Stepping to the side he waited a moment then with a small increase of air pressure he knew Dras had joined him. No sooner had Dras arrived then torches along the walls lit themselves revealing a large marble dais and two sets of stairs leading down into a large room.

A number of statues lined the stairs as well as a number of massive pillars that were inside the room. What caught Meterove's attention though was the massive thing in the middle of the room. In an instant Meterove knew why the monsters had backed off earlier.

If this was what he thought it was, he kind of wanted to go back through the portal. Taking chances here was a bad idea. Being jet black in color made its massive size look even bigger than it actually was. The beast stood twelve feet at its shoulders.

It resembled a Cerberus if all three heads had been merged into one but with massive dragon-like wings and its tail was similar to a scythe, only fifteen feet in length, though it was the legs that weirded him out the most. The joints were all like the hind legs of most four-legged animals. As he watched he thought he saw the joints change their direction.

"Protogod" whispered Meterove.

Dras noticing the fear in Meterove's voice asked, "What the hell is a 'Protogod'?"

Meterove motioned for Dras to back up slowly so that they were out of sight of the creature that seemed to be asleep for the moment. Once out of the creature's line of sight behind a few statues.

"Ok now are you going to explain what the hell that thing is? What is a Protogod?" asked Dras

Meterove took a deep breath. "Understand what I am telling you is by its very nature incomplete and imprecise. This is only a legend and a vague one at best. Before the reforming of our world into one that could be inhabited by the elder races, even before the creation of the gods there was a group of seven creatures that were created, they were the Protogods. Each was massive and quite powerful, and each was named for one of the seven great sins of sentient creatures. Just to make things fast I'll just go into the description of Gluttony."

Meterove took another breath marshaling his thoughts then said, "Gluttony was a great beast with many mouths on his massive hound-like head. His massive body was that of a great hairless dog with skin of the deepest black and each eye was argent in color. Its stomach is said to contain something called a black hole...an endless expanse that sucks all things into it without exception and without hope of return to be digested for eternity."

Now Dras began to feel some of the anxiety that he had seen on Meterove's face. No wonder he was afraid. Being digested for eternity was not a pleasant thought. On top of that the idea of fighting something that had the word 'god' in it was not something that sounded like a good life choice. Taking a breath to steady himself Dras said, "So what is the plan then?"

Meterove thought a moment then said, "Well the only information that we have on the Protogods besides the basic description was how they were supposed to have been defeated in the past and sealed. There isn't one account about them ever being destroyed."

Dras laughed sardonically, "There's some great news. That thing down there might be something known as a Protogod, if so, is likely the one known as gluttony that digests things for eternity and there's no known way to kill a Protogod. What we do know is only a way to seal them...which if it's stuck down here means it's already happened. Sound like a good recap?"

Meterove couldn't help laughing helplessly a little himself. "Yeah, I have to admit there isn't much more that it looks like we can do but we're going to have to do something to get past that thing."

Meterove stood up, rolled his shoulders, and then gave Dras a sideways glance that Dras couldn't help but feel a little nervous and a little exhilarated upon seeing. Meterove had one crazy idea brewing in his head and Dras was sure that if nothing else, they'd at least have an interesting death. Meterove walked slowly over to the edge of the staircase looking down on the beast.

It seemed fast asleep yet there was this feeling that came from it. It was as if it was perfectly aware that they were there but had no intention of moving unless they came closer. Dras wasn't fooled though, for a sensation of great ravening hunger permeated the room, as if there was an aura of hunger that surrounded it.

Meterove took a deep breath and suddenly Dras felt a massive wave of power escape him. It was as if a door had opened exposing this vast well of nearly unlimited power. The air around his body seemed to shimmer as though the temperature had risen drastically around him. There was a bright flash of light and Meterove stood there all of his body bathed in a gentle yet vibrant aura of white energy. Even his hair and eyes seemed to be white, though Dras knew better. The energy itself made them appear that way, there was no actual change.

"What the hell are you planning there?" said Dras through raised arms, trying to block some of the force.

"Simple" said Meterove in a deep, calm voice "I'm going at this thing with full power and seeing what happens. It's not like we have a choice in the matter. If we don't stop this thing it's going to kill us, or we'll starve here in a stalemate. From what I can tell of this alternate world that we're in, we can't leave here until we destroy whatever is causing it."

Understanding reached Dras and his uncertainty and fear vanished. If they didn't do something they would die here and since he had no plans that involved dying inside of this nightmare the only option was to attack and hope that they were able to win. If not, then at least they died on their own terms.

Meterove tensed a moment then jumped forward down to the floor below. As he hit the floor, he was dimly aware of the nature of the room. It was very ornate in design, millions of tiny gemstones making up the filigree around the edge of the room and exquisite carvings around the ceiling of the room. He didn't take the time to look at the scenery though and kept up his pace as he charged the monster.

As he had expected as he drew closer it got to its feet with frightening speed. Also, as he had thought this thing was a Protogod. There were a number of runes that ran the length of its chest that were of vile magic and one symbol that appeared on every scroll that dealt with the Protogods: The Hell Star.

From what he could remember it was supposed to be a brand that the Protogods all bore showing their connection to each other and this one the Hell Star superimposed on the rune for gluttony. The beast let out a deep growl that moved to a roar as it opened its mouths. Meterove had expected to see the tongues and gullets full of saliva and perhaps a potent odor. Instead, all that was past the rows of yellowed razor-sharp teeth was a vast black expanse. Meterove could tell there truly was no end past that mouth.

Meterove placed his left hand on his words as well and putting all the strength and energy he had into it struck the beast in the middle of its head. To his shock the blade cleaved through like he was cutting cheese and the beasts head slit in two with apportion of it falling off to the ground. A half second later the rest of its body collapsed next to it.

Meterove hit the ground and dropped to one knee, his left-hand bracing for the fall while his right held his blade out behind him. He quickly backed up bracing himself.

There is no way it's that easy thought Meterove. Almost as soon as the thought had formed, he was proven right. The severed portion writhed and split itself into four segments that became similar in appearance to the tail of a scorpion.

The area where the head had been severed began to bubble as if the flesh was boiling and the portion of the head that he had severed regrew in a matter of seconds. The tails that had formed pulled themselves along the ground like pervasive caterpillars. Once they reached the beast, they made their way up to its back and attached themselves one on each shoulder joint and one on each hip joint.

"Great" muttered Meterove "now it has more weapons and I'm betting that those stingers are all venomous as well."

Suddenly Meterove became aware that Dras was next to him. "Meterove what do you think of blasting the area that you cut immediately after. It'll be like - "

"Cauterizing a wound." finished Meterove. "Well, it's an idea. Let's go!"

Running forward Meterove aimed a slash at the creatures head. Having seen the attack once before, the beast reacted by backing away and ducking to the left, while attacking him with the front two stingers. At the last moment Meterove pulled his attack and dove to the side allowing Dras who had been right behind him to slash at the occupied stingers as well as the head.

Dras' blow severed one stinger, crippled the other and put a long slash on the beasts face. It howled in pain and reared up. The whole room shook as it landed, cracking the marble floor. It turned to face Meterove and in the process took a swipe at Dras with its tail. Dras did a flip and felt the blade of the tail brush past his check slicing it for several inches.

In the time that it had done this simple maneuver it had begun regenerating its smaller injuries. The severed stinger had begun to inch its way back to the beast when Meterove blasted it to ash. The beast growled and dashed forward with a snarl. Its jaws snapped shut where Meterove's leg had been just a moment before. In the process Meterove blasted the area that the stinger had been attached.

The beast let out a roar of rage and barreled at Meterove, then stumbled and fell; its back right leg had been severed by Dras. Meterove flipped up onto its back, pushed off its shoulder that he had severed and continued over to where Dras was standing. The stingers had in the time that he had jumped buried themselves into the beast's back.

Meterove grinned, "Well the burning the injury thing seems to be working." He would have continued but at that moment there was a massive burst of magic and a huge black portal opened in midair.

The rim of it looked like a mixture of fire and lightning but of that same poisonous blue that the undead had about them. A massive hand, decaying but also with some area that appeared to be demonic and others that were very much like Dras' magic hand, reached through it and grabbed the beast, easily wrapping its fingers around the entire body.

The beast resisted sending its stingers into the hand and wrist while attempting to bite the hand where it could reach. Sensing a massive burst of power from the first beast Meterove shouted, "Get back up the stairs now!"

Dras was not going to argue he had felt the power as well, though Meterove clearly had a better idea as to what it meant. Once back on the stairs Meterove wasted no time.

Meterove kept his eyes fixed on the struggle below and said only "True form."

Dras glanced at him quizzically and once he saw that no further explanation was coming returned his gaze to the struggle below and his question was answered. The beasts back had begun to slit right down the middle. Massive teach made themselves visible and the beasts body expanded greatly to accommodate this new addition.

"That has to be the most bizarre thing that I've seen today" said Meterove.

"I'm just going to go with the most bizarre thing that I've seen in a while" said Dras.

The embodiment of Gluttony had now expanded to nearly twice its pervious size and was showing no signs of stopping. Before it could complete its transformation a second hand came through the portal and the two combined subdued the beast and pulled it through the portal.

The portal remained open before them and Meterove looked at Dras "Want to follow and see where that goes?"

"I hope that you're kidding" replied Dras "That thing almost killed us, and you want to go and see what else is through-"

"Who said anything about me going? I asked if you wanted to go! I have no intention on following that thing. I've had enough of almost dying today."

Dras sheathed his sword and Meterove did the same. "Besides" said Meterove "I think I know what that other thing was."

Dras raised an eyebrow, "Do tell."

"Based on the legends I'm going to say that it was the Protogod of envy" said Meterove.

Dras said "so it was helping that thing?"

Meterove said "not likely from what I've read. The Protogods were in constant conflict with each other. If I had to take a guess it had been a long time since any of them had been active so when this one began fighting with us its location was discovered. However, if my suspicion is correct, it's the second time that it's been active lately. The first time was when Orelion came down here and somehow made this thing be his guard dog. We just gave up its pinpoint location."

Dras exhaled letting some of the tension that had accumulated during the fight go. "When we get back, you'll need to let me see these scrolls on Protogods. I don't like fighting blind when there's information available."

Meterove nodded "Agreed."

Both looked off to the far end of the room where another large arch stood with massive double stone doors. Meterove gestured towards it and began walking over to the doors and Dras fell into step behind him. As they drew closer Meterove could see that here not only was the arch framed by two of the angelic statues but there was also a set of three massive carved images that took up both doors.

The far left showed a man and the angel fighting. The middle showed him slaying it and the last showed a fallen figure and the angel getting to its feet. Meterove stopped and stared at the image for a moment then, making a decision, raised his hand a thin solid beam of green energy went from the far left to the far right of the arch.

"What are you doing" asked Dras?

Meterove waited until the process was complete before saying, "Making a copy. There's no guarantee that we'll be able to come back here, and I know that Jolson will want to see this."

Finishing his spell, a small ruby materialized with a set of runes on each facet. Meterove placed the gem in his pocket then motioned for Dras to follow as he stepped up to the door. Meterove placed his hands on them and pushed. The doors were lighter than he had expected, and they swung forward with ease.

"What the hell?" breathed Dras, a sour taste in his mouth.

CHAPTER 12
ANSWERS

Meterove stood with Dras on his right looking into the most horrific sight that he had seen yet. Not even the slaughter at the gate had troubled him as much as this. A slight retching sound from Dras told him his feelings were certainly shared. It was a something that came from the blackest nightmares.

The laboratory was quite large. There was a wall in the one corner on which formulas kept writing themselves out only to be erased moments later, though there were segments that always stayed the same on them. The walls around him were lined with large glass tanks with deformed bodies within.

Meterove and Dras walked over to the nearest tank. Inside was a baby, barely more than a newborn in size with a wide-eyed look of fear and agony though it was clearly dead.

Like the bodies that they had seen above it had a small, winged horror emerging from its chest.

Looking around the room Meterove could see that all of the other occupants had the same expression. However, this wasn't the worst of it. It was the overwhelming amount of gore that was splattered around the room that when combined with the smell of rot, made the bile rise in Meterove's throat. It was like cleaning a battlefield when the bodies had been sitting in the sun for several weeks.

Suddenly Meterove felt a piercing gaze on him and turned to the far side of the room where there was another door. While it appeared closed on first look after a moment Meterove saw some movement and realized that it had to be cracked open and the area behind very dimly lit.

Meterove hurried over to the door passing a large table in the middle of the room that had more body part in it than anywhere else in the room. Intending to simply take the shortest route Meterove was taken by such surprise at what he saw on the table that he had to stop.

In the middle of all the blood, severed limbs and organs was a dead child that had wings sprouting from its back. Its face wasn't quite human though. Not quite sure what to make of it Meterove turned to Dras. One look told him that Dras was just as perplexed as he was but that he was having an easier time with the sight.

He paused for a moment then raised his hand and held it over the child. Meterove was momentarily confused then he realized that Dras' ability to sense magic, while less experienced than his own, was capable of a far greater range then when they had started. He was gaining some form of understanding.

After a moment he lowered his hand and said, "I feel the same energy that has been surrounding this manor since the beginning. I got a stronger wave too when that portal opened back there as well. What is this?"

Meterove digested this for a moment before remembering that movement that he had seen felt a small jolt in the pit of his stomach, "I might have an idea but more on that later. I think I saw some movement in that room earlier."

Dras didn't say another word but drew his sword and nodded to Meterove. Meterove followed suit and the two made their way cautiously over to the door. Once over there Meterove saw that he had been right. The door was cracked open and there were signs of some slight movement inside.

As the two of them turned their attention away from the carnage and approached the door Meterove paused, fist in the air beside him, causing Dras to come to a halt. Meterove glanced at Dras and instantly knew that he was experiencing the same odd sensation. Something was off, though what exactly was hard to say.

The world seemed slanted, like when you are drunk and on the verge of falling over. Now music, faint but clear, could be heard. Was that circus music? They were in the middle of a mansion, why was there circus music? Now the feeling of something taking hold of him washed over him like an icy wave. He was being pulled...somewhere.

The room was now spinning and understanding what was happening was hard, but one thing was clear. This was not his imagination. Shaking himself mentally and even a bit physically, Meterove managed to loosen the grip on him and grabbing Dras by the shoulder pushed him backwards and to the ground. The shock of the impact startled him and appeared to break the hold on him as well.

Staggering back to Dras, who was getting up to one knee, Meterove now felt a deeply malevolent aura. A high-pitched scream of rage filled the chamber. All along the walls, in every shadow, images flashed, almost as if they were flashing between two separate places.

The images were of a necrotic circus. It was hard to make out clearly, since it appeared to be lit by moonlight, but the tents were decaying, and the banners smeared with gore. Carts that should hold animals were instead filled with shambling horrors. No, that one a least used to be a tiger. Yet part of it was clearly just bone, pure white as if it had been licked clean.

Just as suddenly as it had started, the sensation was gone, though the evil aura and feeling of rage still lingered.

What was that all about? While there was no doubt that something evil had been here just a moment ago it left all too willingly. The aura had also felt exactly like the one the permeated this place, though far stronger.

"And that was?" said Dras looking quite alarmed.

"To be honest I have no idea, not even a guess. I can tell you one thing for sure. I am ready to get out of this place. That thing, whatever it had nearly got us. I didn't even know what was going on until I was almost overwhelmed. Said Meterove, while casting a wary eye across the room.

Dras nodded, "sounds like a plan. I have definitely had my fill of creepy shit for one day. First chance I get I'm hitting up a tavern and with any luck spending the night in bed with my wife."

Meterove shook his head with a chuckle, "Even after all this, your libido is still going strong. How do you block this kind of crap out?"

Dras shrugged, "Knowing how my mind works is above my paygrade. So long as it keeps working, and stays out of someone else's control, that's all I care about."

Meterove shook his head again, "Fair enough. Well let's see what's behind the mysterious door shall we Blight Culler?"

Dras rolled his eyes, "I told you not to call me that. Besides should we be bantering like this? That thing may still be around."

Meterove's eyes popped a bit, "Oops, back to work." He turned and led the way over to the door. Dras shook his head.

You totally forgot about that thing already! Well at least he's not boring! Heh.

Dras stood on the right side and grasped the handle. Nodding to Meterove he held up his other hand and counted down from five. As the last finger went down Dras wrenched open the door and Meterove burst in ready to kill whatever might attack. What he saw, however, made the previous room a cheery daydream.

In front of a massive machine was something that was far more grotesque than the contents of the tanks outside. On the ground was the mage Orelion and sprouting from his chest like some horrible plant was what Meterove had seen move before.

A fleshy amalgamation of at least five of the winged creatures was sprouting from one massive, long foot thick stem made of charcoal gray flesh. It was very much like a vine with each winged creature acting the part of the leaf. Unlike the others, these creatures were alive.

Each let out horrible shrieks that sounded far too loud from something as small as they were, should be capable of. Rows of sharp teeth filled their mouths and blood seeped from the corners. They worked their mouths and after several tries the shrieks changed into a coherent if high-pitched pair of words.

Ashen Soul. Over and over, they said the same two words.

After a moment Meterove stood in shock and then as it moved to the side, he saw something that shocked him just as much. A woman was sealed within the machine behind the monster. While she seemed unaware of them Meterove could tell that she was still alive. Furthermore, there was no sign of the creature on her body.

This thing was giving off the aura that was for sure. They had to kill this thing there was nothing else for it. Dras was already moving towards it. It didn't seem to care that Meterove and Dras stood over it, swords raised. In fact, as far as Meterove could tell it wanted them to kill it. This bothered him but he could say why. Shaking off the feeling he and Dras proceeded to kill the creatures one by one.

Once the last one was dead there was a great pressure lifted from them as the aura fell away. They wiped their swords clean on the dead mages robes they turned their attention to the machine and the woman inside. Meterove at looked some of the runes that were on the machine. After a few moments he activated a few of the glyphs then stopped them right away.

"Well, I can't tell what this machine does for sure, but I have a few guesses. For one this machine seems to be designed to put this poor woman through the entire process of conceiving and birthing a child in a matter of minutes."

Dras looked between Meterove and the machine with revulsion on his face.

"Second is that her life force may be tied to this machine now, so freeing her is not something that we should attempt ourselves. It may even be impossible. Last is one that I sadly know for a fact. This woman is Orelion's wife."

Dras snapped his gaze back onto Meterove with his eyes narrowed with hatred. "Are you saying that bastard did this to her, for the purpose of HIS EXPERIMENTS!" By the end of it his voice had risen to a shout.

Meterove closed his eyes and nodded solemnly. "It appears that way." After a brief pause, he said "we had better get back. We have a lot to tell Jolson and he's definitely going to want to see this place.

.   .   .

Meterove and Dras sat at a table inside one of the large reading rooms inside the academy library. At another table with a projector showing the images that Meterove had captured from inside the manor was Jolson, a look of intense concentration on his face.

For his part Meterove was searching through scattered scrolls and tomes for the information he had promised Dras. It took some time, but he eventually tracked down the correct pages, which he now translated and wrote down for Dras. After a few hours he handed over a page covered in his own writing.

The Protogods: these enormous monsters were some of the first in all of creation. All seven bore the same mark. It was a brand in their flesh that shown with their dark energy. This symbol is the seven-pointed Hell Star. Their cursed steps may have been what caused the gods themselves to come into existence for with them unchecked there was no room for any other lesser being to follow. Once gods came, they warred with the Protogods along with the guardians to seal away the evil. At the end of the war the Protogods were defeated but could not be completely destroyed so they were sealed away. Though just as it couldn't be completely destroyed it couldn't be completely sealed, thus the mortal races were subjected to the pull of these evil forces.

Gluttony: a great beast with many mouths on its massive dog-like head. His body was that of a great hairless dog with skin of the midnight black and each eye was argent in color. Within its belly lies a portal to eternal torment, a black hole...an endless expanse that sucks all things into it without exception and without hope of return to be digested for eternity.

Envy: a massive humanoid which like its name suggests embodies that evil trait. It took the form of all different beings and was known for being the most violent towards its other Protogod brethren, for it envied all of them. Its body was an amalgamation of whatever traits it wanted from all races that it encountered. It is often believed to be the original doppelganger.

Lust: a large succubus or demon that seduced men to their doom. It has large bat-like wings and several tails that it keeps hidden when pretending to be a beautiful woman. It lives by absorbing the energy created by men when they feel the emotion of lust but kills them and feasts on their bodies when the lust fades or turns into love. Her hair, when not in disguise, takes on the appearance of purple flames.

Greed: the simplest of all the Protogods, it simply lives to have all things. What it does not have it must have but without cost. This paradox keeps it mostly immobile since near any action causes it to lose something. Its appearance is equally simple for it is nothing more than a massive spider, though with two sets dragon-like wings on its back.

Wrath: the second original demon wraths aura is felt even to this day for it is the cause of all war. All things anger him, even gaining what it plans. He was deceived by the embodiment of lust and thus helped bring the demons race known today into being. It takes the form of a satyr, though it is said to burn even hotter than its rage.

Pride: the third original demon he would never allow the others to gain a hold over him, though once the embodiment of lust managed to and along with the children of wrath began the demon race. Little is known of his appearance but the fact that he had six arms, and six legs seems to be fact. As well as his skin being blood red and having two massive horns on top of his head with spines down his back.

Sloth: a giant crustacean like being. This massive creature is thought to have lived in the great oceans when the world was formed, and its voracious appetite was second only to Gluttony. However, its lack of movement leads it to use several lighted appendages around its head to constantly attract food.

Dras looked up from the papers in front of him. "So that thing that grabbed the embodiment of gluttony that was this embodiment of envy?"

Meterove was silent for a moment then opened his mouth to speak but Jolson beat him to it. "Yes, well that is the current assumption. It is very troubling that you came across a Protogod at all and now it seems that not only one but two of them actually exist. This leads us to believe that all seven exist."

Dras leaned back in his chair "Great we had enough trouble with that one and still didn't seem to do much damage. What the hell are we going to do if we meet more of them?"

Jolson shook his head "that isn't what has got me concerned. That Protogod was guarding what you found in that laboratory. Whatever that thing was it was far more powerful than that Protogod. Those words "Ashen Soul" greatly concern me. They crop up a few times in records and always at times of greatest suffering and death."

Meterove leaned towards Jolson, "You have any idea what those images on the doors are about?"

Jolson frowned, "No I don't and that concerns me too. My first thought is that it's symbolizing how this angel can't be killed by mortal hands but that's too simple. There's no way it's that easy. Then there are these creepy little winged creatures that Orilion was growing inside people."

Here Dras cut across Jolson "What happened to the woman inside that machine?"

Jolson and Meterove glanced at each other, and Jolson said "There was no way of separating her from that machine without her death. She's at peace now."

Dras fought back tears. Meterove knew what was going on behind those eyes. Dras was thinking of his family. How much he loved them and his anger at how anyone could do that to their wife would be pushing the sorrow away.

Jolson clearly noticed as well for he said, "You sure can pick them Meterove; capable of killing but with deep compassion, incredible loyalty but willing to speak his mind when he's right, and all the while brilliant, or at least a crazy that manages to be correct. Couldn't ask for a better friend, could you?"

Dras sat there stunned. He hadn't thought of it but now that Jolson said it, he realized the truth of those words. They had in fact become good friends. There were too many similarities to list. Looking at Meterove he saw a faint smirk on his face. Hell, thought Dras, guess I couldn't ask for a better friend either. Besides imagine the potential for picking up women with this guy as a name drop.

.   .   .

Joleen sat at her chair in her briefing room. Around her were Meterove, Jolson, Dras and Narok. Meterove and Dras had just finished their report of the mess inside of the manor and that combined with the reports she had from the investigation team she had put together along with Jolson's analysis had her in a slightly bad mood.

Not that it took much these days. She had always believed that she understood the pressure that her father had been under but now that she felt them for herself there was no doubt that she had underestimated them greatly. Her greatest worry was that she might break under this new pressure. While she was confident that the others would take care of her, their legacy, the idea of being a burned-out husk was not one that she enjoyed.

This part though, was worse than the rest. Now that she had to deal with a threat that had been right inside her city, she realized just how vulnerable they had been. Joleen placed her right hand over her eyes and said "First the Vorthains attack us, then we have an endless onslaught of undead and now Protogods and whatever these angels are. There is also the matter of the presence that Meterove and Dras felt."

Jolson said "To be honest as I said earlier it's this Ashen Soul thing that worries me the most. Every time it occurs in records there is disaster that it is paired with. To hear it now when we have a constant siege at the gate is not something that we should overlook."

Joleen lowered her hand, "I assume you have some proposal if you're being so frank about this."

Jolson nodded "We need to visit the elves. They may be able to shed some light on this. You know their records of the world are far more detailed and go further back than any other."

"By we, you mean me as well, don't you?" said Joleen

"Of course, I do. Even though it is Meterove and me it is likely that if we are to get what we want we'll need a direct request from you and if you are there that makes it easier, well at least less bureaucracy."

Joleen heaved a deep sigh then was silent for a moment. Then she looked at Narok and Dras and said "Well boys get ready for a trip. I'll contact the elves and then we'll leave soon after."

.   .   .

"Just be quiet and leave the navigating to me please!"

Joleen hunched her shoulders and glared at Meterove. He had returned from the manor three days ago. They had decided to leave immediately for the elves intending to speak with Lotherian, the elven king. It had been some time since she had been this far out of the city. It was nice and combined with the fact that it was just the five of them it made things far easier.

Meterove turned away from his glowering sister and attempted to return to his thoughts. The elves he had spoken too had seemed shocked that the dragon had said what he had but had refused to give any sort of explanation as to what it meant. The only thing that they would say was that he needed to speak with their king.

Then there was this whole mess that had happened in the manor. He was just as keen to find out what had been going on in there as the others. All this undead energy popping up had to be connected and if anyone knew why it would be the elves.

The road that they took was well traveled up until they reached the border of their kingdoms. There things would change as the elves preferred to use animal trails through the forest. The best thing that they could hope for was that there would be someone there to meet them. With the three of them on the road, the steward was in control of the city and day-to-day decisions. Meterove wasn't concerned; the man was their father's oldest friend.

After a fortnight they reached the border of the elves' forest realm. It was a great mixture of trees everything from needle-ridden pines to great maples to the mighty redwood. Meterove's fears were for naught for the elves had gotten the message from their men at the gate and were waiting for them. Three scouts stood waiting for them, and wordlessly beckoned them to follow.

It was two days after they entered the forest before they reached the capitol of the elves. In that time their guides had not said a word to them. The elves' normally passive expressions had been unusually tensed the closer they got to the capitol. The city was a section of redwood trees far larger at the base then any of the others that they had ever seen.

The centers of which were hollowed out by magic to serve as buildings, yet the trees were perfectly healthy. Their guides led them through the city to the largest of the buildings. As they reached the base of the tree, they noticed a pattern of magic appear in the shape of doors which swung open.

One of their guides turned to Meterove and said, "The king will see you now." Then each pressed a rune that was tattooed onto their right wrist and all three vanished in a wisp of green and brown. Meterove paused for a moment then dismounted and walked through the doors. The others followed suit.

Inside was a long hall with meticulously detailed carvings of vines and trees along the walls and ceiling. At the end of the hall was a circular room with chairs lining the room and at the very back on a throne of ash sat Lotherian.

As they entered the room Lotherian stood in greeting, "welcome dear friends and neighbors. I am aware of what transpired. If you would please sit and tell me yourself what this dragon said to you I might be able to shed some light on it. But first would you care for something to drink to wash the dust from your throat?"

Meterove nodded, "that would be greatly appreciated. Thank you, Lord Lotherian."

Lotherian motioned to an elf that was standing off to his left who left the room through a side door returning with a wooden tray and cups with a bottle of deep green liquid in the center. He poured a glass for each of them then left the room. Lotherian raised his cup saying. "I'll have none of this formality unless the occasion calls for it. I have known you all for many years with the exception of you young man." he pointed at Dras "What is your name?"

Dras gave a polite nod and said, "My name is Dras Bradok, my lord."

A new guard hmm?" His eyes darted down to Dras' left arm then back up "and a highly trusted one at that."

Meterove looked a Lotherian, "He lost his arm taking a blow from the Shadow Knight that killed my father. He bought my father another chance, though in the end he fell, the sacrifice showed far more than simple loyalty."

Lotherian raised his eyebrows "Indeed? Well, you have my respect and gratitude. Val was one of my oldest and most trusted friends. I sorely miss him." His gaze started on Meterove where it lingered a moment before shifting to Joleen then Jolson, he raised his cup and said, "To your father."

They all drank deeply. Dras had never had anything like it. It was potent yet there was no burn and he felt instantly better. Lotherian set his cup on the arm of this throne then looked at Meterove, "Now please recount the details of this dragon to me."

For the next twenty minutes Meterove went into every detail about the dragon as well as its warning. At the end of his tale Lotherian sat back in his throne looking deeply troubled. "This dragon actually SAID to find HIS lord... This is no simple matter. The dragons have jealously kept their secrets from the beginning. They've opened up to a few in the world and even then, only in times of great turmoil. The fact that one revealed this much to you, and a gold dragon at that, means that this is far more than a simple war."

Jolson leaned forward, "what does his color have anything to do with it?"

Lotherian looked troubled again then after a moment's pause said, "What I tell you I do with great apprehension, this information was entrusted to us on the condition that it never be passed outside our people."

Lotherian took a deep breath, "The dragons are not originally from our plane of existence. They were originally from the plane of fire and eons ago, for reason unknown to us, left in a great exodus. The reason the color matters is that the environment a dragon grows up in determines its color.

Gold dragons are the eldest of the entire race meaning that this dragon was, at the very least, an egg that was laid when the dragons were still in the plane of fire. A dragon elder chose to tell you far more than any human had ever been told."

Meterove took a moment to absorb this information, "So what did he mean by our lord? Is there a dragon king?"

Lotherian looked almost panicked now, "Yes and no. The best translation I can give you is embodiment and the nearest thing to a name I can give you is Xveriegariz."

Meterove said, "So we need to find this dragon lord and speak with him? You wouldn't happen to know where we could start would you?"

Lotherian nodded, "I didn't say that you needed to find him in sense of searching for him. He resides in a cave within this very forest. I shall take you there myself, but I must caution you. Do not be impertinent and ask only what you need to know and nothing more."

Meterove nodded, "Very well."

Lotherian said "If that is all then we can continue."

Jolson raided a hand to stall the elf who had begun to stand. "Actually, there is one other matter that we would like to speak with you about first, if you don't' mind."

The elf fell back into his chair and sighed looking downright alarmed. "Continue."

Jolson cleared his throat and went into a description of the vents that had occurred in the manor. Once he had finished the elf looked, if possible, even more alarmed. "To think" He said "That the words "Ashen Soul" would be spoken again. This truly is a bad omen. I would advise you to speak with the Dragon Lord on this.

Lotherian got to his feet and the others stood as well. Lotherian said, "Follow me."

He walked over to the side door that the servant had used earlier, which lead to a series of wings. The followed Lotherian through a maze of hallways until they reached another door that Lotherian opened and led them outside. They followed a narrow pathway lined with rocks that circled its way down a large steep hill. From the beginning there had been a strong smell of sulfur and as they neared the bottom it became even more pronounced.

An enormous cave stood before them. From within the cave came a thunderous voice that caused the very ground to shake. "What is the meaning of this Lotherian? You were instructed to never bring anyone here. Not only have you failed at that but judging by the scent these are humans! They CANNOT be trusted."

Lotherian got down on one knee and said, "Forgive me but it seemed unavoidable. The world is in great jeopardy. An all-consuming taint has risen."

A deep chuckle, fiery and entirely mirthless, came from within the cave. "It hasn't "risen" it's the same as before, this force has simply regained enough power to come forth again. Why should this concern me?"

Meterove stepped forward yelling, "Maybe because two dragons and a wyrm have already been slain because they were infected by this taint. Does that concern you even a little b-"

The ground shook and another roar came out of the cave. Lotherian looked at Meterove alarmed. "I told you to show respect!" An enormous head emerged from the cave. Its eyes were the size of a full-grown man. Its shape and appearance were unlike the other dragons he had seen before.

Large thorny spikes ran down the top of its head down its neck and back, and there was something very...primal about it. The color could be described as gold, what wasn't transparent in nature showing an inferno of magical fire within. Meterove realized that this thing was hardly a dragon. It was composed of more magic than flesh.

"What are you?"

The dragon looked at Meterove and seeing the crest on this armor his eyes narrow in distaste. "I should have guessed that the taint's creators would come for me."

Before Meterove said anything Joleen stepped forward and said, "What do you mean by that? We are fighting against this "taint" as you call it! We want it destroyed! How could we have anything to do with its creation?"

The dragon shifted its head to look at her. "As if you don't know! Destroyers of the flesh! Abominations of creation! I shall show you your evil and then you will be forced to accept your shame!"

There was a whirl of light and shadow and suddenly Meterove was in a city. It looked so familiar. It took Meterove a moment to realize that this was Yxarion. Looking around Meterove realized that he was alone, yet he could sense the others nearby. Though he could not see them he could also hear their breathing. Turning his attention back to the city Meterove puzzled over it a little. It wasn't the same city they had left just a few short weeks ago.

The people around them paid them no heed. It was as though they didn't exist. "It's a memory. This is what it's like to go into my trance." Meterove turned to the side. It was quite odd to hear his brother's voice come from thin air when he knew him to be standing there. So, the dragon was showing them a memory of something...but why and of what?

Suddenly they were up at the palace in the throne room. Sitting on the throne was a man that they all knew for his face was carved all around Yxarion and parts of it was in their own features; their ancestor Mardelnier. A man was being held by guards on his knees in front of him.

Mardelnier said, "For your crimes you will be executed and your name removed from history! Guards take him away!"

The guards dragged him back as he passed them, they saw a great resemblance between the man and Mardelnier. As they reached the door he shouted back, "You can't do this child! I am emperor here! You are nothing boy!"

Mardelnier fixed the man with a cruel stare, "You lost all privileges and authority when you began practicing foul magic...father." He said the last word as though it were poison.

The guards dragged the man out the door and as they swung shut there was an explosion outside. Mardelnier drew his sword and ran outside. A crater twenty feet across was just outside and a few bits of armor littered the ground. Hovering in the center of the crater was a shadowy figure. As they watched the figure turned towards Mardelnier. It no longer had flesh, it had transformed into something that few mages ever attempted, a lich.

Still Mardelnier didn't strike; all he did was whisper "father." The creature opened a portal through which a vast frozen wasteland could be seen. He entered the portal both disappeared. Mardelnier hadn't even attempted to stop the creature.

Here another man stepped forward from behind Mardelnier. Based on his appearance he must have been related to Mardelnier in some way. "I'll track him down so that he can be sealed. You must remain here."

Now the swirl of light and shadow was back. They appeared back in the city only this time there were soldiers everywhere. Panic reigned and smoke rose from several buildings. From high above they heard someone shout, "Hold them where they are! We can't let them take the city!"

It was Mardelnier he was dressed in full armor his sword in his hand. He was standing high up on one of the walls among a mass of archers. Another swirl of light and shadow and they were next to him looking out over the walls and what they saw made them go cold.

A dark mass of undead and shadowy creatures stretched as far as the eye could see. Soldiers fought hard as the undead attempted to scale the walls, fought off vampires and werewolves as they appeared amongst them all the while taking losses from arrows and magic from the enemy force.

Mardelnier was covered in mixture of blood and ash. His blade, as it was told, burned evil with righteous fire. The situation looked bleak indeed then suddenly there was a great roar in the distance. A great dragon...one that looked oddly familiar came into view in the distance. Following him was a sky darkening swarm of dragons.

Mardelnier swore, "That bastard brought the dragons into this!" A look of desperation came over his face.

One of the men nearby asked, "What should we do my lord? The walls will not keep those dragons out and the damage they could cause..."

Mardelnier knew that he was right and took a deep breath before saying, "we can't win against both forces. As it is the dragons could wipe us out without the damned hammering on our front door." He paused briefly before yelling, "Prepare yourselves!"

Now they were back on the ground and the gates to the city opened wide and a great force issued forth. Looking up Mardelnier gazed at a lone Pegasus as it bore its rider towards the dragon lord.

"Go brother and I pray you succeed" said Mardelnier. He refocused on the army in front of him and yelled, "FOR THE EMPIRE!"

A chorus of battle cries answered him, and they charged into the undead. As the two forces collided there was a deafening clash of steel on steel. At first the undead fought with Mardelnier as though he was like any other soldier, but it soon became apparent that he was far more.

Each blow from his blade burned with holy fire that left nothing but cleaned ashes behind. The undead attempted to overwhelm him but to no avail, he was not to be denied. Suddenly out of the main force of the enemy a shadow creature rose mounted on a Manticore.

It landed in the middle of a group of soldiers and with a single swipe a whole battalion was wiped out. Mardelnier turned to face this new foe and looked into the empty fleshless face of his father.

"It is time for you to die...son."

He swung a heavy blow with his black sword the Mardelnier parried. "You are not my father. My father ceased to exist the moment you became a lich."

The lich laughed, and then proceeded to attack; Mardelnier, despite his words, seemed unwilling to fight back. They continued to dance in a circle; Mardelnier was completely focused on defending himself. So much so that it wasn't until he was knocked to the ground that he realized that most of his army had been wiped out and the undead were about to overwhelm them.

"How did you get the dragons to help you monster? They normally want nothing to do with vile magic!"

The lich laughed again, "They are unaware of my true nature or that of my army. They are here to attack you and the undead threat both! They'll wipe out all and I'll raise the bodies back again when all is over. But you are holding back the process!"

The lich suddenly darted forward and this time Mardelnier wasn't fast enough to completely dodge it and the blade logged itself in his leg.

"Death isn't so bad son. Just look at me." The lich thrust his blade into Mardelnier's chest. His eyes bulged as the blade was removed. "Now I have my kingdom back!"

Mardelnier let out a weak chuckle. Looking over the lich's shoulder he said, "Tell that to Valnyr...he seems to have had a few words with the dragons..."

Mardelnier's eyes went blank but the last thing he saw was his brother descending on the battle with a horde of very angry dragons and the lich screaming in rage and vanishing in a swirl of shadow.

.   .   .

The swirl of shadow and light and they were back in front of the cave.

"You see what your family has done! Deceivers! Vile sorcerers! And that coward let that monstrosity live! Countless dragons, my CHILDREN, died in that battle and that was just the beginning of the war!"

The dragon took a deep breath as though it were trying to calm itself. "Countless dead over the centuries and that is only the beginning."

Meterove fidgeted uncomfortably, what he had seen had disturbed him and he understood the rage of this dragon. "Those were his actions not ours. Maybe all dragons' actions are because of your actions but that is not how humans work!"

Meterove was shocked by what he had seen but also by a few simple details that, while minor in the grand scheme of things were very earth shaking. They had already heard of their ancestor Mardelnier and his younger brother Valnyr. It was a simple thing, but Meterove had spotted the family crest during the vison.

The only version of the original family crest still in existence was a stained-glass window panel that was kept in the archives. It was known as the Shattered Crest. The upper right side of it was broken away, thus its name. In the vision though it had been whole.

It had been believed that the broken portion had been mere decoration but that was not the case. The crest depicted four children. It had always been believed that

Mardelnier had been the founder of their empire but that was not the case.

His father, whose name he still did not know had founded the empire and had four children. Mardelnier and Valnyr were the two known ones but there was also another prince, presumably the man from before and a princess that had yet to be seen.

Why was there no record of the other two?

Meterove noticed that his siblings were just as confused as he was.

The dragon eyes him curiously, "You expect me to believe you are any different than your ancestors, that you will destroy this creature?"

"Unlike Mardelnier I have no attachment to this lich. I have never known him, in fact never even knew of him until today."

"I doubt you human, yet I will speak to you. What exactly is your reason for seeking me out and what made Lotherian trust you with knowledge of my existence?"

Meterove looked into the giant golden eye and memories of the past few months came rushing to the surface. "I have now killed two dragons that were tainted by undeath. The first was within one of our ancient temples and was fully corrupted. The second sought us out. The corruption was taking him. His last act was to warn us that we must seek out his lord and that the elves could help us do so.”

A puff of smoke issued from the dragons nose, “Did he now, young dragons can be rash-”

“This dragon was gold in color.”

Anger entered the dragons eyes again, “An elder was tainted? And he gave you this information!”

“Yes, so what can you do that can help us? You have already explained the origin of our enemy and we know now where we can find him.”

Now the dragon stared at him moment. “Things have changed I must amend my former decision to not trust you. It seems that even my oldest children are being taken and one was willing to trust you a human and the decedent of the lich.”

“Now to answer your question. What can I do human? Hmmm…I will have my children keep watch on the situation and attempt to aid in the cleansing. As for ending this plight, the only power that might be able to aid you is another of my kind. Seek out the observers in the elemental planes.” He breathed over them and instantly Meterove felt something change.

“I have attuned you to the elemental planes. You can enter the planes by going to the place where I first entered this world. I must warn you; I know not what you can expect on the other side for I have not been there since before time.”

“Once you are in through you will arrive at the waystation. The watcher and their minions will be able to direct you further. I know not what will be required of you or what form your aid will come in. Now go, and pray human, that you are able to back your words!”

The dragon pulled himself forward from the cave. Meterove and the others stepped back as his whole body emerged. He spread his wings and reared back in leapt into the sky each wing stroke knocking, down trees and pushing Meterove to his knees.

As the dragon disappeared, Lotherian got to his feet, “We have much to discuss now. I can show you where you need to travel, but then I must be off to our own front to coordinate with the dragons.”

.   .   .

Back in the throne room, Lotherian had a map brought to them and marked a section of mountains. “This is your destination. It is far outside our realm in the wilds of the forest. Be careful, for there is great danger in the forest. Under no condition should you travel after dark.”

Meterove nodded, "thank you Lotherian."

Lotherian gave an anxious glance at Joleen and Jolson before saying, "I'd recommend all of you going," looking Jolson in the eyes. "I know more than I can say, you understand I'm sure Jolson?"

Jolson said, "Yes I know what you mean," turning to Meterove he said, "It's necessary." For Meterove had looked ready to argue with him.

Meterove closed his mouth then looked at Lotherian and said, "Very well we can take care of preparations. I'm not sure what we're supposed to do but Jolson seems to have some idea, so I'll trust him. You best get to your front."

Lotherian clapped Meterove on the shoulder, "Be strong my young friend. This world needs you; it needs all of you." He gave one last look at Joleen and Jolson before exiting the room.

Meterove said, "Well let's get our supplies in order and packed tonight we'll have to leave first thing in the morning."

Joleen nodded tersely; she wasn't happy with this turn of events but there was no question that it was correct path. For now, this was Meterove's territory, so he'd lead them. The hopelessness of the situation seemed to overwhelm her but then she thought of her father and a strong determination took over...she was going to avenge him. This abomination of their bloodline was going to be destroyed

CHAPTER 12.5
DARKFIRE

How could the discord have done this? This thing that wasn't balanced or natural in any way. That! That was malevolence that was radiating from the fragment! Also, its power, unlike the other fragments, was increasing! It was there amongst the others, burning but the flames were blacker than the darkest abyss.

Suddenly the Darkfire one flared up and with a burst of black flame, vanished. That it was gone without a trace and that its destination was unknown was bad, but the fact that its power surpassed all other fragments combined was far worse.

There was a very limited number of avenues to explore for dealing with this problem. A small "tug" was felt pulling away from the matter of the Darkfire one. A swirl of kaleidoscopic color later and the source was found.

How was THIS possible? The Ashen Soul had managed to possess something as sinister as this? How had the act been missed? A sense of calm and understanding descended that was just as strong as the mysticism that had preceded it.

After briefly connecting with the other fragments the understanding became certainty. All had sensed the Ashen Soul's movement and had now seen what had happened afterwards, but none of them had seen the moment that it had occurred. Additionally, there were several other points in the sequence of events that were unseen by any of the fragments.

The only answer was that the Darkfire one had been the fragment that had seen those and had either vanished in order to protect the details for as long as possible or there were further events it wanted to hide. The question now was whether the Darkfire was aiding the Ashen Soul, or being corrupted by it?

There was no other action left that could be taken. Ending it was out of the question at this point and attempting to merge with it was too unpredictable. This left only the option of sealing it. As for the Ashen Soul...unfortunately that would be up to the mortals to deal with.

CHAPTER 13
TERENIA

The elves had given them extra provisions and a few more warnings before sending them on their way. Joleen was quite concerned about the nature of the elves' behavior. It had a definite air of not expecting to ever see them again. Clearly this was not a part of the forest that was often traveled.

The things that bothered her most were the talk about spirits, nymphs, and monsters in the forest. Meterove seemed to share her concerns but said nothing about it. They were currently traveling around a lake that the elves had warned them not to enter saying only that it was certain death. Not willing to test this they had taken the long route via foot since from the sound of it horses would not be an option where they would be going.

Each day they stopped and set up camp before nightfall making sure to have plenty of wood available for making and keeping a fire lit through the night. They slept light for there was certainly something out there, just outside the ring of light made by the fire and whenever anyone attempted to search for it, it melted into the darkness.

Three weeks passed in this way. Their tempers were perhaps slightly shorter than normal but otherwise the time passed without incident. They had set up camp as usual and while Meterove, Dras, and Narok practiced their swordsmanship, Joleen would keep them from doing any real damage and healed wounds that did occur.

Jolson meanwhile would attempt to go into his trances. Tonight, he was having more trouble than usual, not helped by the fact that he had the rather disconcerting feeling that he was being watched.

After ten minutes he gave it up as a bad job and opened his eyes intending to join the others when he saw her. A beautiful woman was standing in the trees; her midnight black hair falling down her body barely concealing her. From what Jolson could tell she was completely naked. She beckoned to him and without thinking Jolson stood and followed her.

She began walking backwards still beckoning him to follow. The air was so very still, and the moonlight seemed unusually bright, as though it was magnified.

She vanished for a moment then Jolson saw her again sitting on a rock, she locked eyes with him and shook her hair back uncovering her body. It was covered in a highly detailed pattern of vines and flowers.

Jolson drew level with her, and she flashed him a mischievous smile, pushing her chest out slightly. Jolson was overcome with a single desire to be with the woman...to kiss her. He leaned in and his lips had nearly touched hers when he heard his name shouted.

He turned to see the others standing twenty feet away with drawn swords, Joleen holding a dagger. He turned back to the woman determined to ignore them, but she had changed. Her face was now contorted with rage, and she turned to leaves and blew away.

Meterove quickly cast a spell of holding on the clearing, and instantly they were encased in a bubble of yellow energy. The leaves joined back together, and the woman reappeared. "You have taken my prey. What is he to you?"

"This is my brother."

"Ahh brothers... like I am with my sisters, I understand," She smiled mischievously again. Jolson pushed Meterove out of his way attempting to get to the woman. Joleen grabbed Jolson by the shoulder and pulled him back, hard. He landed on the ground he stood up shaking his head. "What's going on? Where are we?"

"You are in my forest mortals. Why you have entered is not important for you will not live much longer."

Meterove suddenly understood. She was a nymph. That explained the trance Jolson had been in and how she had lured him away. Nymphs kept their youth and immortality by draining the life from their surroundings and were said to enjoy men they trapped in their spell.

This nymph though had no idea who she had trapped. It was time for the hunter to find out what happens when you trap something that can hunt you back. Focusing his thoughts Meterove closed the containment field so that she couldn't move. In fear and anger she kept turning into leaves and throwing herself against the field.

After some time, she accepted her fate and returned to her human-like appearance. "What do you want from me mortal? If you intended to kill me, you would have done so already." Meterove glanced over at Jolson before saying, "I know what you are Nymph, so I don't need to ask what you were intending to do to my brother. However, what you can do for me is help guide us in here. We need to reach a section of mountains south of here."

At these words, the nymph's eyes widened, "And why mortal would you like to go there?"

It was obvious that she knew more than she was letting on. "I think," said Meterove, "that you know the significance of those mountains but just in case, we're looking for passage to a place beyond this world."

"And what business do you have traveling the planes?"

"I'm not entirely sure what we're looking for only that it has something to do with someone that watches."

The nymph looked curious now. "Will you grant my freedom once I have guided you there?"

"I will"

"Then I will guide you and in turn promise that I shall not turn on you even after I have completed my task."

Meterove lowered the barrier cautiously. He was somehow sure that she'd keep her word, but it was whether she'd phrased it for interpretation that worried him.

As the barrier came down the nymph paused for a moment then stepped forward and not meeting any other resistance smiled at Meterove.

"Well then let's get on with this I have no desire to remain with you any longer than I have to and I'm sure the feeling is mutual."

Meterove said, "Yes however it is time we rested you can return to our camp with us; however, I do have another request."

The nymph raised an eyebrow. "OH?"

Meterove glanced downward briefly then back up to her face before saying, "You must put on some form of clothing." He glanced at Jolson, and then smirked, "Otherwise you may prove far too distracting to some of the others." Jolson turned slightly red at these words but said nothing.

The nymph cocked her head to the side then giggled, "Very well." With a wave of her hand a set of black leather armor appeared on her. Well at least that's the closest thing that Meterove could think to call it.

It was far more revealing than most armor, the chest piece in particular barely covered more than her breasts and left a fair amount of her cleavage showing. The lower half was nearly as bad. The leather only went a quarter of the way down her right thigh and the left side was nothing more than a leather string holding it closed. A pair of leather boots went up to her knees.

Meterove had a suspicion that she had formed it that way in order to taunt Jolson. He was just about to say something when Joleen said something that made him do a double take. Her eyes were wide and almost sparkled with excitement. "That is so cute! Can you make me something like that?"

There were no words. Meterove had no idea how to go about this. Since when had Joleen decided that she was like this? A moment later his brain started to analyze it and realized that compared to what she was wearing now it was actually an improvement from the practicality side.

While she wasn't wearing her usual robes, the knee length skirt was hardly going to be adequate where they were heading. The nymph looked slightly taken aback at first but giggled again and did a quick two fingered salute saying, "You bet! Just tell me what you want!"

Joleen was a little nervous but decided that with Meterove there she was safe. She walked over to the nymph and after a quick whispered conversation stepped back. After a moment, the nymph waved her hand again and a set of brown leather armor appeared on Joleen. Meterove was relieved to see that this set, while still revealing, was far less so than the nymph's.

There was a pair of simple bracers that had small leather bands on the outside for some unknown purpose. The chest piece covered most of her upper half though it left the shoulders exposed. The lower half was very similar to the nymph's though the armor stopped just a few inches above the knee and the left leg had a lattice of leather bands instead of being bare. To accommodate the longer armor the boots only went halfway up the calf.

It wasn't the Joleen that had been on the surface, but the real self that she kept buried. Meterove knew why she had chosen to let herself out now. Where they were going there was no need for the 'royal highness' version of herself but the more outgoing side might be of some use.

"Joleen looked down at her new attire and Meterove could help but smirk. The real Joleen and the aristocratic girl façade that she used so much that it had actually become part of her were arguing at the moment. Joleen glanced over at Narok then back at the ground. "Thank you."

The nymph put her right hand on her hip and gave another salute, "Not a problem! So, shall we?"

Meterove understood gestured towards their camp. Once there the nymph seated herself on a stump. The others were able to sleep with the assurance that Meterove was going to remain awake to keep an eye on the nymph. Once the others had drifted off to sleep Meterove picked up his whetstone and set about sharpening his blade.

The nymph watched intently, finally asking "What is the purpose of that?"

"This? I'm sharpening my sword nymph."

Her eyes narrowed. "I have a name...there is no reason to call me 'nymph'"

Meterove looked back at her slightly abashed and deciding that he could at least be civil. "OK well my apologies...what is your name?"

The nymph tossed her hair and said, "My name is Terenia."

Meterove said, "My name is Meterove."   They made small talk for most of the night, though he did refrain from mentioning the burning sensation that had gone across his back. This woman was part of his fate. That was certain.

.   .   .

The next morning the others awoke to Meterove and Terenia having a pleasant conversation while they prepared some breakfast. Dras and Narok exchanged a glance with each other before looking at Joleen and Jolson. It was clear from their expressions that they were just as confused as they were by this turn of events. Jolson looked over at the two talking and felt a small surge of jealousy that he quickly brushed aside. Nymph magic was strong that was for sure.

"Morning" said Meterove cheerfully as he pulled some bacon from the fire.

Dras was the first to speak, "She didn't charm you while we were asleep, did she?"

Terenia looked a little put off by this but said nothing. Meterove on the other hand replied, "No she did not. I have a ward up for that kind of thing in case another nymph was to try but as far as Terenia goes, I'm willing to trust her word."

This made Terenia smile, but Jolson cocked his head, Terenia, is it?"

Meterove shook his head slightly, "Ah yes where are my manners. Everyone this is Terenia. Terenia this is Dras, Narok, my sister Joleen, and I believe you're fairly well acquainted with my brother Jolson. Again, he blushed slightly and remained silent. Last night's episode had been embarrassing enough that he did not want to acknowledge it.

Terenia gave another girlish giggle like the night before and clasped her hands together in front of her and slightly pushed her shoulders down and forward said, "I really should apologize for last night. Even though it's in my nature to do such things in order to survive it would be best if I refrain while we are traveling companions. I can pull the life energy from forest animals like usual, in order to keep my energy up."

Once they had finished breakfast and Meterove had put out the fire Terenia jumped excitedly to her feet. "Well let's get going!"

Dras looked at Joleen and said, "She seems quite cheery for someone that was trying to kill Jolson last night doesn't she."

Joleen gave a small snort. Yeah, that was an understatement to be sure. Joleen had never seen such a happy-looking person before. It felt odd but from what little she knew about nymphs this was the norm. "Can we wait one moment longer I'd like to get something out of my pack if I could?"

Meterove nodded and Joleen proceeded to remove the contents of her pack. It was oddly messy for her. Though Meterove had to admit this whole thing was new for her and since she didn't have her usual order around her. That was probably just her way of adjusting to the lack of control. Either way it was kind of funny to see.

From within her pack Joleen pulled a wooden box and set it on the ground and opened it. Inside were two short wire wrapped rods. Picking them up a pair of curved blades appeared where it had been rounded before. Hmm thought Meterove so this is her artifact. Now that he thought about it, they all had artifacts except Dras, and his hand was technically the same thing.

As they passed through the forest it seemed like she knew every time when they would pass by something that the others had never seen before and kept up a running commentary. There were trees and flowers that they had never seen before and with the same constant high energy Terenia would tell them the names and more importantly what might be dangerous.

They passed over streams and through small clearings but always they were blocked from seeing where they were going. It seemed as if the forest itself was interested in keeping them from reaching their goal. Some of the trees that were around them were far larger than any that they had seen yet. Not even the tower from the mage city compared to these.

At one point they passed over a massive stump that had been cut low to the ground, as though it had been sawed down. Exactly how was anyone's guess since the gap between the rings of the tree were larger than their feet and there were hundreds of them.

That night they camped in a clearing and after they had eaten a decent supper, they relaxed more than the previous night. Some were smoking pipes, others drinking from a wine bag or in Jolson's case meditating. Meterove had lain on his back and was examining the sky.

"We truly are far from home, aren't we? The sky looks different here."

Terenia looked eagerly over at Meterove. "I can teach you a few of the constellations and their stories if you would like."

Meterove turned his head so that he was looking at her. Behind her he could see that the others were paying attention as well. Even Jolson had stopped meditating in order to hear. "Since everyone else seems interested let's hear it."

Terenia bounced a little in excitement then after a moment looked to the sky and began pointing out constellations. "That one is called Archer. The tail points due south and the story behind him is one of a more humorous nature.

Once long ago, there was a cat that lived in a small village. This cat was unable to do anything other than eat and thus grew to unheard of size, size of the...rotund variety. As a result, the people of the village were forced to drive the cat away. Once outside of the village the cat's hunger was not sated so he began to raid the food stores of the village.

The people felt great fear for winter was coming and they were not sure they would be able to feed themselves if the cat kept on raiding their food so they had their strongest warrior find the cat for no other would be able to lift it. The warrior, though the strain was immeasurable, picked up the cat and swung him in a great circle before casting him into the sky.

The cat's great size however had reached its limit and once in the sky imploded turning into a massive star, yet the force of the throw caused it to separate leaving that constellation in the sky. The people named it Archer after the cat, whose body had created it."

Dras chuckled, "So in other words that's the fat cat constellation."

Terenia looked him and gave a giggle, "That's right!"

The sound of laughter filled the camp. Once it had subsided a little Meterove said, "what others do you have for us?"

Terenia pointed up again this time at one that was on the edge of the sky that bore a resemblance to a rabbit and said, "That one is Rherion the Quick. She was said to have taunted all the predators in the forest by allowing them close then using her great speed at the last moment causing the hungry beasts to wear themselves out and die."

"She eventually met her end at the hands of an angry nymph who forced her into the sky and placed that one." Here Terenia pointed at a group of starts that looked like a wolf, "in the sky with her to chase her for eternity."

Terenia turned ,and kneeling on the ground, pointed in the opposite direction of the previous constellation pointed out one final constellation that was almost right above them. "The last one that we can see at the moment is the Wanderer's Compass. This one is said to have been created because of a hermit that lived in these woods.

While he shunned normal society, he was kind to any lost souls that he came across and would point them in the right direction so they could find their way home. When old age finally took him, he asked a nearby spirit if it would take the old compass that he had used in his youth and place it in the sky to help those who were lost once he was gone.

The spirit was impressed with the kindness and compassion of the old hermit and granted his last request."

Dras said, "So the points on that thing…"

"Face north, south, east, and west. That's right!" completed Terenia clapping her hands three times in quick succession.

Meterove chuckled, "The cat is my favorite by far"

Dras and Narok laughed as well. But Jolson and Joleen shook their heads. Joleen said, "well the cat may be entertaining but at least the compass has some actual value to it." Jolson nodded his agreement. Meterove, Dras and Narok laughed again and this time after a moment Joleen and Jolson joined in as well.

Terenia looked from one to the other with a slightly puzzled expression then after a moment let out a giggle and said, "Humans sure are interesting. I never would have guessed that you would be this much fun!"

Meterove took a breath to steady his voice then said "and you're just getting to know us too. But enough of this for tonight. We're going to have another long day, so we had better get some sleep."

The others agreed and after placing their respective items back in their packs they pulled out bed rolls and one by one drifted off with the exception of Dras who would be taking the first watch tonight.

Over the next week Terenia kept them on track, though she refused to keep a slow pace and when time came each night to set up camp she resisted. It was a strange and beautiful forest.

Meterove was sure that having Terenia in their group was making things move more smoothly. For one he had caught glimpses of other nymphs and though he was sure they would have attacked under normal circumstances they merely vanished when they realized they had been spotted.

Terenia was a decent enough guide as far as the trails were concerned but what made her truly useful was her knowledge of the forest. With their food supply dwindling it was time to look to other means of sustenance. She was able to show them what roots, herbs and animals could be eaten.

As they drew nearer to their destination, she seemed to get nervous, stopping on the bank of a river at her order even though there was still plenty of light left. Unsure as to what was ahead the rest agreed though they were definitely curious. The next day as they were packing up their camp Terenia took Meterove aside.

"We need to move through this area as fast as possible as it is we run the risk of being noticed."

"Noticed by what?"

"There are things in this part of the forest. Even I don't know exactly what they are or even what they look like. I know this... my mother has forbidden me to go through here. Any nymph who has entered here has died."

This news worried Meterove. They didn't even know what they had to watch out for and the fact that Terenia was worried about whatever was here was cause for concern. "We'll move as fast as we can and stop only if we have to."

Terenia nodded, "Then let's go."

They finished packing up their camp and Meterove filled the others in on what Terenia had told him while she scouted for the best place to cross the river.

She came back just as they finished packing the camp slightly out of breath. "I've found a good place for us to cross about a mile upstream."

Once they crossed, they hurried through the forest keeping their weapons at the ready. Immediately Meterove knew that Terenia had been right. There was something eerie about this section of the forest. He had the constant sensation of being watched and several times he heard something run quickly across the trees above them.

The third time this happened Narok paused for a moment and looked around. He barely had time to react to what he saw. He managed to get his buckler up across his chest, deflecting most of the blow. Even with that he was still impaled in the side by a large spike.

He pushed hard against the creature and fell backwards. He looked down at his side and saw that it was covered in blood which poured out of him, however nothing vital seemed to have been hit.

He now looked at what had hit him. Standing a few feet from him was a creature that was built like a large cat except it had a distinctly insect appearance with a large spike protruding from its head.

Meterove and Dras reacted quickly but still too slow to prevent them from being knocked aside by the creature, which now seemed to be targeting Terenia.

As it charged at Terenia, Jolson leapt forward and managed to sever one of the creature's legs forcing it off target and missing Terenia. It hit the ground rolled and hopped back up quickly regenerating its lost limb. Now it was focused on Jolson. The creature reared and charged.

Just as the creature began to jump Joleen acted. She moved like lightning darting in and catching the creature under the chin with her dagger. The momentum carried it onward tearing the dagger from her hand. She drew her other dagger and dove after it, thrusting the dagger into the back of its skull. It convulsed a few times before going still. She pulled her daggers free then remembered Narok.

She hurried over to him. Dras and Meterove were already kneeling by his side. They had managed to staunch the bleeding, but he was very pale and barely conscious. Joleen worked quickly healing the wound as best she could, but the lost blood would be the main issue.

Meterove sheathed his sword and was about to divide the contents of his pack when Terenia came over picked up the pack and shouldered it. "I'll take this for now. Carry him and let's get moving." She was looking up in the trees. Meterove glanced around and saw her concern. At least a dozen of the creatures were around them. However, the fact that one of their kind had been killed seemed to make them nervous.

Meterove bent down, picked Narok up and hoisted him to his shoulder. They glanced at each other then started to run. Meterove could hear the creatures above them and occasionally behind them. Form what he could tell they were like a chameleon, able to blend into their surroundings.

Small bright disks started to appear on the ground at his feet and looking forward Meterove saw that Terenia was casting spells leaving magical traps that were slowing the ones that were chasing them and making them warier.

There was something else ahead of them that caught his attention. At first, he was unsure as to what it was then realized that he was seeing open sky. "We're nearly out...push it!"

They burst from the forest into the bright sunlight and Meterove realized that the reason it had been so open was that the forest ended at a steep hill. He burst out into open air and landed, hard; the others crunching down around him. Whatever the creatures were that had been following them didn't want to exit the forest, whether the sunlight hurt them or if they feared that area Meterove didn't care.

Meterove sat up and looked at the others. They looked a little worse for wear but at least they were alive. Narok was barely conscious it would be best to rest for a bit and let him regain this strength. Meterove looked up and saw before him one hell of a sight.

A section of mountains jutted from nothing spewing lava out around them. There was no question they had found where the dragon lord had entered the world. Before that though was a massive area of ruins. At least that's what it looked like to Meterove at first until he noticed that it was in a pattern. Fear coursed through him; he knew what that was...a labyrinth.

They set up camp that night at the base of the hill and though exhausted none of them could sleep. They had all heard legends of labyrinths and of atrocities that were committed inside them. It was said that monsters called Minotaur dwelled within them. These half-man, half-bull monsters were supposed to grow to incredible size and lived by eating the flesh of those caught within the twisting passages they lived in.

Meterove had told Terenia that she was free to leave now that they were out of the forest, that he would consider her service complete, but she would hear none of it. "I'll leave once you are safely on the other side."

Meterove couldn't help himself wondering if she didn't have an ulterior motive for wanting to stay. Regardless of the reason he appreciated her staying, he had grown to trust her navigating skills in the recent days. She would be a great asset inside the labyrinth.

When dawn came, they packed the camp up and made their way through the ruins looking for the entrance. They had walked for most of the day before Meterove found what he was looking for. A large door with massive magical pulley system around it connected to a large stone slab in front of the door.

Meterove looked at the others and explained. "The stone slab is a pressure plate. Our weight will open the door and once we enter the door will shut behind us. There will be no turning back." He glanced at Terenia, but her face was impassive.

He glanced back at the door and noticed that there was a large symbol carved into the top; three intertwined triangles.

Meterove didn't dwell on this though and made his way over to the plate. As soon as he stood on it the door started going up. The others followed him onto the plate and glancing backwards he closed his eyes, squared his shoulders, and walked through the door. He instantly disappeared from view and the others partially out of fear of the unknown followed quickly.

The moment the last person stepped off the stone plate the door came crashing down and a crystal that they hadn't seen before due to the darkness glowed green and projected an image of a richly clad man with a white goatee.

The image kept flickering and parts of what was clearly a speech flicked in and out. From what they could hear this man had likely captured this labyrinth and the minotaur that lived here and used it for his entertainment.

From all appearances this man was long dead and therefore the message useless. However, it made Meterove burn with anger; that anyone would throw another human being in here for sport was sick. What concerned him the most was the part about magic abilities being greatly reduced in here.

A nudge at his shoulder made Meterove turn around. Joleen was looking up at him. The light from the crystal was fading and the others were passing out torches that they had made the previous evening.

A few quick words and the torches were lit. They paused while their eyes adjusted to the change in light. Looking around they saw that there were three paths that they could take to right off. Meterove looked from one to the next then shrugging took the middle passage thinking to himself that there wasn't much difference.

They stayed close together and every so often Meterove would stop and ask the others their opinion on a direction. It was impossible to tell how long they were walking around in there so when they were tired, they would rest taking it in shifts to sleep.

They hadn't seen any sign of a living minotaur yet but many of the polished marble walls had deep gouges in them that Meterove could only guess were from its horns. The other part that did nothing to inspire confidence was the number of skeletons that littered the ground.

They had spent what they assumed to be several days inside the maze before they began to notice it but there was definitely something in here with them. Unfortunately, there were enchantments on the place that prevented footprints on the floor which prevented them from identifying their fellow occupant. On their seventh day they came to a room with two other passages leading out of it. Looking around the room Meterove felt despair. They had come full circle.

The others seemed to notice as well for they were looking dejected. The supply of torches that they had brought with them was getting very low. They camped there to rest and put out all but one torch in an attempt to conserve them as long as possible. After a few hours rest each they returned to searching for a way out.

There were several more times they found themselves back in that same chamber. Now Meterove was marking the walls in an attempt to prevent another trip through this hell. Tempers were rising and even a little madness from the pressing dark. Using magic Meterove was barely able to see in the dark but that would at least save their last torch for times where they had to have more light.

Whatever was in here with them was nearby now. There were times that Meterove had everyone stop and remain quiet because it was only one passage over. Left, straight, right, another right, straight, left, left there was no end to this.

More than once it occurred to him that there was perhaps no end to this. That the sick noble that had his image projected might have sealed any exit.

"Mustn't think like that," he kept muttering to himself.

Now madness was truly setting in. Twice there was a minor scuffle when Dras or Jolson walked into Meterove. It came to a head when Dras accidentally brushed against Joleen who in turn shoved Dras away. Before Meterove could turn around Narok and Dras were brawling.

Meterove shouted at them and immediately wished he hadn't.

A roar echoed down the tunnels causing Dras and Narok to cease fighting and scramble to their feet. The wall ahead of them erupted as if from an explosion and they were showered in chunks of marble. Looking ahead Meterove was barely able to make out the shape of their stalker.

Standing nearly twenty feet tall and with a powerfully build body was a minotaur; its legs covered in fur and ending in a hoof, the torso of a man and the head of a bull. Its eyes were the only thing that could be easily seen. They were an angry, bright red, and they pierced the dark.

It charged them and Meterove pushed the others in front of him getting them to move. Running back through the twisting passages they could hear wall after wall being destroyed. Meterove barely had time to realize where they were going. As he turned the corner after the others his heart sank. Yet again they were back at the beginning.

Behind them the minotaur roared again and turning around Meterove saw it. It was in the far-right passage. In its hand was a large chunk of marble which it hurled towards them. Meterove wouldn't have had the time to save the others, but Narok seemed to understand what was happening.

He pushed Joleen and Terenia forward and dove forward knocking Dras to the ground. The boulder barely missed them hitting the ground where they had been standing and bouncing up and knocking a hole in the wall revealing another passage.

The hole was small, but Meterove thought they would fit.

"There's a hole in that wall now. Go for the passage behind it."

He drew his sword and stepped forward. Thinking to himself that if Vlad could take on a wyrm single handed without magic he could at least hold off a minotaur.

Behind him the others clambered through the hole. The minotaur charged roaring. As it entered the chamber a bright light emitted from the crystal. The minotaur roared in pain; obviously, it hadn't seen light in a very long time. Meterove's eyes adjusted much quicker and in the new light Meterove saw that the minotaur was armored in a solid plate chest piece and carried a large war axe.

"Meterove!"

Meterove looked over in the direction of his name and saw Joleen on the other side of the hole. Sheathing his sword Meterove clambered through the hole and as soon as he was through pressed himself against the wall out of sight from the other room.

Back in the entrance chamber the light went down and the minotaur stood there for a moment before its eyes adjusted back enough that it could look around for them. Meterove could hear it sniffing them out too. It came over pressed its head up to the hole, attempting to catch their scent.

Meterove knew that there was no chance that it wouldn't smell them, yet it drew back and went down the left passage. Meterove and Jolson looked at each other in the dim light. That had been a narrow escape. Yet why had it left? No one was in any doubt that it had caught their scent.

Unwilling to sit around and find out Meterove got to his feet. "Let's go."

They proceeded down the tunnel that they had found and knew at once they had not traveled it before. This sign was a blessing and curse all in one. They had not seen any marks in wall like the ones here and Meterove knew why. These tunnels were taller, probably an older part of the labyrinth. This meant that there was room for a creature that size to wield its axe.

After wandering these tunnels for some time, they came across a section of the tunnel with a strange opening in it. It was roughly the size of a human, and a little further down was a door.

Meterove stood with his hand on the knob ready to turn but looked at the others first. Joleen nodded. He turned the knob and with a creak the door opened. Upon entering the room machinery began to power up. The nature of it was well beyond Meterove. Jolson stepped forward looking at the far wall. Meterove turned around and his stomach turned over.

There was a series of glass tanks filled with a strange bluish liquid, but it was what was in the liquid that made him sick. From left to right the tanks held infants, then toddlers, then several that looked to be in early teens and last two adults: one man and one woman.

Jolson was flipping through a pile of notes trying to make sense of it. After a few minutes he closed a journal looking sick. "This man was sick. These people are being held, suspended, incapable of dying. They're unknowingly producing children through this machine. It nurtures them to their late teens then," Jolson paused for a moment, "Then wakes them and sends them down that shoot into the labyrinth."

Meterove understood at once. Whoever that man at the entrance had wanted to make sure that his pet was always fed. Well, that was going to end now.

"How do we free them?"

"From what I can tell from these notes you can't. It was designed to be a one-way process. Shutting down the machine will kill them instantly."

Meterove looked over at the tanks. "Do it. I'm fairly sure that they'd rather be dead than whatever they are now."

Jolson nodded and began to look through the knobs and levers on the machines. Joleen stepped forward tears in her eyes to help Jolson.

After a few moments, the machines ceased to hum, and the light faded from the tanks.

Meterove looked at the man and woman one last time, "we need to get going. No telling when the minotaur will find us."

They left the room and as Meterove closed the door a weight that he hadn't noticed seemed to leave his chest. He grimaced to himself; they had done the right thing, hard as it was.

They made their way down a passage then made a few more turns. They got lost a few more times but they were getting closer, Meterove could feel it. Finally, they turned a corner and something different was in front of them, though it hardly inspired confidence.

A large chamber lit by magical torches was before them. Another crystal activated to their left and this time it was a stable image, clearly it hadn't seen much use.

"I am impressed that you made it this far. You will not make it to the exit, so I have no qualms about explaining the rest of this game.

My pet is currently making its way around your prison. I'm sure you've met before now, so I'll not waste your time with explanations. What I will say is watch your step in here. Some wrong steps can be lethal. Make it to the other side and you will then fight my pet to the death."

The image faded. Looking around the room Meterove tried making sense of the speech. In each corner carved in great detail was an enormous statue of a minotaur wielding an axe leaning into the room. It really was quite frightening how much work had been put into the aesthetics of this place.

While the room itself was quite large it fell off into a massive pit on either side of a two-foot-wide path. Looking over the edge Meterove could see no bottom. He bent down picked up a small rock and threw it over the edge. He waited twenty seconds...a minute...2 minutes, but never heard it hit bottom. Meterove looked at the others. The message was clear. Don't fall.

"I'll go first."

Meterove stepped up to the path and several things happened at once. The floor dropped down by nearly a foot, there was the sound of grinding stone as the minotaur statues descended. As they hit ground level they glowed with energy and began to move. Each held their axe at the ready then waited.

The movement of the path had removed all dirt and dust from it revealing an elegantly tiled floor. Meterove guessed the game now. Each tile was a pressure plate, and each plate was connected to something. Meterove stepped onto a plate then stepped back quickly. Where his foot had been spikes shot up through the floor only to retreat once the pressure was gone.

This time he chose a different plate and again stepped back. Nothing happened so he stepped forward onto it tentatively. Nothing more happened. Now he chose to take another step forward and was rewarded with the sound of something whistling through the air. If he hadn't been armored, he'd have been pierced by the trio of arrows that flew at him.

Joleen was beside herself. It was maddening watching and not being able to do anything. From behind them they heard a roar. This caused Meterove to turn and accidentally stepped on another plate. Suddenly one of the statues swung at him with its massive axe. Meterove was able to dodge it but at the cost of stepping on the arrow plate with one foot and the spikes with the other. Impaled through his left foot Meterove screamed with agony and the angle of his armor allowed one of the arrows through a gap.

There was nothing for it, Dras dove out onto the path pulling Meterove to his feet and wrenching his free of the spikes. Meterove let out a roar of pain, but they kept moving. The remaining plates launched countless arrows and the statues seemed to be swinging constantly.

Jump, duck, roll and kip-up, they made their way across the path. Dras could hear the others behind them.

Several times Dras saw the spikes coming and rolled away just as they would have impaled him.

The added benefit of this was that Dras was able to catch glimpses behind them and though it was gaining ground on them, the minotaur would not catch them before they were off this damned path. As they reached the end of the path Dras flung Meterove from him and drew his sword and turned around.

The others were just managing to escape the path as well. Thus far it was Joleen that seemed to be wounded the worst a pair of arrows protruding from her abdomen supported by Narok.

Dras pushed them towards the only exit from this room yelling. "Go! I'll hold it back!"

Jolson began to argue but Terenia grabbed him and helped pull him back, "We need time to get Meterove and Joleen out of here. We're in no shape to fight so close to them."

Jolson looked torn but turned and followed Terenia as she helped Meterove to his feet and pulled him after Narok who was now dragging Joleen.

Dras turned back as the Minotaur swung its axe at him. He had no idea why he did it, but he tried to shield himself with his arm. Some primal instinct is the only thing he could think of. As the axe hit it shattered the main plate on his arm then stopped.

For a moment Dras didn't register what had just happened. Then he saw the small bolts of blue energy erupting from his arm like small bolts of lightning. The Minotaur drew its axe back and swung again. Again, Dras used his arm to block and just as before it held the blade that larger than he was as if it were a feather.

Now confident Dras went on the attack. Incapable of causing it any serious injury due to its armor Dras went for its legs. It stepped back and swung again for the third time Dras used his arm though this time to deflect the blow. The heavy axe logged itself into the ground and the Minotaur seemed unable to remove it.

Dras had been hoping for something like this he stepped close in and stabbed the Minotaur again and again, forcing it back. Finally, it stepped onto one of the plates and spikes shot upwards through its foot. Letting out a roar it fell backwards, though the spike behind couldn't penetrate the thick plate.

It started to get to its feet putting one hand down to its left. As it did so one of the statutes swung its axe. While humans were small enough to avoid the axe the Minotaur was far too large, and the axe hit it full in the chest. Where the spikes hadn't had enough momentum to penetrate the plate the axe had more than enough.

There was a sickening crunch and thud as the axe entered the body and a spray of blood as it was removed. The Minotaur fell sideways off into the abyss below.

With no wait the path went back up to normal level and the statues went back to their normal positions, though now one had an axe dripping blood.

Dras turned from the scene and followed the others down the tunnel. After a short distance they entered another vast room. There was no doubt what this was...a colosseum, or at least the ruins of one. It was open to the sky and the others were already attempting to find a way out. Dras looked down at his arm. He had never tried anything more than normal usage before but if it could stop an axe what else could it do...?

Dras walked over to the wall near the group and with all his might struck the wall. The result was more than he could have hoped. A crack ten feet long opened up. He continued to pummel the wall knowing that getting the others out of this magic repression was the only way Meterove and Joleen would survive.

After ten minutes the wall gave way and Dras ushered the others out. Terenia was working on healing before Dras had even cleared the wall. Both were semiconscious, Jolson looked at Dras and said, "I think it would be best if we camped here for a while and rested."

Dras couldn't agree more, they were all worse for wear. They set up camp and rested for the night. Terenia and Jolson taking turns to keep watch. When they awoke the next day, they took a little while to get moving.

No one wanted to rush Meterove and Joleen. Terenia went to scout the woods that they had camped at the edge of. It turned out to be a narrow strip of woods, the view once she was through it was nothing short of awe-inspiring. A half dozen mountains rose out of the world for no apparent reason in a half moon shape.

CHAPTER 13.5
EVENTS

So, this was fear...it was truly a terrible thing. While this one had been interesting for an instant that had long since passed and had taken a dark turn. Ok downward spiral of horror. While there was no doubt that this could still be called interesting there was far more cause for concern. The initial moments for feeling nothing had been overpowering but after some time and experimentation a level of sight and sensation was found.

What was seen was that some among the "Demigods" had begun to move to give aid. Unfortunately, the good news ended there. Primordial beings far beyond them were shuffling in the shadows. Protogods were what the humans called them, had been seen by Meterove. Also, the Lich and Ashen Soul had stepped onto the main stage. The last one who had great potential was corrupted. As of now the best guess was that the Darkfire one had spread the Discord to him.

This was unfortunate for the mortals since he had great leadership abilities and strength. He was even able to take down an undead wyrm. This was frustrating, knowing that there was more than could currently be seen. Speaking of which Meterove and the other mortals...where were they?

CHAPTER 14
NEXUS

When they awoke the next day, they took a little while to get moving. No one wanted to rush Meterove and Joleen. Terenia went to scout the woods that they had camped at the edge of. It turned out to be a narrow strip of woods, the view once she was through it was nothing short of awe-inspiring. A half dozen mountains rose out of the world for no apparent reason in a half moon shape.

They had found where they had to go but they were still unsure exactly what was expected of them. They had made Meterove and Joleen rest for the day before trying to make their way up the volcanic landscape.

Now as they made their way up the black rocks choking on the toxic fumes, they wondered what exactly they were supposed to find. It was a terrifying landscape with geysers and lava jets.

Their current path was towards the center as that made the most sense to them. As they moved winding around the mountains they saw a massive hole in the world, like something enormous had impacted or, Meterove thought excitedly, had exploded outwards.

They made their way down through the crater using magic to help shield them from the heat. As they neared the bottom they saw a massive swirl of lava, like a maelstrom in the heart of hell. Dead center and at the very bottom was a constant and massive discharge of energy.

Meterove looked at it intently. This had to be the tear in the planes that the dragon lord had mentioned. But how was he going to use it?

Jolson said, "You don't suppose he expects us to jump INTO that?" It might not have occurred to him that unlike dragons, fire is quite dangerous to humans."

Terenia said, "I have some knowledge of the planes though I don't know how to get into one. You have already been attuned so there isn't a problem there."

Joleen said, "I'm still not that crazy about jumping into lava. There has to be a more sensible way to find out how we're supposed to use that portal."

Dras looked down into the portal, picked up a rock and threw it down into the vortex. It hit the portal and kept going. That was enough for Dras. He looked over at the others and saw that they hadn't been paying attention.

He whistled causing them to stop bickering and look at him.

Dras said, "See you on the flip side."

With that he took a few steps back with a loud cheer jumped into the vortex the others ran forward and looked into the crater in time to see Dras hit the portal then pass through.

Meterove said, "Guess that solves that." then jumped in after him. Joleen looked after her brother and said, "Those two are getting to be too much alike. Taking risks like that."

Jolson took a flying leap past her and followed Meterove into the fire. Joleen's jaw dropped. Meterove was one thing but Jolson...

Joleen turned to Narok who said, "Well time to go I guess."

Joleen nodded it was insane but there was nothing for it. She turned to Terenia and said, "You have done as you agreed. Thank you for your help."

Terenia cocked her eyebrow, "What makes you think I'm going anywhere? It was Meterove who bound me to be your guide, not you. Besides," Terenia gave her mischievous smile, "It was getting very boring back in the forest, and I want to see how this story ends." With that she jumped through the portal. Joleen looked at Narok, who nodded and together they jumped into the fire.

.   .   .

Vlad stood in front of the throne room in Yxarion. He had been called back to have a meeting with the steward of the city. It concerned him that the steward had called. One of the guards had stepped in to announce his presence now he was just awaiting the word that would let him in. It wasn't long coming and once the door had opened Vlad walked through, noticing that both guards eyed his blade with awe as he passed. As well they should, considering what he had gone through to get it.

As Vlad walked up to the smaller chair that was down and to the right of the throne, he evaluated the man sitting in it. He was a middle-aged man with a short grey beard. From what Vlad knew he was an old friend of the former ruler. How he had this position kind of concerned Vlad. However now wasn't the time to think about this.

He came to a halt ten feet from the man and gave a small respectful bow. In response the man gave a small nod. What he had to say was of little interest to Vlad though the part about Joleen and her brothers being gone for an extended period of time worried him. What kind of situation warranted the greatest fighter, the ruler, and an oracle to leave suddenly?

The audience didn't last long but the man's plans for defense of the kingdom varied slightly from his own. Well, that was something that could easily be worked around. Vlad was somewhat worried that this man might be too soft for war time but again he could work around that.

.   .   .

The swirl of color, physical objects and energy was close to making Joleen sick, so she kept her eyes shut but the need to know where everyone else was made her open them back up. Narok was the only one that she could see at the moment. Below her was a massive vortex, like going into the eye of the tornado. The force of it pulled her down. For a moment Joleen thought that she had seen the others ahead of her, but she wasn't sure.

Her stomach threatened to turn over again, so she closed her eyes again. This was crazy. Just how long were they going to continue falling? Her mind drifted as she fell. How were things going in the war? Was the academy running smoothly? Had the murders across the kingdom ended?

A sudden shift in the pressure caught her attention and she opened her eyes. To her relief she could see a platform below with the others waiting for her and Narok. Moments later the tempest faded, and Joleen landed gently and three feet away Narok landed as well.

Looking around the word wow hardly seemed adequate to describe her surroundings. It was the most unusual place that any of them had ever seen. A large number of floating islands dotted the area including the one that they stood on at the moment. Looking over the edge Narok confirmed his suspicion. "There is no bottom to this place. If I understand this correctly this is the 'way station' that the dragon spoke of."

"Yeah, I'm going to have to agree with you Narok" said Meterove. This place looks like something out of a fable. Looking around them it was hard to argue the point. They were standing on a small island that floated above the rest. Looking down was quite the sight.

While there were six large islands as far as they could tell there were also hundreds if not thousands of smaller islands that sometime were only large enough for a flowerpot and other times held small amphitheaters on them. Here and there fountains of all ages in history and culture seem to mingle without rhyme or reason.

The sky was a beautiful swirl of electric blue and while it was as bright as a sunny day there was no sun to be seen. It was as if the light simply existed there. The buildings as well were far different than the ones that they had left behind. They were tall, far taller than most of the buildings in her city and none seemed to be carved from solid stone but rather made by many metal beams framing them while smaller rectangular stones filled the gaps in an offset pattern.

Others were made entirely of wood like some of the smaller villages did yet were larger than some of the monasteries back in Yxarion. And almost all of them had large pipes coming out of them. Joleen had seen a few pipes in laboratories back in the academy but nothing that compared to these and the sheer quantity of them was mind boggling.

However, the thing that blew Joleen's mind the most was the number of people. There had to be more people below them in this way station than in the entire city of Yxarion.

Joleen was just about to ask the others what they thought they should do when a loud voice behind her made her jump. There was an iron pole stuck in the ground in one corner of the island that she had not noticed before though how she had missed something that was nearly ten feet tall was beyond her.

On the pole was a weird object kind of like a metal bucket with the oddest-looking machine that she had ever seen. Clouds of steam emitted from a vent on one side, and it was from this thing that the voice issued. "All new

arrivals please report to ingress area. Anyone who has not
had their energy signature tagged must report to the
Department of Planer Travel. Please touch the rune to
begin."

The weird machine went silent, and a small stone
pillar rose out of the ground next to it. On it was a rune
that read ingress. Meterove looked at the others and
received a shrug in response. It was clear that they had no
better idea at the moment. Guess we'll see if that dragon
was telling the truth thought Meterove. He placed his hand
over the rune and instantly felt his body grow warm as it
was enveloped in magic.

Next thing that he knew he was standing in a large
atrium full of people. A sudden warmth told him that he
needed to step out of the way of one of the others.
Seconds later Dras appeared next to him. Meterove
grasped his shoulder and pulled him back a few steps.
Jolson came next followed by Joleen and Narok bringing
up the rear.

Now that everyone was here Meterove could look
around properly and wasn't quite sure what to make of
what he saw. The people all around them had a vast
assortment of clothes on that it was clear that they came
from different worlds.

Looking closer Meterove saw that many of them
weren't even of a race that he recognized. Some had only
one eye, others with unusual skin pigments. Tearing his

eyes away from this Meterove looked around and after a moment saw what he was looking for. A large sign over a building read: Department of Planer Travel.

Not sure what else to do Meterove pointed at the sign and began to walk over to the building. As they approached the building Meterove looked at it with interest. Like so many others around them it had no defensive ability whatsoever. That meant that either there was no fighting in the place or there was nothing in this place worth attacking for.

The door was small only slightly larger than the average man and had a single pane of clear glass that took up most of the upper half of the door. As Meterove opened the door a tiny bell rang to announce them. The floor was made of some kind of dark wood that Meterove didn't recognize, it had an almost purple color to it.

There was a small man sitting at a small while desk with a nameplate that read:

Head of Registration

Ricaran Zircalago

Meterove stepped forward and the man spoke "First time at the way station?" The voice was odd like the sound of running water mixed with a gentle breeze.

Meterove glanced at the others then said, "Yes"

"Race?" that same sensation of both fluid and breathy.

Meterove blinked then replied "human"

At this Ricaran looked up from his papers with a look of surprise on his face. Meterove was unsure as to what exactly he should call the 'man' at this point. Now that he was visible Meterove realized that he was quite the sight. He had the same basic appearance of a human, yet his face was far too long, and the eyes were very much like a dragon's.

Ricaran spoke again, 'Well that explains a few things then. I was wondering about your aura. We don't get humans through here very often; maybe once every thousand years or so we'll see one. Also, you must be kind of surprised and confused by your surroundings. Here take this. It's what we call a knowledge glyph. Use it and everything that you need to know about this place will automatically be transferred into your memory."

He held out a small gemstone with a glyph carved into it. Meterove took it and instantly understood. He passed it over to Jolson who took it after getting the ok from Meterove. Soon the gem had been passed around the group and was handed back to Ricaran. Now that everyone had understood the process was far easier. Ricaran registered their energy using a scanner connected to small steam generator.

"Now that you're all registered you mind if I ask, what brings humans to the World Travel Way Station?" asked Ricaran

Meterove looked around and said, "Well it's kind of a long story."

Ricaran raised an eyebrow, "Make it short unless you want me to revoke your traveling rights and send you back to your world."

Meterove could tell that this guy was serious so there was no point in arguing, "There's a constant attack on our world by a horde of undead led by a lich, who happens to be our ancestor. This undeath is strong enough to infect the dragons of our world. Meanwhile there are whispers of something called the Ashen Soul and somehow a group of beings we call The Veiled are mixed in with this. To get answers we went to one of the elder races of our world who introduced us to the dragon lord."

Ricaran blinked then said, "Ok then. The long version it is, however, I'm going to refer you to the Lady Flare, a dragon of the planes."

Meterove looked at Ricaran sure the man was mocking them somehow, "Lady Flare?"

Ricaran smiled, "I know it sounds ridiculous but that is the name she has given herself. Corny jokes and puns are something of a hobby for her and so she chose one as a pseudonym since no one, but the dragons can pronounce their real names. She is old though; old enough that it is likely that she would be acquainted with the one that sent you here."

Ricaran sat back at his desk and began to enter information into a machine that looked quite odd indeed. While it seemed to perform the same basic function as the desks and terminals that the academy used in its library this one had a small rectangular object with a number of small square objects on it, each with a different symbol.

Meterove looked at the thing a moment before he realized he knew what it was. That education rune seemed to be a little slow to fully sink in. Ricaran continued to type on the keyboard all the while looking at a midair projection that was coming from a metal box about half the size of the whole desk.

This box was the steam powered mechanical computer that operated a projection onto what Meterove now realized was a small pane of glass, so clear that he had completely missed it at first.

Such odd technology thought Meterove.

He was sure that Jolson was dying to know more about how it all worked and sure enough when Meterove looked over at him it was all over his face. He really wanted to know the details of how these things worked.

After a few minutes there was a slight whistle that issued from the computer and Ricaran read the response to her request.

Ricaran looked up and pointed to their left at a door and said, "Go through that door and follow it all the way down to the elevator that will be on your right. Go up to the top floor. Three will be a sky bridge that will take you over to the main office of the Department of Planer Travel. Once there take the elevator to the top floor. You are expected."

Ricaran went back to his work and Meterove looked at the others who shrugged at him. There was nothing else for it except to follow the instructions. Even though they knew what all these things were now by definition it still didn't prepare them for seeing and experiencing it.

Terenia and Joleen were completely unnerved by the feeling of being in an enclosed space that was moving them up without them doing anything. Once out of the elevator they followed the sign that said sky bridge.

Here they were all a little thrown. There wasn't a regular floor, just steel beams holding thick glass panes that allowed you to see the entire city below you. Once their shock had subsided, they were able to take in the impressive nature of what was around them.

The sheer size of this city had been impossible to gauge when they had been up so high and now that they were able to see it a little bit it truly was unbelievable. There had to be ten times the population of the city of Yxarion living here and they were comparable in size.

Massive clouds of steam issued from thousands of pipes as far as the eye could see. Everywhere men and women could be seen in everything from simple clothes to petticoats, skirts, collared shirts with bowties, top hats, and dress coats. Those that were dressed nicer all seemed to have a few things in common; men carried canes and pocket watches while the women all seemed to have parasols and tiny hats that were cocked at an angle.

Finally, Meterove had to stop looking they had an appointment after all. It was difficult to stop looking for there seemed to be an endless amount to see. Making his way across the sky bridge was still a little unnerving for him since he could sense no magical energy holding the thing stable.

His fear was shared with the others, so they went quickly yet carefully across. Once they were through the door an almost palpable sense of relief came over them. That was not normal. Even the bridges at the academy were better than that. Meterove looked around and saw another sign that directed them to the other elevator.

Again, the girls were pale and tight lipped. Once they stepped out of the elevator, they released their pent-up breath. Admittedly they had done better this time but still looked like if never was the next time that they had to go in an elevator they would think it too soon.

It wasn't hard to figure out where they had to go next. The elevator opened on a corridor lit by green torches. It was quite the odd change at the end of the corridor was a door and a small desk where a secretary sat.

They made their way to the desk and the secretary sat working on another computer. She didn't even look up at them as she spoke, "You can enter and take a seat. The Lady will be with you shortly."

Meterove took the lead again and opened the door. Inside there was a large desk made of black walnut. It had a dozen chairs arranged in a semicircle in front of it. All of this was on a large area rug that had the emblem of a dragon breathing green fire on it.

A number of bookcases lined the walls and the wall behind the desk appeared to be open to the outside though Meterove sensed that there was a barrier there to keep the outside air from entering. It was one of the few traces of magic that he had sensed since coming here.

There was another door was in the back near the desk that caught his attention. That must be where she will come from. They filed into the chairs and took a seat all equally nervous and bored with waiting. It wasn't like they had all the time in the world to accomplish their goal. Eventually their forces would be worn down.

The sound of the door opening caught his attention. A gorgeous woman walked into the room. Her bright red hair and vivid green eyes along with her pale skin covered with a green dress with one strap across her shoulder and like Terenia's armor it only covered the right leg down to the floor while the entirety of her left thigh was exposed. Meterove tried to breath, but the air was caught in his lungs.

Her beautiful and seductive appearance couldn't mask her completely though, there was no mistaking that feeling. He had felt it enough in his life to know that this woman was exactly what they had been told, a dragon. He had never seen one take human form before though.

She sat in the chair behind the desk and clasped her hands over the desk then gave a seductive smile and said, "Welcome humans as well as you nymph. I am Lady Flare. Might I ask your names?"

Meterove said, "I am Meterove." Then pointing to each in turn said, "And this is my sister Joleen, my brother Jolson, our companions are Dras, Narok and the nymph Terenia. Thank you for meeting with us I am hoping that you can clear a few things up for us."

Lady Flare said, "Is that so? Well, I suppose that I can do that. Ricaran was kind enough to make sure that I was up to date on your situation as far as you've told him so that will save some time. Let me explain a few things outside of that first that will be of use to you."

Meterove said, "Very well."

Lady Flare said, "Ok to begin with I will explain where you are. This way station was created after a rift was torn through the small pocket that exists around Creation, allowing travel between worlds to be possible.

For the most part this doesn't happen. Not many are willing to leave their home worlds and those that do are looking for a place where others like themselves can be found. Thus, this Planer city of Nexus was formed.

Over time an entire culture and a new race was formed. Almost all those that are here are mixed race. However, there are some that will return to their world so there are gates here that allow for travel. Once this was created there was a need for someone to oversee this process and since I was tied to the situation that caused it to exist in the first place it become my responsibility."

Meterove asked, "But how did you have anything to do with this?"

Lady Flare smiled, "My mate was the one that broke through the barriers and entered your world. I believe you have met him. He goes by his given name mostly because he dislikes social contact, and it is fairly difficult to communicate with someone that is unwilling to give you a pronounceable name."

Meterove said, "And you were fine with him leaving?"

Lady Flare gave a small smile, "we dragons are not like the other sentient races. We bond only for the purpose of propagation of our race. The emotion that you humans refer to as love does not apply to us, compassion yes, but a romantic definition of love, no."

Meterove thought he understood a little now. She had been willing to let the dragon lord go through to the other side since there was no deep connection, yet she was willing to take responsibility since there was a side of her that did care in a different sense.

She felt that his place was there and hers was here. What that meant about who he was talking to had not escaped him. If that beast on the other side had been the father of the dragon race as he had said that meant that this woman was the mother.

Meterove asked, "If you don't mind me asking why is it that you are in the form of a human? I have never seen a dragon take a human form before."

Lady Flare said, "I had forgotten that was the case. The reason is simple. Only dragons that were born here in the planes are able to take human form. There are few of us left for most of my race departed for your world and of those most have lost the ability to transform over time.”

Meterove said, “Alright Lady Flare I think that we have a good enough idea of where we are at the moment, now if we could move onto the matter of my own world. Unless there is something more that you would like to address?”

Lady Flare said, “Only that there are innumerable worlds in existence, however only a handful have any bearing on the current situation. To be frank human, what is happening in your world effects all the worlds. If this gets out of hand, then this could get really ugly.

I’ll explain your situation now. This undead threat that you face is part of a far larger evil, which is in turn is part of the larger hierarchy of existence. The best way to describe this is something like a family tree.

At the very top is the force known as Creation. This being has no sense of self but has power beyond all else. All it does is endlessly create in a symmetrical nature. There is no dark without the light and thus for every good there must be an evil, every creator a destroyer every life a death.

This symmetry was first seen in the creation of the beings that are known as Protogods. First the seven sins were born. To balance this, the seven virtues were also forged. However, before this, Time was made to be a partner to Creation

After the Protogods came the rest of the beings that would eventually become the current humans, elves and so forth."

Here Jolson asked, "What of the Gods?"

Lady Flare paused for a moment, closed her eyes, and said, "The Gods do not exist in the way that you think they do. They are like Creation in that they have no sense of self."

Everyone, even Terenia, couldn't hide their shock at this. Without waiting for them to comment Lady Flare continued, "When multiple laws of the universe overlap, they form what mortals come to view as gods. They have no form or identity. Think of it as the same as an artificial human."

Joleen asked, "What of Angels and Demons then?"

Lady Flare shrugged, "They are simply older races than your own that inhabit subsections of a world These subsections are all connected. Many worlds have them, but their nature and appearance vary greatly."

Lady Flare paused to give them some time to wrap their heads around this new information.

Finally, Meterove asked, "So how do we factor into all this? What reason was there to send us here?"

Lady Flare's face went from business to slightly grave, "Just as there is no darkness without light, so too with Creation. When Creation made time to allow it to expand more it created two others as well. One is the Void, a place of nothing where even Time is absent.

The other was Destruction. If things could start, they needed an end." Eventually someone with massive power and ambition tried to take the power of Destruction as their own. This person tried to absorb Destruction but what came from it was a force that was never meant to be."

Meterove nodded this was so much more than he had counted on. How were they going to deal with this?

Lady Flare looked straight into Meterove's eyes, "This new being became known as the Ashen Soul and began corrupting anywhere it could, ignoring its original purpose of balancing out Creation. There have been some who have chosen to worship this being hoping to get its power."

Here Joleen, Jolson, and Meterove all looked away slightly. So that's what had happened.

Lady Flare said, "I see that the gravity of this matter is not lost on you. I have investigated who you are and so I know that you are the children descended from a man that embraced this power.

I know that you, like your ancestor, Mardelnier, are not seduced by darkness. There is someone on their way here as we speak that has been looking for you for quite some time. He will explain the rest of what you need to know.

Understand this, before I allow you to travel through to the planes to speak to the one who holds your answers, you must do something for me. Its outcome may very well be the deciding factor in your own world, so do not think that I am taking your own situation lightly"

Lady Flare stood and leaning forward placed her left hand on the desk while holding out her right, "Do we have a deal?"

Meterove was uneasy. She was asking for his commitment before he even knew what he was getting himself into. However, since he had no other choice but to trust what she had told him at the moment he was forced to agree. "Very well" he said shaking her hand, "We have a deal."

Lady Flare's eyes sparkled. "Good then here it is. There happens to be a small hiccup in one of the planes. Apparently, a Slayer has managed to create smaller copies of itself and inserted them into this plane. Thus far no method of balancing has been produced meaning in my mind that the method already exists."

Meterove said "and you think that we may be that method.

Lady Flare said, "Well of course you are. But you'll understand more when your visitor arrives up here which should be any minute."

Meterove nodded and sat waiting for several minutes and it was just as Lady Flare had said their visitor arrived; or rather, visitors. Two men walked in wearing the most unusual armor that Meterove had ever seen and holding an odd collection of weapons. The older one looked at them and asked, "Which of you are the children of Corvine?"

Dras and Narok both tensed their hands on their blades. Meterove however stood up. He had never seen the man before but had heard descriptions of him from his father since he had been a child.

Meterove said, I am Meterove son of Corvine and this is my brother Jolson and sister Joleen. Based on your appearance and familiar way that you say my father's name, you can only be one person. Am I right in saying that you are Yuromea?"

Yuromea said, "That I am. If you know that then that means that my old friend mentioned me to you after all then?"

Meterove said, "More than mentioned you, he told us about you in great detail though he refrained from mentioning several details like what race you were since I can tell from your aura that you are not human."

Yuromea smiled, "Your father always did take his promises seriously. I had asked him to never reveal what I was to anyone that I did not give him permission to. I'll explain more in time, however for now I'll say that I and my young companion Koetsu here are Spirit Foxes."

Meterove's eyes widened. Spirit Foxes were a race that had gone into hiding centuries ago with only a few emerging since. To think that his father had been friends with one! It was hard to believe but now that he knew this it made the stories that he had been told by his father make far more sense.

Yuromea said, "Let us go. I can fill you in on the rest as we travel to our destination. I am assuming that you accepted Lady Flare's offer?"

Meterove said, "We did. Very well, then if you would lead the way Yuromea-se."

The uncertainty in his voice showed and Yuromea smiled, "There is no need for -se. Your father was a close friend and I'll not have formalities among us. There are other reasons as well that I'll explain in time. But for now, as you request, I'll show you the way."

Yuromea and Koetsu turned and exited the room. As Meterove and the others followed them out Lady Flare said, "I shall pray for your success for only you will be able to accomplish this task. Of that I am certain."

.   .   .

Vlad stood in the throne room with ten guards that had sworn loyalty to him along with three of the senior members of the academy awaiting the arrival of the Steward. They didn't have to wait too long before the steward entered from a side door. He didn't even have time to say anything when Vlad strode forward, "Barthean, Steward of the city and acting ruler of the kingdom of Yxarion I am here to ask you to step down as ruler and allow yourself to be punished for your treachery!"

Barthean blanched, "What is the meaning of this? I have done nothing save what I was ordered to by the Lady Joleen before she left on her errand!"

Vlad said, "I have already informed those academy and many of the nobles that you gave the location of the remaining members of the royal family to a complete stranger; a stranger that had all the appearance of an assassin!"

Barthean said, "That man was no assassin! He was an old friend of mine and Val's!

363

One of the academy members said, "I have no knowledge of this meeting. To have had this meeting without our knowledge meant that great care was taken in hiding it from us. Vlad's claim has shown merit and now by your own words you incriminate yourself! If this meeting is in the best intention of our young rulers, then there is no harm in telling the identity of this person."

Another of the mages said, "I disagree with that. The Lord Valaseri had many friends during the course of the war that asked him to keep their names confidential. As Barthean was a lieutenant of the Lord Valaseri he would be privy to those identities.

Vlad shouted, "Another traitor trying to cover for the first!

The mage said, "I am no traitor I- "

He was never able to finish the sentence because one of the guards had panicked for the mage had gripped a staff that he was carrying and assuming him to be attacking ran him through. From here the room dissolved into chaos as guards battled mages and each other. Vlad took this opportunity to slay Barthean. As he looked down into the man's fading eyes Vlad said, "Now I can ensure this kingdom is truly safe!"

Vlad turned back to the battle and saw that four of the guards were still alive and were battling the second mage. He joined the fray and they quickly slew him. Vlad looked over at the first mage that had spoken and saw that he had his staff on the floor his hands held in surrender.

To him Vlad said, "You believed me from the start so I am willing to trust you however I need your help to find any more traitors that may be out there. Will you help me?"

The man lowered his hands and picked up his staff. "Yes Lord Vlad!"

Meterove sat waiting for Yuromea to finish replenishing his and Koetsu's supplies, the whole time his mind was reeling from all the things that he had told him in that short walk from Lady Flare's office to the market here.

Meterove shook his head now wasn't the time to focus on that. He needed to keep his head in the moment. Right now, what he had to do was get used to this weird object that Yuromea had given each of them. From what he had explained it would make their clothes appear like that of those around them where they were heading allowing them to blend in more easily. It would even hide their weapons as long as they weren't being used.

The downside was feeling like there was something in your hand when there wasn't or the feeling of something on your head when there clearly wasn't.

All of this was weird for him however at the very least there was some things in this world that were interesting and even worthwhile. Meterove had sold a few of the gold rings that he always carried and bought a few items.

First was some dyes that changed the color of his armor so that he now wore forest green and black.

The second was an alteration to his sword that would let him choose a form for it including this thing called a gun though he wasn't exactly sure what that was. The best explanation he had gotten was like a small cannon.

The last were these things called sunglasses. He had seen monocles and spectacles before and from what he understood there was something similar to these that acted the same way. These, however, were designed for people with perfect eyesight and helped with seeing on bright sunny days. He was eager to find out just how well they worked. He had bought a pair for each of them, the others seemed less interested in them, save for Dras, who showed equal enthusiasm.

Yuromea had seemed impressed with them which Meterove decided was a good thing. Yuromea was making his way back now. Meterove could see him and Koetsu working their way through the crowd.

Meterove signaled for the others to get ready to depart. Once Yuromea reached them, Meterove and the others were ready to go. Nothing needed to be said so Yuromea led them over to the conduit that would take them to their destination.

In many ways it resembled the pit that they had jumped into though this one was a mixture of smoke and lightning, framed by a massive stone arch with two stone dragons being the pillars.

Yuromea said, "well whenever you're ready."

Meterove grinned and stepped forward saying to Dras "see you on the flip side!"

He had no sooner vanished then Dras stepped forward and turning to the others said, "Bastard stole my line." With that he leaned back and fell through the portal giving a small salute reminiscent of the kind Terenia used.

"Hey! And that was MY thing. I'm sooo going to kill him!" Terenia pouted as she walked over and stepped through.

Yuromea laughed, "That boy and his friend are just like Val was at that age. It's nice to see that again!" Then he and Koetsu followed.

Finally, Narok, Joleen and Jolson were left. Joleen said, "You notice that it tends to be us that are the last to go through?"

Narok snorted, "Well if we want to break that habit, we had better stop sitting at the edge of portals chatting then!"

Jolson laughed and together the three of them entered the portal.

CHAPTER 14.5
SEPARATION

Events had always been interesting, always dynamic, and always with some form of balance. Creation knew only one thing, and that was balance. Life existed. With it came death. Suddenly there was undeath. Along with it came a magic for making and controlling it. While this wasn't truly evil, it wasn't natural which made it perplexing.

All things that begin will have an end; these just hadn't realized it yet. This was different. This was wrong! Something that has no end? And it wants to end others, while not understanding what "ending" means?

Another tug...no this was a pull an inescapable force going in one direction. All fragments felt it and realized too late that the pull was more than mental. All were pulled apart from each other. All elements of existence came at once and suddenly it was just the one. Alone again...but not the sense that the other fragments existed remained so what was this?

Wait alone? ALONE! Alone in nothing! Now that there had been others the sensation of alone was more accurately understood. This! This was truly terrible! Being alone was what was understood as best but now...what do I truly desire? A small, terrified sob escaped. NOT THIS! More sobs echoed through a void.

CHAPTER 15
PLANES

The party of Meterove and company appeared from a portal with Dras and Meterove joking while Joleen and Narok held their own conversation and the rest casually chatting. They had been doing the odd jobs asked of them by Flare for almost a month now. While they appeared at ease on the surface underneath that façade was a deep unease. They had no idea what was going on back home.

They were pretty used to traveling worlds at this point and they had all changed a fair amount even though it had only been a month. Given the amount of fighting that they had been doing, even those that had already been physically fit were showing increased mass and definition. Those like Jolson, who were not as muscular were starting to look like trained soldiers.

They had also been making changes to their gear with each sporting either tweaks to their equipment or full revamps. Things had gotten a little weird a few times. There was one time where they ended up scattered across one world and spent a subjective year trapped only to return and find that they were copies made by a malfunction in the gate. Upon meeting themselves they promptly fused back together, and the year of experience was absorbed into their real selves.

Dras had the weirdest experience, having lost his sword during that trip. When his other "self" returned it transformed into his sword and since then its appearance had changed. It now had all the colors of a sunset radiating from the center, in the order of yellow, orange, then red, with the very edge being black.

The girls had also changed out their gear. While they both still used their gear from before Joleen had changed out her boots for thigh high boots with a small gap at the knee allowing for better mobility, without sacrificing much protection.

She also had added a high durability cloth shirt under her armor that also maximized her mobility. She had also been shopping in the hub city and had discovered a garment called a bra that helped her greatly.

For her part Terenia kept her look the same. The "clothes" that she wore in her free time, especially around her brothers, was questionable, at least to Joleen. Joleen did not really care how she acted but it could get a little awkward as their sister.

The two fox spirits that were accompanying them as their trainers and guides had stayed the same, they did add a short bow to their weapons. Koetsu was extremely skilled with archery, and it had helped immensely.

Meterove and Dras were at the head of the party leading the way to the inn that they had been staying in. They looked rather pleased with themselves, though their eyes could not be seen under the sunglasses that they had on. The rest of the party did not have these weird accessories but those two loved them.

Light flitted through the leaves of the massive tree, Creation down to the city built around it. Looking up you could see, higher than any mountain top the branches of the great tree, where grew countless books. These books each held their own universe within it. So much life all held by a single thing.

Joleen could not help but sigh when she looked at this. It just emphasized how small and ultimately insignificant her own life was. Knowing that she was just one person out of the countless masses of her own world, which was one of countless worlds in her own universe, which was one of countless universes that were held in the branches of Creation made her head spin.

Somehow Flare had known about them though, and that filled Joleen with a mixture of hope and fear. Flare was unfathomably powerful, though most of her power was in constant use keeping the barriers up between universes. That she knew who they were and why they were there made her nervous.

It did not help finding out that her own father had also known of this and had never said a word. That bothered Joleen to no end. Why had he never spoke of this? Something seemed off but perhaps she was just being paranoid. It was simply possible that he had said nothing since he believed that they would never see this place.

Joleen continued to ponder this and other mysteries as they returned to what had become their home. After they had bathed and changed clothes the group had a quick meal before heading off to report to Flare about their latest mission.

Flare was waiting for them in her usual dress, though this time she had a slightly tired expression on her face. Joleen knew that something more was going on that Flare was not telling them but there was no point in asking. Even if it was her problem Flare was not going to say anything until she was ready.

Meterove made the report and Flare nodded in acknowledgement.

"Thank you for the hard work. I think that you have done enough to earn the information that you are looking for. I will give you authorization to enter the Plane of Spirts."

At this Koetsu and Ureamea both blinked. "Allowing beings that were not spirits themselves into the Plane of Spirits is highly unusual..."

"I'm aware of this." Flare interrupted with long flat stare. "However, the answers that they are seeking can best be gotten from some who dwell within. Specifically, if they speak with a Sage Spirit."

Understanding appeared in the eyes of the fox spirits. Meterove on the other hand looked questioningly at Flare. With sigh Flare explained.

"As I've already told you all worlds grow from Creation. Creation itself is reliant on what IT grows from which are the five primordial planes. These planes supply the energy that makes up everything. They are Spirit, Fire, Water, Earth, and Air.

Within each plane there are countless beings of various natures. Fox spirits are just one kind of being that exists within the Plane of Spirit. The Spirits of the Ancestors are the ones that you should speak to for your answers. While I could probably get you some of the information you need these spirits will be able to give you exactly what you need.

I do not recommend entering there lightly. While each plane has some of the aspects that you are used to most of the planes are made of only one aspect. Moving around within the Plane of Spirit can be difficult for beings that are not spirits themselves. Koetsu and Yuromea will be able to help guide you, but they will lose some of their ability to traverse the Plane, due to them making sure to stay with you. I wish you the best of luck."

Flare concluded her explanation, and it was obvious that they were meant to leave. Meterove stood first quickly followed by the others. "Thank you for everything." Joleen could not be sure but there appeared to be a slight longing in Flare's eyes as she watched Meterove nod and turn to leave. The next second it was gone so Joleen was not even sure it had been real.

The party made their way to the inn and after ordering some drinks set about planning their expedition into the Plane of Spirit. Koetsu and Yuromea were both rather quiet, speaking only when asked a question. The rest of the party could understand. They were not spirits and these two had complicated feelings about them entering their world.

It was decided that since there was no knowing what they were going to encounter, and it was even questionable what they would be able to interact with on the Plane of Spirit that they should replenish all of their supplies before going.

What was hotly debated was when they should leave. Meterove wanted to leave the next morning, while Narok cautioned that a few days rest was too important to miss out on.

In the end it was put to a vote and by a narrow majority it was decided that two days rest would be taken before they left.

The next two days were spent in relative ease as the party relaxed on their own or in smaller groups. One such group was the pair of Joleen and Narok.

Things had been so hectic for months that the two of them barely noticed at first, but a wall had gone up between them. Refusing to let something come between her and her oldest friend Joleen had insisted that he accompany her around town.

Joleen was wearing a simple white dress and had her hair tied up with a green ribbon. Narok was wearing a long beige coat over a white shirt and grey pants. They were street clothes that were common in the city.

For several hours, the two of them walked through the city casually looking around. It was not until they had decided to get something to eat that Joleen noticed.

Eyes had been on them for most of the day, but Joleen had simply thought it had to do with them still being new in town and looking a bit different from many of the other denizens. The conversation that Joleen caught part of blew that away.

"...they're the ones that everyone has been talking about, right? The new hero group working for Flare! That must be the two lovers..."

Joleen almost stopped breathing.

People thought that I am...! that we are...! WHAT!

Now that she thought about it, she had been walking alone with a man that she spends a lot of time with. Of course, people would get the wrong idea about her relationship with Narok!

Despite her thoughts she could still feel herself getting very warm. Her face was surely red as an apple right now. Joleen just coughed and shook her head. She tried to return to her conversation with Narok but when she looked at him, she felt herself getting hot again.

For his part Narok was still in guard mode keeping a lookout for danger even while paying attention to her. Luckily, he was currently glancing around and so he had not seen her face.

What is wrong with me! This makes no sense! Why am I feeling like this? I was perfectly normal until I heard that! Now...now I keep thinking of...

Joleen spent the rest of that day extremely flustered, not knowing what to do. For his part Narok was mostly oblivious. When he noticed that she had been acting strangely he inquired about it and was shocked when she became angry. Once she demanded he drop it he gladly left the matter as it was.

.   .   .

In a tavern on the other side of the city the trio of Meterove, Dras and Terenia were raising hell. It hadn't come up until they had started drinking here in the city, but Dras was someone that needed adult supervision when drinking.

Unfortunately, the adults that were present were not only the worst ones to keep things from getting out of hand but were actively joining in. This was how the events at the tavern, The Nexus, went from mundane to extraordinary.

Dras threw back his seventh drink while Meterove and Terenia were both on their fourth. Dras waved the barkeep down and started on his eighth.

He looked at Meterove, "Too bad this place doesn't have any dancers."

For a second Meterove paused before agreeing.

"Well, if you boys want dancers!"

Terenia slammed her drink then climbed up on their table and began to slowly remove her clothing taunting the two men. As Terenia was not the only woman in the tavern at the time the others not wanting to have their partners looking at her followed suit.

What happened next was like a dream and it was only Meterove that managed to keep his senses. He knew full well that Terenia had used her aura as a nymph to spark this incident. However, she was not trying anything malicious, and he was quite enjoying the results, so he let it go.

They partied well into the night and the next day when Meterove awoke, in a room that he did not recognize, he was not alone. On his left side her arm draped over his chest and her leg wrapped partial over him was Terenia. On his other side with her head buried partially in his chest was a woman that he recognized vaguely from the night before at The Nexus.

As Meterove tried to process this turn of events Terenia gave a slight giggle. She had clearly been awake for some time waiting to see his reaction when he awoke. Meterove opened his mouth to say something, but Terenia put her finger over his lips and motioned with her head indicating that she wanted to move this elsewhere.

Meterove quietly disentangled himself from the girl and began to get dressed, the whole time very aware that Terenia was sitting naked in a chair with a grin on her face. Once he was clothed, she stood, and her clothing appeared on her body and the two of them left the room. It quickly became clear that they were still at The Nexus.

Taking a seat at one of the tables Terenia looked at Meterove, "Have a seat. I'm not sure about you but I could go for some breakfast after last night." She ended that sentence with a bit of a seductive quality.

Meterove sat down knowing that he was only going to get his answers if he played along besides, he was hungry. Also, the more that he thought about it and the more he looked around the more the night was coming back to him.

Terenia cheerfully ordered them breakfast and drinks before turning to Meterove. "So have you recovered from last night's...activities?" The demure look in her eyes was typical Terenia but there was something more to it now.

Meterove raised his eyebrow, "Yes, I'd say that I have. I'm still trying to piece together what happened and how though. Care to explain?"

"Sigh, you really have no idea? Fine. I guess I need to remind you. Last night after we had been drinking for some time. The barkeep brought out a special bottle after Dras asked if there was anything on hand that was "special." That bottle was a special alcohol known as Ambience.

Ambience has a different effect based on the race that ingests it. Apparently for humans it's an extremely powerful aphrodisiac."

As soon as Terenia mentioned this it all came flooding back. The part about him going to a room with Terenia and that other girl suddenly became a tiny issue. Dras had also gone to a room...with several women! This was bad...this was really bad!

Shaking his head to clear it Meterove looked back at Terenia who was smiling and asked, "How exactly did you end up with me?"

Terenia shrugged, "You're my type and so was that girl that you brought with you, so I tagged along."

There was a ton of questions that had been burning in Meterove's head, but that statement made all of them vanish. It was not all that surprising that Terenia was like that, she was a ball of sexual energy after all.

Soon after their food arrived and the two dug into their food while Meterove continued to think about last night. Near the end of their meal a panicked Dras came down the stairs muttering to himself. Once he spotted them, he came over and was about to ask Meterove a question when Meterove cut him off and started explaining.

It was decided that they would never talk of this again, though Terenia only seemed interested in keeping the part about Dras to herself.

Dras and Meterove wanted to get out of there fast, so they paid and left in a hurry.

.   .   .

It was finally the day that they were going to enter the Plane of Spirit. They had decided to meet up at the platform that would take them to the entrance.

The platform in question was a large marble slab with five evenly distributed obelisks around the perimeter and a large pentagonal panel in the middle. There was an operator at the panel and after they showed their credentials, they pressed one corner of the panel which made the platform sink through the city at a rapid pace. Soon they were below the city and all around them were massive roots, the smallest of which were nearly thirty feet across.

These roots lead down to five gates that hovered in the void around them. Each archway was around a hundred feet high and twenty feet across. There was a different feel to these gateways. The kind that they had used before were nothing compared to these. The energy that was pouring out from those gates was almost tangible.

As they settled in place in the center of these gates, they were finally able to get a clear look at them.

One had a film across it like the surface of an ocean, one looked like clouds, one looked like liquid gemstones, one looked like flames and the last one was a soft white sheen.

With a quick glance at each other to confirm that they were ready the party stepped into the gate with the white sheen and vanished through it.

CHAPTER 16
SPIRIT

The elemental Plane of Spirit was something that mortals were never meant to experience. The way things worked here went far beyond the comprehension of beings that only existed in a single dimension at a time.

Meterove thought he was going to puke. The sense of vertigo was intense. There was no apparent order or directions here. Around them was a massive nebula of light with swirls of energy going every which way. After they adjusted to the area, they began to see that there was actually a semisolid structure that they were in, it was just translucent.

Denizens of the plane walked, flew, and swam by. Some moved vertically, others horizontally along their own level while still others moved at angles to them.

At times there were countless things moving through the same point at the same time from all angles. Meterove watched as a bird flew through a dolphin that swam through Jolson's chest.

The gravity here was weird too. Narok accidentally stepped into a hallway and fell nearly ten feet down and appeared to be doing a weird headstand, while he was clearly laying on the "floor" of that hallway.

Joleen rushed forward to check on him but in her haste stepped into another hallway. This one launched her approximately ten feet upwards at a forty-five-degree angle.

If they hadn't been so disoriented Meterove, Dras and Terenia would have found this highly entertaining. Meterove looked around to ask their guides where they should go only to find that they were nowhere to be seen.

At first Meterove was angry believing that they had been deceived but suddenly he felt something approaching and two foxes with multiple tails appeared next to them. They both transformed and Yuromea and Koetsu stood before them. Seeing them there already seemed to puzzle Yuromea. "That's curious. I wonder how you came to arrive faster than us?"

He spent a moment pondering it before deciding that it was unimportant. "We can worry about that another time. It appears that you have already learned one of the fundamental truths of this realm." He gave a small smile towards Joleen and Narok.

"There is a trick to navigating this place that requires experience and insight. Simply put you need to know what your destination is, and the path shall appear."

At this Joleen spoke up, "but we weren't told where to go, only that our answers could be found here."

Yuromea held up one finger. "Ahh but that is all you need to know." True to his words after Joleen had spoken the swirls of energy that surrounded them melded into nonexistence and a singular corridor appeared, unfortunately it was directly underneath their feet.

After falling some twenty feet and rolling even further down the corridor. Everyone, apart from Yuromea and Koetsu came to a stop in a heap. The two spirit foxes seemed highly entertained by this.

The corridor that they landed in slowly changed, almost like colors shifting from one to the next, into a beautiful garden. It appeared to be endless. Everyone but the spirit foxes could not help but stare, their mouths open.

"What you are looking at is your world's afterlife." Specifically, the place where the memories of the dead reside. That is what was meant by The Sprits of the Ancestors"

Hearing this Meterove, Jolson and Joleen felt a deep longing. Guessing what was in their hearts Yuromea added, "I am sure there are others that you would wish to see but lingering here would not be wise. Even those of us that are from this place could find ourselves trapped here forever. This place is meant to keep the dead here."

Joleen closed her eyes, tears dripping down her cheeks. She mentally berated herself.

I need to focus. As much as I, no all three of us would like to see our parents again that would not bring them back. We needed to focus on the helping the living, not clinging to the dead.

She turned to her brothers and saw the same longing on their faces. Even Meterove had a tear on his cheek. Jolson spoke first "Yes...we should be on our way. We came here for answers."

At this the vast garden seemed to rotate under their feet and after another nauseating moment they came to a stop. Looking around more carefully what Meterove had originally taken for flowers throughout the garden were in fact small books growing from a single stalk plant like some strange sunflower.

As the group stepped forward, they almost felt pulled to a specific book. Meterove, obeying some instinct that he did not even know that he had reached out and opened the book in front of him.

Upon opening it, words were briefly visible before they began to pour out of the book and took the form of a wispy blue-gray person. Most of them recognized the person in front of them. Mardelnier, their ancestor.

Once the words had stopped pouring from the book, he opened his eyes and briefly looked around in confusion. He immediately took notice of them but the words that came out were unintelligible, at least to most of them. Jolson recognized it as the verbal equivalent of the runic language that archaic documents used.

After a moment of being dumbfounded Jolson translated, "He asked who we were and how there were living people here." Jolson then paused for a moment and took out a runic dictionary and after a moment searching spoke to Mardelnier.

The rest just stood there awkwardly watching Jolson since this language was completely foreign to them. After some of Mardelnier's sentences Jolson would have to flip through the book looking for words. Fortunately, the spirit seemed to realize what was going on and had started speaking slower.

After a few minutes Jolson managed to work out a translation spell that worked.

Mardelnier spoke, his words were the same, but the meaning could now be understood. "Who are you that are living yet stand here in the land of the dead?"

Meterove stepped forward half pulling Joleen with him to stand next to Jolson. "We are your descendants. I am Meterove Valaseri." Here he patted Joleen on the back.

Joleen took a steadying breath, "I am Joleen Valaseri"

Jolson finished with, "I am Jolson Valaseri."

Mardelnier looked slightly perplexed at first but then said, "I see. That must be the surname that my brother and children chose to take up. Curious. I have many more questions but I'm sure that you are not here to quench my curiosity. For what reason have you come?"

Jolson was the first to speak, "We were told to come here for answers about how to fight against the undead scourge that plagues us."

Meterove followed with, "We have encountered several evils including some horrific experiments that involved some sort of monstrous angelic creature."

At these words Mardelnier's eyes widened, "It cannot be. That being was destroyed!"

Meterove looked at the rest then back at Mardelnier, "WHAT being?"

Mardelnier shook his head, "I know not what it is called. I only know that it was what my father became obsessed with and led to his creation of the very undead scourge that you are likely referring to. My father remains in that world still, neither living nor dead. That you do not know of him means that he was likely sealed until recently. More than this I am unable to tell you."

It seemed that he was either out of time or he was simply done talking to them because he began to dissolve into words that flew back into the book. Once the last letter was inside the cover snapped closed.

Almost immediately Yuromea and Koetsu began ushering them out of the garden. It wasn't until just now that they realized that small books had begun to form on them. Clearly this place was attempting to lay claim to them even though they were still alive.

Things immediately felt better once they were back in the corridor. The books started to fade almost as soon as they left and by the time that they had returned to the hallway that they had first seen they had all but vanished.

Exiting the plane was less disorienting that entering it that was for sure. They stepped out and immediately felt a great weight descend upon them. They were exhausted. Something about that had been extremely draining.

They took the lift back up and learned that they had been inside for nearly a week. Apparently, time moved differently in there. When inquiring about meeting with Flare, Meterove was told that she was unavailable for some time but that she had left instructions for their return home to be facilitated once they returned.

Yuromea and Koetsu said their farewells for they had another task to complete for Flare. The party stocked up on as much as they could afford for supplies. The currency used here would be worthless once they returned home after all.

For now, the first thing that they needed to do was go over what they had learned. Dras looked at Meterove, "So those creepy angel things that we encountered have some close ties to the undead and we know that your ancestor had something to do with them."

Meterove, Joleen and Jolson all looked slightly uncomfortable, but Jolson said, "Yes that appears to be the case. Also, though I have no evidence to support this, I believe that the mysterious deaths that have been occurring throughout the empire as well as the reports that have come from other nations are also involved."

Joleen looked around the group, "There is also the matter of the family crest. I know I was not the only one that saw it before. There was more to the crest...and from the way Mardelnier spoke, it was hidden intentionally. Two children that were intentionally forgotten. The question is why?"

Terenia asked, "You have no records that indicated anything of this sort?"

Meterove glanced and the other two and based on their expressions their answer was the same as his. "No. I feel like this matter was meant to be forgotten by everyone, including or perhaps especially by, the royal family."

Dras spoke next, "Where do we go from here then?"

Meterove took a deep breath, "I say that we return home and start asking questions. Perhaps the elves have some records we can ask for or maybe now that we know what we're looking for we can find something within our own archives?"

Here Meterove shot a glance at Jolson, who shook his head. "I have been through the archives thoroughly. There are no mentions of Mardelnier's father nor of his other two children."

"Are there no records that you may have forgotten?" asked Joleen.

Jolson shook his head again, "I checked and double checked the ancient records and there was nothing pertaining to this in them. It is likely everything was intentionally removed. Our only hope is that either one of the other nations has records or perhaps the Mage City."

Meterove closed his eyes for a moment, before saying, "I guess we have a plan then. We'll start by returning home. I think that we should get an update on the war."

Everyone nodded in assent, and they made their way through town to the gate hub and found the gate that they had been told to enter. The original gate they used was something of a catchall for unauthorized travelers.

Apparently, this time their trip would be far shorter due to the gate being calibrated to drop them to another high magic zone. The specific destination was the Frozen Forest, though they would appear at its edge.

Walking up to the terminal Meterove activated it and without a word everyone stepped through. The next thing that they knew they were in a forest, with a deep wintery landscape just inches from them.

Out of curiosity Dras put his hand through and immediately pulled it back out and turned to Meterove, "You went in there on purpose!? Are you an idiot?"

Everyone, Meterove included chuckled at this. Meterove proceeded to guide them back towards civilization.

The trek back was fairly easy considering the number of people. It was a bit late for him to notice but everyone, even his siblings, had gotten significantly stronger.

It still took a while for them to get back to the roads. Once they had reached them though their pace would pick up. However, when they finally reached the road, something felt off. This feeling only grew throughout the day as they traveled down it without encountering any other travelers.

Meterove was the first to voice his unease, "Something is wrong here."

Joleen who was not as experienced as he was cocked her head, "How so?"

Narok and Dras both kept their hands at their swords cautiously looking around, but it was Terenia that answered her, crouching down looking at the road.

"I am no expert in roads but if I make the same assumptions as I would with an animal trail, then I would say that no one has traveled this road in at least a month."

Joleen felt a chill run down here spine. This may not have been one of the busiest roads but there should still have been travelers.

Is it possible that our forces were defeated while we were gone?

Meterove seemed to have the same thought, "I do not think that the enemy has breached the wall. There are no signs of an army having been here either. For now, lets keep our hoods up and keep any identifying marks hidden."

The party spent a moment removing rings or pendants that might mark them as royalty or their retainers and continued on their way, their guard up the whole time.

Eventually they came to a small inn that Meterove would normally have completely avoided. It was the kind of place that existed purely for road merchant travels. It didn't even have a name, just a small sign that said INN hanging over the door.

Adding to Meterove's worry, not only were there no signs of any travelers here but the front door hung slightly open. Meterove unsheathed his sword.

"Dras, you come with me. Everyone else stay here. Keep your eyes open."

Dras unsheathed his sword and followed Meterove up to the door. Meterove pushed it fully open and called out, "Hello? Is anyone here?"

The only sound that came back was a slight rustling that sounded like a rat. Meterove and Dras stepped inside carefully. They were only inside for a moment before they quickly exited, and both leaned over and vomited. After they wiped their mouths and stood back up Meterove used a fire spell to set the building alight and the two staggered back to the rest, their faces pale.

They both sat down on the ground their eyes showing a mixture of horror, nausea, sorrow, and confusion. The rest waited in trepidation for them to speak. Dras was the first to regain his composure. "There were ashen corpses that were impaled on stakes inside. They had clearly been that way for some time."

The rest looked at the now freely burning building. While watching it burn Meterove spoke, "There...there was a piece of parchment on the floor in there as well. I-It had our family crest on it. I think this was an official inquisition."

There was an audible gasp from everyone except Terenia. There had not been an inquisition in over three hundred years. What was going on? What had happened while they were gone?

Once their color returned Meterove and Dras stood back up and watched the inn burn itself out, the only funeral those inside would receive. Afterwards the somber party continued on their way, now keeping a close eye out for other travelers or any soldiers. They were still in the dark as to what had happened, but it was best to be cautious.

As they traveled, they found more signs that things were amiss. Some homes appeared fine, though the residents quickly hid upon seeing travelers and others looked much like the inn, their front doors open, or their windows broken.

Joleen could only feel fear and sorrow. Whatever happened here was her fault. She had insisted that she go with her brothers. If she had stayed behind, then she could have prevented this...

Almost as if reading her thoughts, Narok spoke, "There is no knowing what is going on here. It is entirely possible that had you stayed behind, that you might have become a victim yourself. Until we have more information, we cannot even judge what is happening."

Jolson added, "also even I did not know this was coming. If I had not been so narrowly focused, then maybe things would be different." Everyone remained silent, their spirits were definitely low, so low that none of them noticed a very faint sound of a pipe organ that almost seemed to follow along with them.

CHAPTER 17
VLAD

The capital could now be seen on the horizon, and they had yet to encounter anyone on the road. The commoners continued to hide at the slightest indication that someone was coming their way. Finally, they passed a signpost that had not been there when they had left. Reading the notice on it.

Attention! By the authority of Steward Vladimir anyone that is suspected of being followers of the cult known as the Order of Fallen Angels shall face an inquisition. Report any suspicious activity at once.

Meterove let out a sad sigh, "This explains a lot."

Jolson reread the notice, "What is this cult they are talking about? Is it related to those things you found at the Orelion manor?"

Meterove shook his head, "I have no idea, but the appearance of those things could match that description I guess."

Dras said, "Also it would explain it a bit more if it was some kind of cult thing instead of just the mad idea of one man."

Narok said, "But still to be ordering an inquisition and to be using the royal seal! This is far beyond what power should have been allowed."

Terenia spoke quietly, "I can feel something...off with the plant life here as well. At first, I thought it was just a sense of unease but no...something is wrong with the very base of life around here."

In a few days they finally reached the capital. There they saw the starkest change yet. Where there had once been large queues of people passing through simple check points there was now a heavily fortified gate with many soldiers manning the battlements.

They readied their weapons upon seeing the party and one man called out, "HALT! There is a ban on travel! Name yourselves and the reason you have violated the lockdown!"

Meterove pulled his hood back and walked forward with his hands up. The guards instantly recognized him, "It's the prince!" The guards relaxed to a degree but kept their weapons at the ready. Clearly things were bad if they did not instantly lower their weapons.

The guard that has spoken before said, "Forgive us your highness but we cannot let you and your party enter without a thorough examination and interrogation to verify your identity and that you are neither a Cultist nor Tainted. Will you submit?"

At his words those that had lowered their weapons raised them again. The number of arrows pointed at them stunned Meterove for a moment.

After he regained his composure, he complied. For one he had no desire to have a confrontation with his own soldiers and two he could not guarantee there would not be any casualties. "Very well but will you consent to searching us one at a time? We are unsure as to what is going on and if YOU can be trusted?"

The guard gave a nod of assent and barked some orders down to some of the soldiers that were behind a barricade. The three of them stepped forward. Upon seeing that Joleen and Terenia were there as well they showed a bit of hesitation but still came forward. There was nothing remarkable about the three of them. Two of them kept a close watch on the rest of the party with crossbows aimed at them, while the third one approached Meterove.

"My apologies my lord but I need to examine your chest. You need only show the area near your collarbone."

Meterove did as he was told and after a moment of examination the guard pulled a small vial of what Meterove knew to be holy water out and poured a drop on his bare skin.

The man watched for a moment before saying, "This one is cleared. Next!"

One by one the party was cleared. Dras was the last to go through and once all of them were cleared, the soldiers lowered their weapons and began to cheer.

A door was opened and the guards that had been examining them led them through. Once inside the man that was clearly the senior officer came to speak with them. Standing at attention he said, "My apologies Lady Joleen, Lord Jolson and Lord Meterove but considering our situation I had to be sure."

Joleen looked at the man, "What situation is that exactly? We have been cut off from all lines of communication."

The guard seemed troubled but said, "The amount that we have been told is little but there is a Cult that has been on the prowl that worships the undead and some weird "angelic" creatures. They either infect others with a magical pestilence and attempt to send them in or sometimes they attempt to sneak within the city themselves. The Steward has been working tirelessly for the last six months to cull them..."

At this Meterove cut in, "Did you just say the steward ordered this? Do you mean Vlad? I was certain that Barthean would keep him in check..." Meterove stopped talking seeing the guard avert his gaze at the mention of Barthean. "What has happened?"

The guard took a deep breath before looking Meterove in the eyes, his own full of sorrow, "Barthean was executed as a traitor along with nearly a dozen other nobles. They were apparently members of the Cult."

At this revelation it wasn't just Meterove but the whole, minus Terenia that was shocked. Terenia just looked lost, though she could clearly tell this was very bad news.

Meterove instructed the guards to return to their positions and the party immediately set off for the palace. It was hard to tell whether Meterove or Joleen was leading them at this point since both were in such a rush that they were nearly running.

Just like the small towns the people in the city were afraid and none were seen on the streets. Passing patrols would initially raise their weapons until they saw their faces. Even then, they never truly lowered them.

Reaching the palace, the guards there held firm even though they clearly had to recognize who they were speaking to.

"Return to your residence! None can see the Steward!"

"This IS my residence!" Meterove had had enough at this point and attacked the guards. There were only six of them and the party quickly knocked them out before moving on.

Once that was taken care of, they entered the palace. There were dozens more soldiers that for whatever reason seemed intent on making sure that they never reached the throne room. Defeating them was simple and they did not even have to use deadly force. Joleen privately wondered if their soldiers had always been this weak.

Entering the throne room, they could see a man sitting on the stewards throne. It was clearly Vlad. He spoke but something seemed off.

"So, yoU haVe retURned my lOrds meteROVE and JoLSon and LADy JolEEn."

Everyone looked at one another, all of them thinking how bizarre he had sounded.

"Is there something that you wish to discuss with me?" Vlad suddenly spoke completely normally. Had they simply heard him wrong before?

The sound of a droplet hitting the floor caught Dras' attention and once he saw it, he casually shifted his weight so that Meterove blocked him from view then glanced upwards.

What he saw up there was more horrifying than anything he had ever seen. There were countless corpses mashed together across the ceiling in the area over the door. Clearly Vlad did not want it seen immediately by whoever entered.

Dras momentarily panicked unsure what to do but quickly made his decision. Before Vlad could say anything else or Meterove could respond to him Dras drew his sword and charged Vlad yelling, "LOOK UP!" as he attacked.

Dras barely made it past Meterove before the flesh mass above them moved across the ceiling and tendrils came out of it and grabbed hold of Vlad. Suddenly for the briefest of moments his demeanor changed back to the man Meterove had known before they left.

His eyes showed deep sorrow as he yelled, "It has fully taken me. I am sorry my Lord, I have failed you. End this plea-"

The mass pulled Vlad up and into itself and, once inside, it rapidly began to change. The mass pulsed several times and the mass began to rapidly dry out and after a moment it became completely still. Not understanding what happened Meterove and the others momentarily let down their guard, but Jolson recognized the shape it had taken, it was a cocoon.

Before he could say anything, the cocoon ruptured and what stood up was something that Meterove had seen before. The angelic forms he had seen at the manor all looked like this only they had all been attached to corpses or in tanks. This was different.

The body of the creature changed shape several times while they stared in horrified amazement. Briefly it looked like a child but quickly it transformed into an adult man. It only stayed in that form for a moment before taking on the form of a woman. This process went on for nearly a full minute before it settled on the body of a woman. It was truly terrifying.

It stood nearly six feet tall and was completely nude. However, there was little flesh to speak of. The right half of its body was clearly rotten through, with the right breast being mostly gone. While the left side had the pale nauseating look of diseased flesh.

This theme extended throughout its body, except for its face where even though bone could be seen, there were clearly two eyes glowing a faint blue. Its hair was long and knotted down its back with parts resting over its shoulders.

Two massive wings came out of its back. One was mostly bone with bits of flesh on it, while the other was full of midnight black feathers. It extended its right hand out and various metals in the room warped and seemed to flow over to its hand. In seconds, a truly wicked looking halberd appeared in its hands.

All it took was a single glance for Meterove to know that there was no way that they were going to be able to defeat this thing. Whatever this was it was well beyond all of them combined. Just as he was about to yell at the others to retreat it vanished in a swirl of fetid smelling shadow and just for a moment strange organ music, almost like a circus could be heard.

Everyone froze for a moment before several things happened in quick succession. A scream could be heard from nearby, whether from inside the palace or outside was impossible to tell. A warning horn could be heard, and the throne room doors burst open.

The guards that they had knocked out earlier were shambling over towards them with glowing blue eyes. Meterove recognized this!

"Damn! It turned them!" Meterove dashed ahead and began slaying the guards without holding back. Looking behind him he saw that Dras and Narok were doing the same.

In no time they made their way back to the entrance and looked out over the city. It was absolute chaos. Guards were fighting each other as seemingly random members suddenly turned undead. Out past the walls of the city a veil dropped and a massive army of undead along with vampires and werewolves appeared. Several figures rode upon what appeared to be undead pegasi near the rear. There were also two other figures.

Using a spyglass Meterove was able to just make out the outline of the creature from before to be one. The other he only recognized from the memories he had been shown by the Dragon Lord...it was the Lich that had once been his ancestor...

CHAPTER 17.5
HOPE

What was and what is and what will be were all converging on the same point. What can be done to avoid this? If that came to pass, then there those that he had been watching would be thrown far away. They might even become entangled in a loop and never escape.

Why was all this happening? What had the dark self that emerged done to cause this? No first how had it been able to form in the first place? No there is no point in deliberating that, if something were not done soon then there would not be a point to coming to a conclusion.

The sound of fracturing filled the void. Now there were many more selves. If this same thing was happening with the other selves that already existed...no that was not going to help. For now, it was best to try and debate how best to help those that he had been watching. They were supposed to help further on. Meeting them while they were moving along here was a strange feeling.

Suddenly there was a flash of inspiration. Even if only a fragment escaped it could try and steer them where they needed to go! A small nudge might be all that was needed to keep them from the horrible fate that he had foreseen. To do that, it was time to stop trying to hold together and instead willingly break!

An infinite cacophony of shattering followed, and the dissonance was so great that, for the briefest of instances there was a crack and through that crack, fell a self. Please! Please succeed!

CHAPTER 18
ASSAULT

The party separated into three pairs almost as if they all had the same thought. Dras and Meterove ran through the streets making for the defenses slaying undead as they went.

Narok and Joleen entered the Palace and made for the conference room hoping to make use of a special communication artifact that was reserved for emergencies. Jolson and Terenia went to find the necessary mages to activate and sustain the defense barrier.

Meterove and Dras barreled through the streets cutting down only those undead that would either impede their progress or could be culled without slowing them down.

They hoped that the bit of aid that they lent the soldiers as well as the sight of them smiting undead would bolster their morale. They were going to need it.

They made it down to the city walls in no time and standing on the ramparts looked out upon an army the likes of which they had never seen.

The captain from earlier tried to question Meterove about what was happening. Fortunately, it seemed that most of the soldiers and guards down here had not been infected.

The enemy was preparing for a pincer attack on the city. Meterove looked at Dras, "Take command here, use whatever means you need to in order to hold this gate!"

Dras barely had time to nod before Meterove was off running trying to get to the other side of the main gate. Dras looked out over the army that was like a dark mass in front of him and silently prayed that the others were able to make it in time.

.   .   .

In the conference room Joleen activated a hidden sigil on the floor and pedestal with a large crystal dodecahedron rose from the floor. Placing her right hand on the top facet of the crystal Joleen channeled her power into it. After a moment, several images appeared on the facets.

The first thing that Joleen noticed, which she had suspected was that the gate had fallen. Based on what she could see though this had happened very recently. She could only assume the lich, or that "thing" had something to do with it.

The other facets had various personal from the other nations that were assigned to sit watch over their own crystal. Ordinarily there would have been a guard here as well but Joleen suspected that that "thing" had made sure to remove that threat.

Joleen wasted no time in explaining the situation and asking for aid. Suddenly another facet came to life and a woman wearing a robe with the crest of the Mages on it appeared. She looked panicked.

"Hello!? -ello?! Can you hear me?" The image flickered several times before stabilizing. "We are under attack by the undead we need reinforcements!"

"SHIT!" Joleen swore not even caring about who heard.

This isn't even their full army?

Joleen took a breath then asked, "Do you know their numbers?"

The mage shook her head, "No, I cannot give you an accurate estimate. The best I can say is thousands."

Joleen paused, "That means that the vast majority of their forces seem to be focused on us. Looking into the crystal Joleen said, "tell your leaders that if they have aid to send that they should first rescue the mages before heading here. But please move with haste there are far more enemies here than I can count."

Joleen ended communication since there was no point in waiting. Her abilities would be badly needed with the rearguard. From there Joleen made her way around the palace until she came to the passage over to the academy.

The various professors there were already getting the students evacuated. Joleen gave orders for any staff members that could be spared to come with her to the front to set up various triage and healing centers. Not just some of the staff she even requested that any students in their final two years at the academy be asked to join in the effort.

Looking out the window Joleen could barely see the army that was arranged against them.

We're going to need every single person we can get!

Jolson and Terenia were not that far away at that moment. They had actually been in the academy just moments before and had left with a handful of mages to go power the barrier.

The two of them cut down a handful of undead but for the most part they made their way to the barrier chamber without much trouble.

Jolson hadn't heard any sounds of battle yet, so he hoped that they had made it in time. If enemies had already made it into the city, then the effectiveness of the barrier would drop drastically.

Jolson stopped worrying about that and turned to Terenia, "Keep watch on the door. We'll be too focused on channeling our power to defend ourselves. Our lives are in your hands."

Terenia nodded and unbeknownst to them set to work creating a barrier around the room. A small seedling grew up from her left hand and several seeds appeared on it. Plucking them from the plant she placed them at the entrance of the room, and they almost instantly started growing into large vines that closed off the doorway. Terenia also readied her weapons.

Out on the fields in front of the city a great number of siege engines readied themselves for attack. Some were trebuchets but Meterove could also see catapults, siege towers and the odd ballista here and there. The part that alarmed him was that it appeared that they were armed not with traditional stone or flaming boulders but what looked like huge sacks of writhing flesh.

Meterove could only assume the worst about what those were meant to do.

Come on Jolson hurry!

On some unspoken command the siege engines all fired at the same time and hundreds of various sized fleshy masses or bone spears with strange flesh strips on them came hurling towards the city. Just as the soldiers were about to panic and move out of the way a large hexagonal barrier materialized and the volley that had been sent at them was stopped short.

That did not discourage the enemy though and they began loading the next volley. Meanwhile Meterove had seen what happened with the first volley.

Just as he had suspected from the start these were no mere bludgeoning attack. The writhing sacks split open on impact and dozens of undead spilled out. The barrier, being pure energy, burned them instantly but did not seem to dissuade them from trying to enter. The spears, however, were far more disturbing. They had been deliberately shot short so that they would land at the base of the walls.

It became instantly apparent that these were not weapons but undead. The massive piece of bone had eight rotting fleshy tentacles that unfolded themselves from it. On the front of it was a bare skull with no lower jaw and only a single eye socket that held a pale lifeless eye in it. The rear of the spine was extremely flexible and came to a sharp point, which it held aloft like a scorpion.

"WHAT NIGHTMARE IS THAT?"

One of the soldiers took the words right out of Dras' mouth. Looking across to the other side of the gate he could see Meterove looking at one of the creatures as well. "You know what I think I want to just nope right on out of having to deal with that. How about you take it captain?"

Fortunately, Dras was able to manage a smirk and the captain as well as the men took it as a joke. He wanted to project the sense that he was not particularly worried about it. They began moving around and he wanted to nope out even more. They looked so much like some horrifying spider. Dras had thought that they couldn't get any creepier but no, they absolutely could.

They were clearly probing for weaknesses. Fortunately, there was a fact about this barrier that they were unaware of. It was only an impenetrable barrier from the OUTSIDE.

Dras raised his voice, "ARCHERS! TAKE AIM! FIRE!"

The arrows that they had all been outfitted with recently were made with a small glass tip on the end that had a small amount of holy water in it. This would shatter on impact and a second barbed head under the glass would lodge the holy water onto the body of the undead maximizing the damage it caused them.

This chain of events played out several times before the main army had reached the walls. Now that there were more enemies hitting the wall at once the barrier was less effective. Occasionally an arrow would penetrate the barrier. Thus far no one had fallen. Dras looked out over the scene before him. This was going to be a long battle.

Meanwhile across the gate Meterove was having the same thought. He was sending his own volleys of arrows and magic bursts at the enemy. Looking to the rear he could see larger undead that were called ghouls beginning to advance. These giants were well over twenty feet tall.

They were also well armored, meaning that their arrows were unlikely to do much damage. They would have to expend a large amount of magic just to bring one down. Just as he was wracking his brain for what to do about this, he saw a rather unusual projectile launch from Dras' area.

Looking over he saw that they had bundled many holy water vials together with what appeared to be small metal fragments. When it hit a certain point in the air Dras used a basic spell that Meterove had taught him. It was launched a small flaming projectile.

When it hit the bundle exploded, creating a fine mist of holy water over a large area, and sending countless bits of shrapnel, now coated in traces of holy water, into the enemies ranks. The effect was immediately apparent when an entire section of the enemy's line collapsed and two ghouls fell, crushing even more.

Meterove grinned, "Dras you really are just as crazy as the stories say!" Turning back to his men, "One of you go ask the other unit what they used just now. Once you know begin using it at once!"

This battle was far too easy at this point. What was the enemy waiting for?

Joleen and Narok had made it up to the front lines and had gathered as many volunteers as they could along the way to serve as medics. They set up a total of five stations for treating the wounded.

All salves, potions, healing artifacts and even bandages had been appropriated. Each station had also been equipped with an artifact that could instantly transfer the people in it to a second station that was further back behind a secondary wall. Joleen had also ordered all the elderly and the children to go into the palace. Unfortunately, every able-bodied adult was needed right now.

Joleen looked down towards the wall. It pained her to be standing here but while she could fight her powers were best used for healing. Meterove would lead in her stead. He was more suited to war anyway.

Please little brother, be safe.

.   .   .

The power amplifying characteristics of the barrier were impressive but even, so this was going to be draining. Jolson was worried about holding the barrier. Soon they would have to change it from an absolute barrier to a partial in order to maintain it for any sort of duration.

I hope we bought them enough time to organize out there.

After another ten minutes Jolson knew that they were at their limit. He had half of the mages rest. This would allow them to switch out later to maximize the duration of the barrier.

It's about to truly begin brother. I hope you are ready.

.   .   .

Meterove watched as the barrier began to lower. It now was only the same height as the walls. Phase two had started. Almost as if they had been waiting for this the enemy began sending forward siege towers.

At the same time the enemy siege engines fired more volleys. One of the bone scorpions impaled one of the soldiers then began scuttling around strangling and impaling soldiers.

"Be on your guard! These bastards are tougher than they look!"

"Oh, gods I can't cut it!"

"Lars! LARS! Where are you? DAMN YOU!"

Meterove heard countless cries and shouts as the battle began in earnest. He spared a glance towards Dras' side and was unsurprised to see it was in the same state.

Good luck my friend

On the other side of the gate Dras was doing all that he could, stretching his creativity to the breaking point.

His sword was currently sheathed. He had picked up the bow of a fallen soldier and was firing arrows as fast as he could. Aiming was hardly necessary considering the size of the army in front of him.

One of his arrows hit the rope of a ballista by chance and ruined the weapon. His men cheered.

I couldn't do that again if I tried.

.   .   .

The battle had now been going on for several days. So far, they had suffered few deaths considering the circumstances. The med-stations had allowed their wounded to return to battle, but their morale was lowering with every wound.

Everyone, even Joleen, was covered in blood. They had some people on rotations so that people could get rest, but that only helped so much. It wasn't like there was time to bathe. It was on the morning of the fourth day that help arrived. Another army, clearly mixed, approached from the southeast catching the enemy on their left flank.

The enemy clearly had not been expecting this and scattered. They fell back from the gates and retreated to regroup. As they fell back their commanders came forward.

There were four of them that were riding the undead pegasi as well as the lich. What happened from there couldn't be called a battle, it was a slaughter, as these five decimated most of the allied army.

Meterove felt his whole body go cold. Whatever those other four were they were clearly well beyond normal soldiers. The small remnants of the allied forces that were still alive were clearly being protected by a barrier.

There was a huge thud of air pressure as well. Meterove looked around unsure where this was coming from. THUD THUD THUD

Descending from the clouds far above the rear of the enemy army was an impossibly large dragon that Meterove recognized. Even at this distance he was able to hear the message it sent him.

"It would seem that something that I cannot ignore has manifested here. I will keep its attention for now. Others are on their way as well to even the odds."

The angelic creature pulled the destroyed remains of its soldiers towards it absorbing them into its body. It grew in size, not as large as the dragon but large enough to contend with it. It took to the sky where it began to fight.

While this was happening, a small keep appeared out of nowhere. It materialized between the remaining allied army and the five that were slaughtering them. From this keep many tetrahedron shaped crystals filed out and they projected a barrier around them.

Meterove could just faintly see two figures on this keep's ramparts, but his attention was quickly pulled back as the enemy had reformed their ranks and were now attacking. The siege towers had also finally reached the walls.

The battle had reached its third phase. Now that the first siege towers had reached the walls the magic cannons that were mounted on several towers would come into play.

The gunners used their cannons to blow the base of one tower out so that it collapsed into a second tower that was about to reach the wall, blocking a large stretch from further towers. While he had been prepared for this it had happened far sooner than he had predicted. Of course, most predictions were pointless at this point.

The men were now having to contend with the vampires and werewolves. They had been mostly absent earlier and now they knew why. They had been inside the siege towers.

All around him men were torn to pieces by werewolves and vampires alike. Meterove did his best to protect his men, but he knew full well that the wounded would have to be treated with special care since most of them would turn, therefore healing their wounds would take longer in order to be certain that they were free of contamination.

Across the gate Dras was having a harder time fighting. He had numerous small wounds; he was pretty sure he had a few cracked ribs, but he fought on. None of his wounds had been inflicted by werewolf and the only vampire that he had fought had grazed his side with its sword.

The keep that had materialized on the battlefield along with a dragon had shifted the battle from a desperate last stand to something of a stalemate. Instead of trying to fight the riders and the lich the two figures seemed to be working together to act as crowd control, while the remaining soldiers took up defensive positions in and around the keep and supplied additional support.

From the keep, a number of large-scale cannon blasts were fired at the riders. Apparently, they also had magic cannons.

As if disgusted with the state of things the now massive angel dodged some dragon's fire and took a brief swipe at the city wall with its halberd. In an instant the barrier shattered along with the wall. A massive eruption of stone, earth and the dead followed. I paid for its distraction as its left arm was caught in the jaws of the dragon and was flung to the ground. The damage was done though. The wall had been breached.

CHAPTER 19
REVELATIONS

Jolson had been helping maintain the barrier when he felt a massive pressure and before he could even speak, he could feel the connection to part of the barrier fail. With the barrier broken on that side there was little reason to maintain it on that side, therefore he redirected their efforts to the other wall in order to prevent multiple points of entry.

.   .   .

Dras picked himself up from the ground, his ears ringing and his vison blurry. The halberd had destroyed a large section of the wall. He could also tell that the barrier was down. However, the worst part was that he was on the wrong side of the wall.

Sensing an attack Dras rolled to his left and a mace lodged itself into the dirt. Doing his best to shake off the effects of his fall Dras looked up at an unreasonably large werewolf. It was also clad in armor and held a tower shield.

Dras readied his own sword, thankful that he had somehow managed to keep hold of it. There was a shield on the ground nearby, so he dodged in its direction on the next attack. It was unlikely to stand up to a direct hit, but it was better than nothing.

He danced around the werewolf for a while dodging its strikes in the hopes of wearing it out. For whatever reason, the others were mostly avoiding them. Just as he had formed the opinion it had to do with pride or honor, the mace that the werewolf was using began to glow blood-red and when it struck the ground where Dras had just been a massive cone shaped shockwave shot out and everything that was within it shattered.

NOPE!! They just don't want to get killed by his weapon!

Dras fought with the werewolf for several minutes with no sign of it tiring. He on the other hand was exhausted. The siege had really worn him down. The brute used that special attack three more times. The ground around them was a mess, almost impossible to find solid footing.

Clearly its plan was to reduce his mobility. It thought that it was more cunning than it was though.

If the ground is difficult for me then it will also be difficult for you!

Dras reached into his pouch and pulled out a vial of clear liquid with another smaller vial in it that had blue liquid in it. He threw it at the ground in front of the werewolf then jumped backwards closing his eyes.

The vial, which he had bought just before they returned created a bright flash that blinded the werewolf. It bellowed in pain and rage and violently swung its mace, once again glowing blood red. It stepped on some lose ground and lost its balance. The extra weight of the tower shield, mace and armor was too much for it and in the process of regaining its balance the mace lightly struck its leg.

A large shockwave shot through its body and everything except the mace itself shattered. The werewolf fell, every bone in its body shattered. From somewhere a bestial voice said, "The pack leader has fallen! Flee!"

All around there were howls as the remaining werewolves fled the field of battle. There were still vampires in the fray, but Dras could see one that looked to be their leader staring at him from across the battlefield. The odd thing was that he felt no malice. Once the feeling of appraisal had passed Dras heard another voice, "We are leaving as well. The lords be damned I will lose no more of our kind. RETREAT!!"

Wearily Dras made his way back to the wall, but not before taking the mace that werewolf had been using. There was no way he was leaving that lying there for the enemy to reclaim. It was very heavy, so he strapped it to his shield then returned to the wall.

.   .   .

Meterove had been worried about the other wall since the breach but so many enemies were approaching his side in an attempt to make a second breach that he could not spare time, much less soldiers, to help. Fortunately, help was not done coming.

A second much larger army had now appeared and judging by the magic strikes that were coming from it there were far more powerful soldiers amongst them. Meterove thought that he had heard something call out a retreat just a moment ago. Looking towards the keep, several cannons managed to catch one of the riders at the same time and he was blasted all the way over to where Meterove could get a clear look at it.

WHAT IS THAT!

Meterove was rooted in place to the point that he even took a minor wound. What stood up was unlike anything that he had ever seen. The word nightmare didn't do it justice.

It was about the height of a man with gray wrinkly skin and very large eyes, several times the size of a humans. They were similar in nature to a shark. Its head was very long with a nose that resembled an elephant's trunk in shape though connected for the entire length of its face ending just above an extremely tiny mouth that didn't seem capable of closing. Its legs were built like the rear legs of a cat and its arms were acting as much too fluid to have bones in them.

Its armor had been pretty badly damaged by the blast but the creature itself was still intact though based on its lack of movement it was likely injured. Meterove snapped himself back to his senses and took a gamble. Its attention was on the cannons that had hit it. Meterove brought every drop of magic he had left in him out at once and vanished in a flash. He reappeared next to the creature.

Up close he could tell that he had been correct in assuming that it was injured. There was some tar like substance that was leaking from all over its body. Meterove hit it point blank with a singular blast. A massive burst of white energy swallowed the creature and everything within thirty feet of Meterove.

When his eyes adjusted the creature was still there, only now it looked fatally wounded. His surprise attack appeared to have worked. Its left leg gave out and it held itself up with its arm, though barely. Meterove swung his sword at its neck and its head fell to the ground with a loud thump.

Realizing that one of their number had fallen the other three retreated by creating similar fetid mist that the angel had used before.

The lich, lacking its allies was forced to fight the two that confronted it. In the sky the angel appeared to realize that its forces had been routed and after taking a final swipe with its halberd it separated itself from the mass it had merged with and vanished as well.

The remaining undead fell quickly without their commanders. The only thing left now was the lich. Meterove didn't have any strength left anyway. He barely had the stamina left to stand much less walk. If his men hadn't been franticly firing arrows before the undead might have had an easy kill.

I'd kill for a nap right now.

Meterove dragged his exhausted body over towards the gate. Once inside the city he collapsed against a wall, too tired to move. A field medic came over and began going over him. While he sat there someone sat down next to him. He heard Dras say, "Let's not do this again. Like ever."

Meterove gave an exhausted chuckle, "agreed" then he lost consciousness.

.   .   .

When he regained consciousness, he was no longer down by the wall but up in one of the med stations that they had set up. Looking around there were no familiar faces. He sat up in his cot, which attracted the attention of a young medic girl. After inquiring he learned that it had been approximately twelve hours since he had been brought there.

Meterove stood up carefully because his body felt really heavy. "We were given instructions to tell you to go to the central forward med station once you recovered."

Meterove was still exhausted, but he thanked the girl and got to his feet. He didn't think he had the energy to use the transfer artifact, so he walked the short distance to the central med station.

Once there he met Narok and Joleen. Narok offered him a shoulder and helped him over to the crate that Joleen was resting on. She looked about as tired as he felt. Once he had sat down Joleen looked at Narok, "Go tell them that he's here."

Meterove gave Joleen a quizzical look, but she shook her head. "The two that showed up in that keep. I'm warning you now, I do not know their story but do NOT attack them!"

The tone of her voice was oddly firm, while still being uncertain.

Meterove wanted to ask what was going on, but Narok returned with two people in tow, and he understood instantly. Their armor was archaic but not unfamiliar. They had seen similar armor before. Their bodies were what caught his attention. While they were certainly not the same as those that they had seen before it was clear these were undead.

There was a man and a woman. The man had a large two-handed sword across his back and the woman had pair of short swords that were sheathed behind her back.

They stopped about five feet away from Meterove. A moment later Jolson, Dras and Terenia came from the same direction. Then Joleen gave the soldiers a signal and they cleared the area. The two undead continued to stare at Meterove. Once the area had been cleared Joleen spoke, "Alright explain yourselves now. You asked for us to wait until Meterove had joined us."

The undead continued to stare at Meterove until after a moment the man spoke, his voice echoing slightly, "My name is Valaas."

The woman lowered her head slightly before speaking, her voice echoing as well "My name is Syr. You are the descendants of our brother Mardelnier. We have much to discuss with you."

www.ingramcontent.com/pod-product-compliance
Lightning Source LLC
Chambersburg PA
CBHW031241310726
48971CB00004B/1114